Monstrous Ties

SHINA JAMES

WRITER'S TREE / SAN ANTONIO

Writer's Tree Publishing

P.O. Box 875

Helotes, TX 78023

First Edition: October 2016

Monstrous Ties is a work of fiction. All of the names, characters, organizations, and events portrayed in this novel are either products of the author's imagination or are used fictitiously. Any resemblance to actual events or persons, living or dead is entirely coincidental.

ISBN- 978-0-9961221-2-2 (Paperback)

Hold fast to dreams

For when dreams go

Life is a barren field

Frozen with snow

Dreams

Langston Hughes

BOOK 1

"Bram"

Prologue

They've waited for this moment…this hour—this minute—this second. All they had was time, which was not on their side—until now. Each one stares earnestly into their enemy's eyes. Each one muses about the murder, the last breath, and the impending silence, because nothing will ever be the same. They will gladly take on all of the chaos and monsters of the world if it means they can be free of their enemy.

He will savor every moment like a maggot savors decay, and Amelia will relish the agony.

If revenge is a dish best served cold, then it will be the coldest dish ever consumed—and how sweet the taste upon their lips.

Chapter One

Amelia stares at the luminous light, unable to imagine what fool would have the audacity to walk away. There is nothing behind her but gloom and utter darkness—the scary kind—the kind where you know that there are horrible and unimaginable things to follow. Only she's not *completely* sure. Her only certainty is that she loves Aaron and that she can't be without him. She shades her eyes with her hand and steps closer. She glides slowly, gracefully on weightless feet. The pain she once felt in her chest is gone, but her heart still thumps loudly in her ears, so she's positive she's not dead.

All she has to do is walk into the light and end her sadness and worries forever, but the reality is she didn't come this far to die—or live for eternity. She just wants Aaron and somehow knows he's not in there, yet. As her traitorous feet continue to move forward in the direction of paradise, she is flattered to know that Heaven awaits her. As she scans to her left and then her right, she finds herself ambivalent about how to resolve her plight.

In a flash, her feet lift off the ground, but ironically, she's not afraid. If anything, she's liberated and excited as the light gets brighter and brighter. She glides ahead, and then abruptly pauses mid-air. *Am I to be taken away within the blink of an eye, or do I have a choice?* She wonders. "What do I do?" she whispers.

Without warning, the finality of her decision almost knocks the wind out of her. She breathes in the sweetest air as beads of sweat stream from her armpits. Suddenly, small creatures scurry out of the light. They flutter all around her, making her laugh until she's brimming with happiness. She slowly reaches out her hand to touch one, but they quickly move away. She is almost engulfed in the light feeling at peace when her subconscious awakens—she can't remember if there was something she was supposed to do.

As she lets the tiny angels guide her toward divinity, she is moved to want to share this experience with someone—then Aaron pops into her mind.

"Huh!" she gasps as if someone just slapped her in the face. She immediately snaps out of euphoria and lands on her bottom.

"Ouch!" Tears pour out of her eyes as she realizes she was just about to give up without even knowing it. "I'm sorry but I have to go!"

She leaps up, rubs her throbbing tailbone, and runs away. She sprints so fast her legs barely have time to adjust to the speed. She keeps running until she's far away from anything resembling Heaven. Her worries and most terrifying thoughts skewer into her mind, which forces her to stop and catch her breath. As horrible as she feels right now, away from the light, she knows she's one step closer to finding Aaron—and that makes it all worth it.

There's a long journey ahead of her, but she feels empowered to start her assigned mission. She speed walks into a slight jog through plumes of dark mist until she embarks upon a frightful existence. Now, every nerve in her body awakens as if each ending was purposely set on fire. Her skin stings from head to toe as the familiarity of her surroundings sink in. It dawns on her that this is where she saw Aaron for the first time. "I'm in the swamp," she whispers. She treads forward, crosses her arms over her chest, and then she stumbles upon a gathering of rodents. An all-black one stops chewing on a carcass and stares at her. She flinches as it's beady eyes dig into her almost as if it could see her soul. A cool squall releases a strong odor of decay and she holds her breath. Pinching her nose, she reluctantly braves the smell and slowly moves away.

"H-hello! Is there anyone here?!" she hollers. She stops and turns in every direction so fast she gets a dizzy spell, but fear of the unknown keeps her alert. She does a double take when she sees an all-white landscape of snow plummeting to the ground to her far right. Crystals the size of golf balls continuously plunge onto mounds of frozen matter. The chilly anomaly before her causes her teeth to clatter. A few flakes drift towards her and melt. She hates the snow and searches for a way to distance herself from it. She squats down and looks up at the rolling clouds that have created a blanket over the gloomy creation. They thicken until the last glimmer of the murky sky is concealed. Another round of rumbling thunder sends shockwaves through her body and transforms her legs into jelly. Her shaky hands are invisible as the dense atmosphere has turned everything into night.

She covers her ears, inhales and counts to ten. Suddenly, a bolt of lightning crashes down in front of her. A loud shrill escapes her lips but is subdued by another encroaching blast. She gets down on all fours and blindly crawls away until she feels the rough edges of tree bark. She desperately tries to find a stable branch as she digs her nails into the wood until warm fluid seeps from her fingertips. She leans up against the tree, wraps her arms around her knees, and buries her head as the chilly rain beats down on her back.

Blinded by darkness and completely drenched, Amelia lifts her head, which feels heavier than it should. She wrings out her soaked hair, swings her head in a clockwise pattern, and massages the aches in the back of her neck. As the last few droplets of rain ceases, the clouds begin to break away into cotton-like masses. But the blue sky she's accustomed to seeing is charcoal gray. She senses that there is nothing normal or safe about this place and wonders if she's in Hell. Creeek! She pivots from the sound, lifts herself off the ground, removes her hair from her face and sees a very tall, slender man in front of her. His olive-toned complexion is impeccable and his straight raven hair dances around his shoulders in the wind. He's wearing a cream-color button down shirt and black slacks. He strolls away from a maple tree and stops seven feet away from her, forming his lips into a hard line. His amber eyes stare into hers as every sound imaginable becomes eerily silent.

Amelia smiles and turns on her heels when an intoxicating essence of peonies infuses the air in a warm breeze. Her hair slowly dries and her skin is now cool to the touch. She bites her bottom lip and looks over her shoulder at him.

"You needn't be afraid," he whispers with a smile.

Against her better judgment, she faces him. "I'm not afraid. I'm just looking for someone—and you're not him," she sighs.

A low, deep chuckle rises from his chest and out of his mouth. "I'm sorry to disappoint you." He clasps his hands together and steps closer just as Amelia takes a step back. "I can help you find your friend."

"How so?"

"Let's just say I have connections," he says.

Amelia takes a step closer and crosses her arms. "You can help me? I-I don't even know your name."

"What's in a name?" he asks and leans against a tree. He studies a red rock before tossing it away. "I find it troublesome that a person needs to know a name. I'd rather they get to know *me*—as a person. If I told you my name was Watson, whether it be true or not, would you really care?"

"I suppose I would. I see it as our first truth, a gift we're given when entering this world…that stays with us until the day we die. Some have the luxury of changing their name, but our birth name is indelible." She lightly runs her fingers along the rough edges of a sapling. "Would you have me call you a fool?" Amelia asks.

"Ha! Ha! You're a clever girl. But, I still prefer anonymity," he says.

Amelia bites her lower lip and looks around at the grim matter as it floats through a sweet and tasty breeze. "You know, I think I'll take my chances on my own." She turns her back to him.

"Wait, are you sure I can't help?" he asks again and takes a step closer.

"I'm positive."

The hairs on the back of her neck stand as she slowly walks away. With every step she takes, she is certain he's getting closer to her. A hot, burning gust of wind brushes against her back. She balls up her fists and spins around—but he's vanished. She saunters to where he was standing and can't find a single footprint. The air has returned to a stinking humid calamity as her body assumes the sweaty mess it was before.

BUZZZ!!

AAHH!!" Amelia screams and falls onto her hands and knees. She looks back and spots a fly the size of her head spinning around and rushing back towards her. She leaps up and hobbles to an oversized bush and hides behind it.

She wipes the sweat from her forehead and peeks through the leaves as her body trembles.

Sssss!

Oh No! She forces herself to become completely stiff as the weight of something slides across her feet. She looks down and spots an all red snake as it slithers across her legs. She covers her mouth to stifle a scream and slowly scoots backwards, carefully removing her legs away from the red creature. It needles through the bush and disappears beneath. When she realizes the fly has moved away from her vicinity, she crawls towards another nearby shrub and pauses in case it comes back. No one is in sight, which makes her all the more afraid as she fans her flushed face with her damp shirt. The fresh powdery scent of her deodorant is soothing as she tries to brave the amalgam of decay and humidity. To block out the scary memory of the snake, she tries to envision Aaron's face and his warm hands. She could almost feel the warmth of his touch when the ground starts to shake.

That's an earthquake, she thinks as she wraps her hands around some honeysuckle vines and hopes she makes it out alive. After moments of being shaken to the core, she bites her bottom lip and wiggles her nose. Her intense need to sneeze is stronger than her resistance. "Achoo!" she wipes her nose and sighs.

"Who are you?" someone asks.

She cranes her neck and jumps up when she sees an extra-large groundhog that stands almost two feet tall on it's hind legs. It's human-like magenta iris's remind her of those beasts waiting in the bushes where all you can see is glowing eyes in the darkness. She blinks twice; *Am I having a massive hallucination?* she wonders.

"Did... did you say something?" Amelia asks.

It hops closer to her and gawks. A light breeze brushes across his chocolate fur as he wiggles his black nose. "You smell delicious," it croaks as saliva drips from its furry mouth. It projects its purple tongue and savors the taste of the air.

With her mind racing, Amelia takes a step back. "I'm Amelia. I'm looking for someone," she whispers in a shaky voice. In the corner of her eye, she sees two more creatures coming from behind the other shrubs.

"Well, you certainly don't belong here. I've never smelled such sweet meat in my life. Oh, pardon me," he says as he bends over. "My name is Roki."

"Hello—um Roki. You're right; I don't belong here. I guess I'll be on my way now. See ya!" She runs towards a dirt trail only to find her escape short-lived. Twenty more monsters have popped out from every direction. They have her surrounded.

Uh oh! She lifts both hands. "Listen, I just want to get out of here and find Aaron! I'm not here to hurt any of you!"

They all gaze at each other and then back at her. The largest one is about three feet tall and hops over to her.

Shoot!

"Who are you?" The large one asks.

"Like I told the others, I'm Amelia and I'm here to find my fiancé. His name is Aaron."

"I am Masacus, and this is our home you have intruded on my friend." He sticks out his purple tongue, sniffs loudly, and snorts.

"Oh, I am so sorry. I was just passing through and didn't realize you were living…h-here," Amelia says.

"Well, we don't get many intruders this side of the woods. Nonetheless, you will pay for disturbing our rest."

"Disturbing your rest? Look, I'm sorry for trespassing, but something was chasing me," Amelia whispers.

Masacus laughs and bares his extremely sharp teeth.

Amelia grits her teeth and runs past him, willing herself to run faster than she ever has but they're quicker than she anticipated. "Get away from me!" She kicks one of them out of her way. She looks back and notices that Masacus is right behind her. His crimson eyes have turned a shade of orange and his sharp teeth are inches away from her thigh. She sucks in a gulp of air and runs faster, but tires quickly. The thin atmosphere is making it harder for her to breathe, but she's determined not to give up without a fight.

"Get her!" Masacus pants. He too is out of breath. Two creatures rush under her feet and trip her. She goes down, face first, into the black, gooey mud. She quickly wipes the mud from her eyes and attempts to rise. Everything is a blur. By the time she can see clearly, five of them surround her and lift her body off the ground as if she's weightless. She kicks and squirms, trying frantically to escape, but they have a tight grip on her legs and arms. As she's being carried back to doom, she can't believe how strong her new enemies are.

"Let me go you disgusting fur balls!" She twists her legs and hollers for freedom but they ignore her antics and continue to carry her back to their village.

Masacus toddles back to his previous spot and patiently waits for his minions to bring Amelia forth. "So you thought you could escape, my delectable friend."

"Look I don't belong here. You need to let me go," Amelia demands, still squirming.

"That's not going to happen you fool! Especially now!" One barks.

Feeling defeated, Amelia says to Roki, "Listen, I sense you have a kind spirit. Tell him to let me go."

"Masacus is my father," he admits as he sticks his tongue out again, besotted with the taste.

"Well listen Roki, I know you think I smell delicious, but I am not food! I'm a real person." She glances at all the others while they stand around enjoying the show. As the words flutter out of her mouth, she knows they carry no weight as the creatures can't see past their own desires.

"Enough talking! Prepare her for the feast!" Masacus demands.

The lurid squeals from their tiny lungs startle her. A cold rivulet glides down her face as her heart pounds against her chest. They transport her to a nearby tree, tie her against it, and then force her to sit and watch as they prepare a huge fire. She desperately tries to break free without being too obvious when Roki slowly strolls over.

"Don't worry. I doubt you'll feel a thing," he says.

"Is that supposed to be funny? You things want to burn and eat me alive! I'm pretty sure I'll feel it."

"We need your blood so that our mother the queen can live," he explains. "We knew you were special when you woke us up."

"What are you talking about?"

"You have a pure heart and you've been untouched. When someone like you treads on our land, it awakens everyone. You're special. We could sense it right away in the atmosphere, and your scent can't be overlooked."

Amelia sniffs her armpits. "My scent?"

"What's your favorite food?"

"Pepperoni pizza," she replies.

Roki scratches his head. "I don't know what that is but I imagine it is tasty. Multiply that times a hundred and that is what your scent tastes like to us. To *not* feast on you would be an egregious mistake. My mother is very sick and the wise ones from the Crying Forest told us that she will survive if she feasts on a pure heart. She has to eat your heart." His tongue escapes his mouth again. With a sigh, he looks away to restrain himself.

"You have got to be kidding me?!" Amelia shrieks.

"I don't expect you to understand; you're just a mere vessel." Everything stops and the others quiet down when a fragile all-white creature is escorted out and placed next to the fire.

"Is that her?" Amelia asks.

"Yes, that is my mother, Crima." He peers at her with sad eyes.

"Roki, I'm really sorry about your mother, but you have to let me go. You can't just feed me to her, and what if you're wrong? What if she doesn't get better? You'll have killed me for nothing," Amelia pleads.

"I wouldn't say for nothing, but, please don't make this any harder than it already is. We will feast on you and that's final. Besides, my father is the King Gobblewit and there's no going against his rules."

"Gobblewit?"

"Yes. That's what we are, dwellers beneath the land and trees," he explains. He walks away and tends to Crima. He caresses her flawless white fur and rests her head against a makeshift pillow made out of a pile of leaves. All the while, Amelia has been rubbing the ties against the tree bark. While Crima preoccupies their attention, Amelia finally gets her hands free and quickly unties her feet.

"Get her and bring her to the fire!" Masacus says.

"Shoot! Now it's too late," she mumbles to herself.

Four Gobblewits carry her to the fire and tie her onto a long wooden stick.

There's no use in trying to escape; they'll just catch up with me, anyway. Besides, even if I do get away from them, something or someone else will catch and kill me. Reasoning is the only card she has left to play. "Please guys, let me go! This isn't right," she begs.

They ignore her and proceed to lift her body and hang her over the fire, as if they're roasting a pig.

She immediately feels the intensity of the heat on her back and the smoke is making her nauseous. She looks up and stares at the sky. When they lower her body closer to the flames, she purposely visualizes her parents' smiling faces, then Aaron's and Navid's. *I didn't think this is how I'd end up, but I'm not surprised. It would be just my luck to die at the hand or paw of Gobblewits.* She's more embarrassed than scared. "Aaron, where ever you are I love you."

Tears roll down her cheeks as she feels the heat on her shirt. Her mouth has gone dry. She recoils and waits for the pain to amplify, hoping it happens quickly. Then, she hears a sudden crack and realizes the stick is breaking. *Oh no! I'm going to fall directly into the fire!*

The Gobblewits are all gazing at her with watery mouths, waiting to taste her burning flesh.

Amelia begins to feel a sense of hope that she might be able to survive this.

Crack! The stick breaks just as she maneuvers herself away from the orange blaze. She scorches her hand in the process. Roki hobbles over and ceases the fire that's erupted on her pants. Her first reaction is to kick him away, but when she sees all the smoke she assumes he's attempting to save her life. She starts to cough vigorously and scoots away from the blinding smoke, all the while amazed that she's still alive.

"Roki, what are you doing son?" Masacus roars.

"Nothing father… she was on fire."

"That's the point!"

Amelia stands up and backs away slowly. She winces from the pain of her burned hand and holds it close to her chest.

"Father, maybe this isn't right. I think this is wrong," Roki utters with his head down.

"She is no one! This person can save your mother's life you fool. Now get another stick and tie her to it!"

Roki looks at Amelia and then at his mother, apologetically. Amelia is stunned by his compassion.

With a somber look Roki whispers, "No."

All of the Gobblewits gasp loudly, in disbelief. Amelia has to admit she's a little frightened for Roki too. Within three seconds, Masacus rushes over to him and stabs him with his spear. Roki stumbles and lands on his back. Blood spews out of his furry chest. While in shock, Amelia glares at Masacus, trying to contemplate what her eyes have just witnessed. When she snaps out of it she says, "What's the matter with you?! He's your son!"

"He can be replaced. I have no time for this. Crima is dying and she will feast on your heart! We all will!"

Masacus has no regard for his son's life? she considers, infuriated. This very moment reminds her of Leona. She sorrowfully kneels down to caress Roki's soft brown fur.

"I'm sorry. We just met and you already tried to save my life," she says.

"It's alright Amelia. We've been doing this for a long, long time. Killing and eating innocent people or capturing them for the Beast. But I can't do it any longer and if dying is my way out, then I'm glad to go."

"What's the Beast?"

"You will find out soon. Get out of here Amelia, before it's too late. We haven't come across anyone pure in a long time and everyone will want you," he confesses as his eyes close.

Amelia shivers and braces herself. She slowly stands and takes her chances by sprinting away, but three Gobblewits are right behind her.

"Ugh! Get off my face!" she hollers. She furiously pulls one off her head while keeping a fast stride. "I can't go back! Help me!" she shouts, even though she knows that no one can hear her. She trips over a rock and falls into slimy greenish-brown goo. By the time she wipes her face, eight Gobblewits have her surrounded. "Just leave me alone!" she cries. She buries her head between her knees and waits for them to carry her away. When someone touches her hair, she looks up and sees Aaron. Her heart drops into her stomach and suddenly there's three of him. "Aaron is that you? You're here?"

She rises up and gazes into his eyes. Instantly, she realizes that something is wrong. The smile on her face fades and tears of disappointment erupt. The green eyes she longed for aren't there, indicating an imposter. She angrily crosses her arms and waits for an explanation when before her eyes, Aaron transforms into a girl who looks to be around her age. Amelia slowly steps backwards and bends down to pick up a stick. She guards herself until she's backed up against a massive Sequoia tree.

Chapter Two

"Who and what are you?" Amelia asks.

"My name is Carys. I thought you needed some help," she utters shyly.

"Where are the Gobblewits? They had me surrounded." She glances at the nearby shrubs, curious to their whereabouts.

"I took care of them. I scared them away."

"How?"

Carys strolls towards Amelia and reaches out her hand. Amelia firmly presses her body against the tree with her hands glued to her sides. She proceeds to draw away from the strange girl but Carys smacks her teeth and forcefully takes Amelia's hand.

"Huh! Whoa!" Carys shrieks as she quickly lets go.

Amelia sniffs her hands with concern. *Do I have cooties?*

"We have to go now!" Carys demands as she grabs Amelia's hand again.

"Where are we going?"

"I know what you want and I have to get you to the Crying Forest," Carys declares.

"What exactly is that?" Amelia asks while trying to break free from Carys's grip.

Carys ignores her queries and continues moving. Amelia remembers what Roki said about people wanting her and gets frightened. She frees her hand and runs away, sprinting through tangled webs and fog until she reaches a giant wall. She hides behind it while trying to catch her breath. When the smell of rotten vegetation fills her nostrils, she puts her hand over her mouth to keep from vomiting. After a few slow breaths and quick meditation, she observes a field of leafless trees and dead flowers. Giant tomatoes and decayed lettuce heads cover every inch of the ground. She looks up at the rolling clouds that dance across the mustard colored sky.

To gather her thoughts, she sits down and ponders how Carys could look like Aaron and then transform into someone else. *Has she seen him before?* She angrily throws an old stick towards the unkempt garden and whispers, "I don't know what makes me think I can save Aaron when I can't even save myself." She mopes in silence, accepting the fact that she was almost killed by the Gobblewits and that the only person who could save her was an imposter.

She obsessively looks over her shoulder, completely terrified by what could be on the prowl. She bites her nails and taps her foot while thinking of a way to find Aaron and make it out alive. With a long sigh, she realizes that Carys is the only one who can answer her questions and possibly help her. She rolls her eyes and reluctantly stands. "I guess it's now or nev… huh! AAHH!"

For a split second Amelia thought she was dead, she certainly feels like she is. Earth and matter continuously alight onto her, slowly burying her alive inside of a dark hole. She shakes her head at her luck, confounded as to why she can't seem to keep her feet on solid ground, literally. She makes an attempt to sit up, but her arms feel like they've detached from her body. While trying to give herself time to adjust from the fall, she ponders how she's going to find Carys and not the tangible reason as to what the massive hole is really used for. Just as she thinks her luck can't get any worse, a giant bee makes it's way inside. It descends into the dark abyss in a perfect spiral. She tries to move, but can't, and is forced to watch the stinger aim right for her immovable body.

"Close your eyes!" Carys shouts below.

Thank God! Amelia squeezes her eyes shut and tries to wiggle her numb fingers. Lurid buzzing sounds echo in her ears and vibrate her entire body. With all that has happened, she doesn't know how much longer she can hold on to her sanity. The ominous noises of the insect continue to ricochet off the rock walls as dirt and matter bury her. The pungent flavor of spoil and decay brushes across her lips. With blinded eyes, she listens to the commotion and wonders, *What's taking Carys so long to save me?* She hears what sounds like two bees fighting each other to the death and assumes that the winner will come for her next. Knowing she's not ready to die, she wills herself to move her fingers, her hands, and then her arms. She cringes through the pain and sits up, looking around just in time to see a bee plummeting towards her.

"Whoa!" She rolls over, away from the insect and stays put until she realizes it's dead. While slowly rising to her feet, she gets frightened by it's massive size. She touches one of the wings and rubs the thin crispy surface. *What is this place?* She crumbles it between her fingers as tiny pieces flutter to the ground.

When another round of loud buzzing commences, she freezes, hoping the victor won't come for her. She squints through the darkness to see where the sound is coming from when she spots a huge wasp buzzing around at the top of the hole. "Carys watch out up there! There's a giant wasp flying out!" She walks towards the wall and attempts to climb her way out, furious with herself for letting so much time pass.

"Grab a hold of this!" Carys hollers and drops down a long vine.

Amelia holds on tight as Carys tugs her out.

"Thank you so much, I thought I was done for," Amelia says. She reaches out to shake Carys's hand, but Carys quickly crosses her arms. Amelia ignores her rudeness and glares down at the dark abyss, bothered that she almost died. "Listen, I'm sorry for running away from you, but you really scared me."

"We don't have a lot of time and I need to get you out of here," Carys replies without acknowledging Amelia's apology.

"Okay, but before I do anything you need to explain to me who you are and why you looked like Aaron when we first met? Have you seen him?" Amelia's eyes well up as she prepares to hear bad news.

"Follow me, I'll take you somewhere safe," Carys says. She strolls past Amelia and heads into a wooded area. Amelia's gut tells her she should follow her but she will keep her guard up until Carys explains herself. "You don't have to be afraid you know," Carys murmurs.

"I'm not," Amelia lies.

Carys smirks and keeps walking until they reach a well-lit area with a pond in the center. Olive green bushes adorned with orange and purple berries surrounds the water. "Where are we?"

"Nowhere special, but this is safer than where we were before." They both sit down in the grass.

Amelia looks around, *Why are some places rotting, while some are lively,* she wonders.

"So you're here looking for your boyfriend?" Carys asks.

"Yes, I have to find him and I don't have a lot of time. I have to
bring him back to me before it's too late."

"How do you know he's not already dead?" Carys retorts.

The very thought makes Amelia's stomach turn. She gulps down
warm acidic fluid and concentrates on being optimistic. "I know how
this must sound to you, but I can still feel him. I know in my heart
he's still alive but I don't know for how long. I just wish I knew
where he was. I keep hearing these people begging me to find him,
but they won't tell me how. I'm afraid that I'll be stuck here and
never get to him in time. So, what is this place? This isn't hell is it? I
mean, am I dead and don't realize it?" Her heart pounds against her
chest. *What if this whole time I've been in hell because I chose to
walk away from the light?* "Please you have to tell me before I lose
my mind! Am I trapped?!"

"No you're not trapped... I am." A lonely tears glides down
Carys's rosy right cheek.

"What do you mean?"

"I've been here in Bram for almost ten years."

"Ten years! Bram? I don't understand."

"This place is called Bram. It's where The Beast lives. He's a
terrifying thing to say the least. This is his creation. I don't know
how long this world has been here, but I imagine it must have been
created when he died, which was a long time ago. Sometimes your
mind can conjure up the craziest things, and I assume this place is
here because of him and his unfinished business. He wreaks havoc
on anyone who passes through or tries to escape. He's kind of like a
devil. He himself is trapped here partly because he refuses to let go
of the many souls he's kept here for so long. He'll never let them go
because he gains power from them. He especially preys on the weak-
minded, that's how he stays alive," Carys explains.

"How is that possible? I thought that once you die you either go to
Heaven or Hell."

"Sometimes people, like you, aren't ready to die and choose to
stay in between. Now what lies in between is whatever a person, like
the Beast, can create. I'm not sure if everyone can create worlds
though. I assume only those who are evil enough and in the devil's
likeness. But you never know, so much is unknown and unseen. I
just know that there must be better places out there somewhere.
Wherever there's evil, there is good nearby, right? The problem is
that you can get trapped in horrible places like this so easily. I think
that's why it's smarter to just walk into the light if given the chance

because once you get sucked in here, there is no escape until someone or something destroys the world. Obviously, it hasn't happened yet."

"How do you know so much?" Amelia replies.

"I've been here for ten years remember? Anyway, the Beast can be very deceiving. He promised me that if I capture souls for him that he would let me go. I shamefully held up my end, but he didn't. Instead he kept me here for all these years."

"Carys I am so sorry. So, are you dead or alive?" *I hope she doesn't think I'm being rude. I just need to know exactly what I'm up against.*

"I died five years ago." She looks away and throws a purple rock into the pond.

"How do you know you're dead? You said you've been here for ten years."

"He told me that it would be easier to capture souls if I had special powers. At first I objected, but he kept on pursuing the issue. I eventually gave in and the second he gave me the powers, I knew that I was dead."

"How? I mean you could be wrong?"

"Amelia, put your hand over your heart," Carys sighs, irritated.

With trembling fingers, Amelia obeys and can feel the drum-like beat on her chest.

"When I finally decided to take the powers from him—my heart stopped. You see, I didn't know that I could have left whenever I wanted to. I thought I had to do what he wanted in order to leave, but the truth is that when he touches you and gives you powers, that's when you become trapped and your life is really over. Anyway, it was too late to go back on the deal so here I am. I spent the first five years without powers and I always felt my heart beating, which means that somehow I was still alive, until he touched me. He can fool anyone. That's how he captures the souls. Most people who pass through here are on some sort of a mission, or they're just not ready to die. There is a minority who are actually dead, but most are not."

"May I ask what happened to you? You said that before you took his powers you were still alive?"

Carys drops her head and rolls her eyes. "I was really stupid and took my life for granted. My boyfriend and I were tripping off acid and thought it would be cool to jump off the Golden Gate Bridge. That wasn't the first time we did crazy stuff. We were always getting into trouble and came close to dying on numerous occasions. I won't get into the gory details, but when we got to the bridge, we held hands and were supposed to jump off together. When I leaped off the bridge, I realized I was alone. He chickened out at the last minute and couldn't do it. I can't tell you how sobering that was. As I was falling to my death, all I could think about was how stupid and irresponsible I had been. How my family was going to be devastated because of what I had done. I had no reason to be on drugs or do something so outrageous. Of course in the end, it was too late. I couldn't even tell them how sorry I was and how much I loved them." She wipes away a tear.

"So that's why you're here, isn't it?"

"I wanted to wait for my mother and tell her how sorry I was. I assumed they kept me alive as long as they could. Of course once the Beast got a hold of me, it was all over. I thought if I waited around here she would come looking for me. But now that I'm stuck here, I know that it was dumb of me to hang around. I should've just gone into the light," Carys says.

"Carys, we all do crazy things. Look at what I'm doing. I chose to walk away from the light to find Aaron. You just have to accept what you've done and move forward from here. I just hate that you can't leave. So everyone who passes through here has never left?" Amelia asks, worried.

"No, not everyone. Over the years I've seen only a handful of people who can see right through him and leave on their own, which really angers him. Trust me, you don't want to be around when someone refuses his advances and leaves. But most people give in because he promises you the world and it seems like he knows exactly what to say to entice you," she murmurs.

"That sounds really scary. So I'm assuming that everyone here is dead."

"There is one person here that isn't dead yet. I don't know how they're still alive but I can hear their heart beating."

Having heard enough Amelia asks, "Carys, how do I get out of here?"

"Your best shot is the Crying Forest. They will tell you where to go and what to do, but there are no guarantees on where you'll end up," Carys warns.

"Okay, so I just go to them and they can tell me whatever I need to know?"

"Yes, they have all the answers to anything you wish to ask, but choose your words wisely. It's also heavily guarded by The Beast's army so you can only go when the sky is yellow."

"Yellow?"

"The sky goes through different color stages throughout the day. It's kind of a way for us to know what time of day it is or what is to come. I found out one day when I was staring at the sky and noticed how the colors changed as time went on. It only changes in this area though, not all over. This is called *Hues Pond*. But if the sky ever turns black, you must run and hide because that means that either The Beast or his army is near," she advises. "Never let them see you. When the sky is yellow, they're all asleep and when it's red, they're awake. When they're awake, they roam the entire world, looking for lost souls or for people passing through. The Beast has one main guard that never sleeps so always be on the lookout for him no matter what."

"Who is he?"

"His name is Mortis, and he has a watch dog named Stylot. This dog has four eyes and can see and smell everything. There really is no escaping him once they're on your trail. Mortis has the power of physical manipulation. He can make you do whatever he wants, whether you try to resists or not."

Amelia nods, hoping that she never comes in contact with any of these awful beings. *I thought the Gobblewits were bad, but this sounds like my worst nightmare.*

"Oh no! The sky is turning black! Carys what do we do?" Amelia whispers while looking up at the sky.

Carys doesn't answer her.

"Carys! Carys where are you?" She frantically looks around but can't see her. "Where did she go so fast?" *I can't believe she left me.* Amelia runs over to a nearby tree and hides. She peeks around the large trunk and notices shadowy figures coming closer. Man-sized monsters march across the path with huge torches. *Holy crap!* She kneels down and scoots closer to get a better look.

The monsters resemble large beetles with bulging eyes and black horns on each side of their heads. Their prickly arms and legs are in uniform as they march in pairs, almost as if they've been in the military for years. They're reciting some chant but she can't make it out. As they get closer and closer, they scream: *Execution!* With their torches blazing, she's surprised they haven't set themselves on fire. Now that she has a better look, she notices that there are twenty beetles all together. Suddenly, a surprisingly normal man steps away from the guards and holds up his right hand. All of the beetles stop and turn to look at him.

"Make way for the Beast!" he shouts.

If Amelia didn't know she was alive before, she definitely knows now because her heart is beating so hard and fast its painful. She wonders if they can hear it.

In perfect order, the guards move out of the way and make a hole. They stand as upright as possible and form a parallel line, facing each other. The man walks back and forth and stares at each of them, making sure they look as flawless as statues. He's holding a leash in his hand. "Not now Stylot!" he yells as he holds the leash close to his body.

Huh! That must be Mortis and his dog. Shoot! Amelia starts to sweat, remembering that Stylot can see and hear everything. Stylot breaks away from Mortis's tight grip and makes a beeline in Amelia's direction.

Oh no! She feels lightheaded. Her shaking legs give out and she falls backwards.

"Stylot get back here!" Mortis screams. He quickly grabs hold of the leash and forces the growling four-eyed dog back to his side.

Amelia takes a deep breath and wipes the sweat off her forehead. *That was close.* She crouches down and continues staring. Stylot howls and moans as he tugs on the leash. He growls in Amelia's direction, but can't get away. Amelia wants to run, but is certain that if she moves, it's all over for her. Then, something approaches and the ground begins to shake.

"Guards! Bring me the prisoner!" Mortis shouts. The guards are still standing like mannequins. Two fly-like human beasts appear, carrying a man to the center of the path. His hands are covered in slimy chains. He cries and begs for his life. The two human flies stand on each side of him and growl, revealing thousands of sharp teeth.

Amelia attempts to keep her balance as the thumping in her chest worsens. She sees a distorted figure moving as the guards all stand in position. Out of nowhere, a giant monstrous Beast appears. *Huh?* Her face grows hot and her eyes are glued on the creature. Every hair on her body stands erect. The Beast is the scariest thing she's ever laid eyes on. She hides her face behind the stump with trepidation. Tears continually stream down her face and into the grass. It wasn't until right now that she realizes: *I'm never going to make it out alive.*

I may never see Aaron again. She remembers the curve of his smile and the shape of his eyes; this maybe the last memory she gets to have of him. As his the image falls apart like broken puzzle pieces, she wishes her parents were with her.

"This man has trespassed on our land," Mortis says to the Beast.

Amelia breaks out of her reverie and looks out to view the trial.

"What is your name?" The Beast roars. The vibrations from his deep voice rattle her insides. The leaves on the bushes tremble as he growls, "Why have you come?"

The prisoner's entire body is shaking. A liquid mass forms at the zipper of his pants and travels down to his shoes, and a large rivulet runs from his forehead down to the side of neck.

"Uh, I was just looking for my wife. I'm s-sorry to trespass on your world," the prisoner croaks.

"Your punishment will be death!" he roars.

Within two seconds, every bit of that poor prisoner is gone. After consuming the defenseless man, the Beast's body glows for about five seconds. Another soul is trapped inside the monster, making him stronger than ever. He grumbles loudly and vanishes. All of the guards assume their original position and then march down the path with their torches blazing in the darkness.

Amelia turns back around and slides down into the grass, utterly devastated. Her bottom lip quivers and her ears are ringing. As she sniffles in silence, she patiently waits until the last of the orange flames are nowhere in sight. She slowly moves from behind the tree and searches for a quiet place to rest until the sky turns yellow again.

Her contemplation is interrupted by the sound of barking,

"What is it Stylot? What do you see boy?" Mortis yells.

Dammit! I thought they were gone. She sprints towards the pond and hides behind some bushes. She glares through the leaves, searching for the dog. *I can't die! I just can't!* She knows Stylot smelled her earlier but hopes that Mortis will ignore him again. As she hides in fear, she becomes furious with Carys for leaving her all alone. Once the barking has stopped she peeks to see if they're still there.

I hope the coast is clear, she thinks. She walks out of the wooded area and heads in the opposite direction of the guards. The thought of them finding and killing her is unimaginable. Her main focus is Aaron. *He must be all alone some place, waiting for me.* She refuses to let her fear consume her, although there are horrendous creatures lurking in every angle. She doesn't understand this world or why she came here, but knows there has to be a way out—somewhere.

"Get her!" someone roars. She whirls around and sees the two human flies from earlier running after her.

Shoot! She takes fast strides when a shadow above distracts her. They're soaring over her like buzzards waiting to feed. Green slime discharges from their mouths and lands on the ground in front of her.

She hurdles over the slime and keeps moving, but one of them flies down and blocks her.

"AHH!" she screams. Seeing the creatures from far away was scary enough but being so close to them makes her vertiginous. She stumbles and steps back just as the other one alights down. She has nowhere to run.

"Suko grab her!" She attempts to run but finds herself slowly coming to a halt. The greenish-black slime has interlaced around her ankles. Then, the one named Suko spits the slime onto her wrists, leaving them numb and tingly.

"What did you do to me?" Amelia cries while trying to rub away the slime. It's consistency is a mixture of gelatin and bubblegum. Her legs and wrists burn as she tries to free herself. When she can no longer feel her arms she screams, "I'm paralyzed! Please let me go."

"Keno, you know what to do," Suko says.

"Please um Suko and Keno, you don't want me. I—I'm nobody."

They look at each other and remain silent. Keno reaches for her arm but draws back when he gets too close. He looks at Suko and speaks to him in another language.

Amelia can't imagine what they're talking about. "What are you going to do with me?"

"Nothing compared to what the Beast will do," Keno replies, maliciously. "He's been waiting for you."

"She'll be dead by the next red sky," Suko laughs.

Chapter Three

Millions of thoughts are sprinting through Amelia's mind. *Did I just hear them correctly? The single most agonizing truth this very moment is that I'm once again, someone else's prey.* An eerily sweet breeze springs into her nose and suddenly fades away. Some of her fear dissipates, long enough for her to look her enemies in the eye and ask a significant question: "What do you mean, he's waiting for me?"

"Just be quiet," Suko snaps.

She wishes she had some answers. Her arms are useless and feel weighted down, which means no escaping. She shakes her head and grits her teeth, seething, knowing that the only person who could save her has left her to die. Suko and Keno drag her through a field of prickly bushes adorned with lime colored berries. When they get stuck through a small opening, they pull hard and yank her through, scraping her legs in the process.

"Hey! Do you have to be such an ass?" Amelia screams. Ripples of blood ooze out of her legs.

"Ha! Ha! Ha! She's feisty, I like her," Keno laughs.

"You don't have to pull me so hard! It's not like I'm resisting! Where are you taking me?"

"You'll see, just keep still!" Keno hollers while tugging her along.

"You know if you idiots hadn't paralyzed my legs then maybe I would be able to walk!" Her body tingles and aches in places she never thought existed. She has a moment of nostalgia, thinking about strenuous workouts Mr. Wilkers demanded of her. Her bottom lip quivers as she fights back tears. They drag her along over dirty stumps, rocks, and matter so foul she terminates the need to ask, what it is. Her cheeks are flushed and beads of sweat filter into her mouth, leaving a salty essence across her lips.

After being hauled from one side of doom to the other, they finally stop at an enormous gothic-like castle. It stands about ten stories tall with only two dark square openings at the very top. The gloomy atmosphere is consumed with a brownish-gray haze, making it difficult to see clearly. She looks down at the charcoal slime covered ground and almost convulses as the foul stench of feces permeates the air. Her mouth is watering and the world is spinning, but she fights to keep calm. She tries to recall her scariest nightmares and is certain she's never imagined anything so revolting and atrocious, and yet, this is where she is. This place is where they brought her. All that's missing is a couple of fire spitting dragons waiting to greet her at the door. Instead, she's greeted by two of the beetle guards from earlier. Keno and Suko pull her towards the entrance.

Keno motions for the guards to step aside so he can unlock the gate. They lug her through, into darkness. The further away she gets from the beetles, the more relieved she is to not fall victim to them. She's gathered that Suko and Keno are not a threat…yet. But the beetles would be more than happy to rid her quickly. The entrance door slams shut. Growling echoes through the walls. The inside of the castle is dark and cold and the only lights are the fire torches that hang on the walls. Now that she's inside, she contemplates the thought of never getting out. As she's carried along, she notices there are no windows and wonders if the only way out is through the front gate.

Click! Keno opens another set of doors and walks ahead into daylight.

She tries her luck and pleads for them to let her go, but is completely disregarded. As they exit the castle, they stop so that Suko can lock the large steel doors. If she had feeling in her legs she knows this would be the best time to run. She looks up at the sunless sky and admires the gray overcast. She has always appreciated cloudy days, preferring them to sunny ones. There was always something about the way the clouds cradled the earth right before it rained, which made her feel at peace. As they pull her up a grassless hill, she tries to keep calm while little blue worms with red antennas wrap their slimy bodies around her paralyzed ankles. If there ever was a time to have no feeling in her limbs she's glad it's at this very moment. The greenish-black substance lingers and continues to keep her limbs numb and heavy.

"Here we are girl! Your chambers await you," Suko says slyly.

Amelia peeks around the side of Keno and quickly turns back around in disbelief. The ghastly cell they expect her to crawl in is mortifying. *I wish I could move my damn arms.* Her beating heart races with fear as they kick her ill-fated body inside the cell. They slam the gate shut, causing her ears to ring in protest. She's devastated by the finality of her current situation, realizing that the only way out is probably through death or worse...torture.

It has all happened so quickly. Suko and Keno fly away, leaving her with pieces of her sanity. *I am only a strange creature in this world*, she laments.

The thought of being left there to decay or get eaten takes its toll on her mind. "I'm so afraid," she cries. She starts to rock back and forth while unknowingly pulling out clumps of her hair. She is officially losing her mind and has no idea how to stop it. Her brain misfires as mortal thoughts invade her conscious. She's running, racing from monsters and barrels of blood. Sharp teeth, red eyes, and beetles are getting closer. Everything and everyone is after her. "Help!" she screams. She can't get out of her head. Nothing makes sense. The more she rocks, the more her hair falls onto the cell floor. "Ha! Ha!" she laughs. She cackles hysterically and cries. Warm tears pool her eyes and slide down her cheeks. "Ahh! Help me!" she cries out.

A cool draft enters the cell and causes her to shiver. She rubs her arms and chants, "I'm Amelia Waters; I'm alive. I'm going to survive." She wipes her nose and leans against the wall as her hallucination subsides. "I'm Amelia Waters; I'm alive. I'm going to survive." Her heart slows down and she counts to ten to control her breathing. She rubs her wrists and legs and realizes that she's had control over her limbs. "Somebody help me!" she shouts.

"Are you okay?" A small voice whispers.

"Huh!" Amelia draws her knees to her chest and scoots to a corner. She squints through tears and sees a shadow of someone. "W-who's there?" she asks.

The silhouette moves closer to her, revealing nothing more than a little girl.

She shudders to think why a child is stuck in a cell with her. *What could she have possibly done to deserve this? But then again, what did I do?* "I thought I was alone in here," Amelia whispers.

"I'm Mili," the little girl says.

"I'm Amelia." She crawls a little closer to the edge of the cell to get a better look at the girl. Aside from being covered in dirt, she's flawless. "You're surprisingly normal. I think you're the most normal thing I've seen."

"Same here," Mili agrees.

Amelia rubs on her arms and legs as the throbbing ceases. "I guess the slime only lasts for an hour or so."

"No, the slime from Suko and Keno lasts for at least three hours, sometimes longer," Mili replies.

"How is that possible? They captured me an hour ago, I think."

"Well maybe for you it doesn't last as long, but you've been in this cell for five hours."

"What are you talking about? They just threw me in here about an hour ago."

She shakes her head no. "I'm sorry, but it's true. You were in a daze when they first threw you in here. It frightened me so I stayed in the corner because I didn't know what else to do. It's like the moment they brought you to the cell, you literally froze and stayed absolutely still until just a few minutes ago when you started laughing and crying. You pulled your hair out and screamed a lot," Mili explains.

"I guess I didn't know I was capable of blacking out like that. If what you're saying is true, then I'm doomed. If my mind is that easily broken then what kind of tricks will the Beast use to keep me here?" Amelia says.

"Don't worry. I don't think he'll harm you."

"Why would you say that?"

"The Beast thrives on souls. But you have something far more precious…purity. Purity makes him more powerful, so you would be his secret weapon. He'll want to keep you alive to help him," she assures.

"How do you know I'm pure? Is it so obvious that even weird creatures can sense it?" She thinks about Roki, who also knew she was pure. She wonders again, *How could his own father kill him like that, like he was nothing?*

"More or less, but you have an aura that we can all see. It's a purple glow."

"Purple? You must be kidding. Obviously you've been in this cell way too long."

Mili scoots closer and holds out her hand to touch Amelia's arm but quickly draws back. "Oh no! We have to get you out of here!" she shouts.

"Why did you pull away from me? Everyone who tries to touch me pulls away. Am I poisonous?"

Mili scoots further back from her and stares.

"Mili what is it?"

"You can beat him. You're the one we've been waiting for. You have the gift. That's why they kept you alive; he's been waiting for you so that he can kill you. I was wrong. It's more than just purity with you. You're powerful! He's going to kill you before you can kill him," she explains.

"What?!"

"No one can kill the Beast, but you can. Don't you see?"

"No! I don't see anything and I just want to get out of here! I have to find Aaron before it's too late!"

"Aaron is fine, they're keeping him very happy, but he misses you," Mili assures.

"How do you know? What are you?"

"I'm just a girl, but I can see the present. I can see him, he's cute." She giggles.

"Mili, are you telling me that you are psychic?"

"Whatever you want to call it, but I have an ability of seeing everything without actually being there. I can also feel what people want to know without them asking."

"Okay so how do you know what Aaron looks like? I mean there are a million of them out there," Amelia snipes.

"Because I can see what you want to know. Each person is different. Your Aaron has curly black locks and bright green eyes," Mili says.

"Oh my God, I miss him so much," Amelia cries.

"I know you do. Don't cry Amelia, he's still alive, but very far away and heavily guarded. He's waiting for you."

"So why are you here in this cell? Are you pure too?"

"I'm not pure because the Beast fooled me into working with him. Once you take his powers or work with him, you're tainted forever. At least until we all are set free from this place."

"So is seeing the present a power he gave you?"

"No, I was born seeing everything. He sensed my gift when I wandered through here. I was killed by my mother when I was ten. She got tired of all of the constant negative attention of having "a freak for a daughter" as she put it. She was schizophrenic and went through many bad episodes. My father wanted to take me away from her but she refused to let me go and always kept me locked in my room. When the judge finally gave him custody, she ran into my room and shot me in the chest."

"I can't believe that. I'm sorry Mili. I don't understand why people are so cruel to their own kids. I just don't get it."

"Well, I knew it was coming. I saw her get the gun from a neighbor. She came back into the house, took a drink, and walked into my room."

"Why didn't you run? I mean if you saw her get a gun, then you should have taken off."

"At the time I believed what everyone said about me, that I was an accident and a possessed child. They said that I was a joke and that I should be put away. My mother always told me that I made her sick. She used to tell me over and over that she wished I was normal. I didn't want to live anymore so I chose to put her out of her misery and let her do whatever she wanted. When she entered my room, she didn't hesitate. For the first time in my life I felt free. I was happy to get away from the horrible life I knew. But the problem was, my father showed up just as I fell to the floor."

"That's horrible."

"My mother was shocked that he was there and turned the gun on him. She knew he would kill her so she shot him in the head."

"Oh my! You saw all that?"

Mili nods her head yes.

"Is that why you wandered into this world? You couldn't rest?"

"Yes, I was looking for my father when the Beast got a hold of me first. I've been here ever since…trapped," she murmurs, obviously forlorn.

"Did the Beast tell you to capture souls for him?"

"No, he told me he would help me find my father if I agreed to tell him when another soul was coming. I was his eyes. That's why no one can hide from him. They come to me and ask where the people are. He wanted my powers instead of the other way around, but nonetheless, I agreed to help him and the rest is history."

"Do you know if your father is here?"

"Yes, he is. But I have yet to make it out of this cell. They keep me here locked away for their personal gain…just like when I was alive," she cries. "You know, death is supposed to be better than this." She rubs her nose and wipes her eyes.

"We have to figure out a way to get out, Mili. I will help you somehow. By the way, did you tell them where to find me?"

"No. I couldn't see you. You are the only person in the many years I've been here that I haven't been able to see."

"Well that ugly dog sure found me quickly enough," Amelia grunts.

"Yes Stylot can see and smell everything, but the Beast cloned my powers and gave it to Stylot just in case they couldn't get to me in time."

Poor Mili; what a disaster! I need to try and help her and the others. I can't fathom leaving them here for eternity under the command of a demon. But doing so seems impossible when she doesn't have the resources…or does she? *Mili did say I am powerful. I wish someone would send me a sign.*

The thought of Aaron somewhere out there makes her depressed that she's not with him. *What if I don't make it out alive?* The way they fell in love was such a gift—one she will treasure forever. *I wonder, is my purity just a coincidence, or is it my destiny?* She thought of all those times she tried to make love to him, but it never happened. *Is being here some foretold prophecy that must be fulfilled? This is torture. How long will he be okay?* Nevertheless, she knew she couldn't leave without trying to help these people.

"Amelia, he's okay you know," Mili assures her.

Amelia breaks away from her thoughts, realizing that Mili can sense her feelings. "But for how long?"

Mili shrugs her shoulders, but is obviously concerned. "Try to focus on getting out of here before the Beast comes. I'm sure Keno and Suko are telling him who you are," she declares.

"So what exactly do you think I am?" Amelia asks.

"If you don't see it? I can't tell you. You have to *see* Amelia."

Amelia scratches her forehead, confused. She doesn't know whether to scream or cry. She leans backwards against the wall and ponders how to get them out of the cell. She wonders if playing dead will work.

"I can feel you starting to worry again, try not to let it consume you."

"It's hard not to. I have no idea what I'm doing, and if I'm so powerful, how come no one is running for the hills when they come near me?" Amelia snaps, then rolls her eyes.

"I don't know. I don't have all the answers. I just know that you are more powerful than you think."

Amelia shakes her head in disbelief and lets out a long sigh. "I ran into a girl named Carys and she told me that the sky changes colors and when it turns black that means they're near."

"Yes but the sky stays the same where we are. Only in *Hues Pond* will it change throughout the day. I remember seeing the colorful sky in passing when the Beast was after me," Mili whispers.

"So we have no way of knowing when they're near?"

"I can see the present, remember?" Mili laughs.

"Oh that's right! Well, do you see anyone coming?"

Mili looks straight ahead as if she's in a trance. Her eyes are moving quickly as she searches for enemies. The suspense is driving Amelia nuts as she bites her nails. She stares through the cell bars, hoping that wherever Aaron is, he's thinking about her. What she wouldn't give for his warm hands to touch her face again and then feel his soft lips on hers.

"They're near!" Mili screams. She slides back into the corner and hides in the darkness. A beetle guard stomps towards the cell and stares at Amelia with its mouth open. Amelia slowly scoots back into the dark and stays very still. She looks over at Mili who is practically invisible in her corner and then glares back at the creature. *What does he want? I'm sure the Beast wouldn't approve of this.*

Slime falls from the beetle's mouth as he takes out his keys.

"Mili, when he opens the door we need to run," Amelia whispers. Mili shakes her head no.

"It's our only shot at getting out of here. Trust me."

Mili finally crawls a little closer to her and braces herself.

"What do you want?" Amelia screams, although she can tell by the way he's looking at her that he wants to eat her. Without saying a word, the beetle looks around and unlocks the cell. Amelia's legs are trembling, but she's hoping they won't give out on her when she needs them the most. "Get ready." she whispers to Mili. The anticipation is getting the best of her but she has to get them the hell out of there. *Click!* "Run Mili! Now!" Amelia screams as she kicks the guard out of the way. Mili sprints out of the cell. Amelia leaps up and runs past the guard, but it trips her and forces her to fall into slime.

Mili stops in her tracks and comes back for Amelia. Amelia rises up and wipes the goop from her face. She glides past him when he shouts, "Come back here!"

"He's on our trail Mili! Just keep running!" Amelia yells but it's too late. The guard flies up in the sky and drops down in front of them. Amelia and Mili look at each other, worried.

"What is he going to do with us?" Amelia asks.

He slowly walks towards them, as if he's savoring every moment in defeating their antics. Although he looks like a giant bug, Amelia can tell he has a big grin on his face and she shudders, thinking what's to come. For once she wishes Suko and Keno were there because at least they would stop him, for now. "I'm sorry Mili," Amelia says, tearfully as the guard approaches their fearful bodies. He lets out one last earth shattering roar before he reaches for Amelia's arm. Something hot and electrifying forces her to fly backwards. She quickly stands up and looks around.

"He vanished!" Mili screams.

Chapter Four

"What happened? Where did he go?" Amelia squints to see if her eyes are playing tricks on her.

"He touched your arm and vanished!"

"Is that why no one touches me?" Amelia asks.

"Yes, we can all sense it when we come near you. It actually hurts us to get too close, but I don't think the guard realized it until it was too late. I had no idea you were *this* powerful," Mili says.
"Let's get out of here before the other guards come looking for him. Mili I need you to see if someone is coming."

She quickly goes into another trance, but it's too late. Two guards are approaching them with angry eyes.

"Get them!" One screams.

"Stay put Mili."

"Stay put? That's your brilliant plan? They'll eat us alive!"

"Trust me. I wouldn't steer you wrong." For once, Amelia feels powerful and brave enough to at least defeat the guards. From what she can tell, they don't have any special powers that will overthrow her, as long as she's fast enough. Mili starts to tremble as they get closer, but Amelia's ready to get this war started. The guards are closing in on them and are moving slowly, and without fear. Their torches are fierce and blazing hot, but Amelia's not afraid. Mr. Wilkers always told her to never show fear. That's one promise she's been trying to keep.

"Your punishment will be death for trying to escape," one says as he moves closer.

"We can't do it without the Beast's permission," the other one replies to him.

"He'll never know. We'll tell him that she killed our brother."

"Okay, if you say so. I just think we should put them back in the cell."

Are they seriously arguing in front of us? These things aren't too bright, but I guess they don't have to be.

"What are your names?" Amelia interrupts, stepping closer. She looks back at a frightened Mili, whose close behind her.

"Why do you ask girl?"

"I just want to know."

They look at each other and converse back and forth in their own language. "I'm Brug and this is Dran. For someone's who's about to die, you're very inquisitive," Brug roars.

Dran kicks Amelia down and takes Mili's arm. She snatches away as Amelia gets to her feet, all the while ignoring the incredibly hot torches that could smoke her within seconds. She guards Mili and gets in a crouching stance.

"Well my name is Amelia. I think it's only fair to formally meet the person that's going to send you back to hell."

"What!" Brug shouts. With one touch, the guards have instantly vanished from this world—sent to another. All that's left is a dark cloud of smoke.

"Wow! You are so cool!" Mili shrieks, then smiles at her. "Do you understand the damage you could do to this place? The Beast won't stand a chance," she continues.

"Ha Ha! I feel pretty dominant right about now." Amelia can't believe that she's killed three guards within a matter of seconds. Surprisingly, she's less afraid and wonders if *she's* like the Beast. Carys told her, "the more souls he keeps the more powerful he becomes." With her newfound powers, Amelia is beginning to recognize that the more she kills, the more invincible she is. *Maybe I really can do some serious damage here.* "Come on, let's get out of here."

She searches through the worm infested ground for the keys that the guard dropped. When she finds the keys she rushes to the gate to unlock the castle. She's frantic as she anticipates a herd of guards coming towards them. When she opens the castle door, a huge rush of wind almost knocks them down. With her adrenaline surging, Amelia runs into darkness with Mili trailing behind. "Mili, are you close?"

"Yes, I'm right behind you. It feels so strange to be out of the cell. I can't thank you enough for getting me out of there," she pants.

"Don't thank me just yet, we could still run into trouble." She loathes running in the dark with no idea of where she's going. This moment is all too familiar as it reminds her of the dreams she had about Roland. She slows down and follows the torches on the walls. When they reach the front gate, she braces herself and pushes it open, remembering that there were two guards standing there when Keno and Suko brought her inside. "Mili, do you think the two guards I just killed were the ones standing at this gate?"

"Yes it was them, I saw them," Mili confirms.

"How can you tell them apart? They all look alike to me, like giant beetles."

"I've been here long enough to know the routine and those two guards had green horns."

"Don't they all? I saw them in the dark before I was captured and their horns all looked the same color."

"You can't see it because you don't have the Beasts' powers. It's like a club where the members all have a mark or something that defines them from the others," she explains.

"Ok, well let's hope that we can escape." Amelia walks cautiously through the gate. "No one's here, lets hurry!" she shouts, relieved. They run as fast as possible in hopes of getting far away from the castle. "Just keep going!" Amelia hollers as they scamper into the rain. The warm drops feel good on her skin and it's refreshing to feel normal and clean, if only for a second.

Boom!

They both stop and stare in the direction of the ground shaking blast.

"Mili, I'm sure I don't have to ask..," Amelia begins.

Mili's eyes begin to search for answers. "Run! The Beast is awake and he's just realized I'm gone!" she cries.

Amelia takes off running, envisioning a finish line for her to cross. *Powers or no powers, I'm just not ready to face that thing.* She stops by a large tree trunk to catch her breath.

"How did he find out so quickly? I thought he sleeps most of the day."

"Nothing like this has ever happened before. I think Mortis must have found out somehow because he's the only one who's allowed to wake him."

"What do we do? Where do we go?"

"The only place I can see that's safe is…"

Bark! Bark!

"Hurry Mili! I know that bark, its Stylot!"

"Follow me!" Mili screams. She sprints towards the snowy area.

This is the last place I want to hide, Amelia considers, *but if Mili says so…. I hope she's thought this through because I hate being cold.*

As they sift through the frozen white powder, Amelia thinks about the time when she was a child, playing in the snow with Cash. They built a huge snowman and threw snowballs at each other. She remembers Alexandria coming outside to bring them hot cocoa and warning them to come inside soon. Amelia cried and begged her dad to let her stay out a little longer, even though her face was freezing and she couldn't feel her feet—this time she feels differently about the cold. *I hate this.*

"I can sense that you hate being cold. It's making you angry, but this is a safe place to stay right now. This is the only place where Stylot can't see or smell us," Mili warns her.

"Why is that?" Amelia replies, shivering.

"I don't know what's in the snow, but Mortis comes to me all the time and asks if there are people hiding over here. He knows that Stylot won't find them here unless I tell them."

"Now I wish I had come here the first time I entered this horror show. Instead I walked right into a weird stranger and then I almost got eaten by the Gobblewits."

"The Gobblewits are very pretentious creatures to say the least. They have no mercy or compassion for anyone who trespasses."

"Yeah, I unfortunately found that out the hard way. But one of them did have mercy on me; it actually got him killed," Amelia says.

"Well if you can survive them, then you are definitely a force to be reckoned with."

Stylot's frightening growls are louder and closer.

"Oh no! I thought you said he can't smell us here?"

"He can't, I don't understand what's going on," Mili replies.

"Come on, let's hide behind these trees," Amelia whispers.

They peek from behind a giant tree trunk and spot Stylot going frantically trying to get to something. *What could he possibly be after if he can't smell us?* Out of nowhere, a scared little boy dashes across the road from the rain. He's soaking wet. "Oh no! Mili we have to do something."

"I'm sorry Amelia, but if we leave the snow we may as well ask to
be killed."

"Look at him, he's just a boy. I hope they don't hurt him."

Mortis appears and grabs the boy's arms. "What are you doing
here?!" he roars.

"I, I'm looking for my mommy," he says innocently.

The ground starts to shake and the leaves from the trees fall onto
Amelia and Mili. Amelia's stomach twists around itself and her
lungs barely allow air to pass.

"You know what's coming?" Mili asks.

Amelia nods her head and looks ahead as the beetle guards get into
formation for the Beast. Her legs are starting to tremble and she has
an overwhelming need to curl into a ball. The Beast is too
frightening to look at. She puts her head down and looks at the snow.
She tries to keep Aaron on her mind to get her through the calamity
that's getting ready to take place. *I can't...I won't witness the
slaughter of another innocent soul...someone who by chance
wandered through to find his mother.* She forces her mind to
concentrate on Aaron. *Think of Aaron Amelia. Think of his beautiful
green eyes and his perfect lips that kissed you every day to assure
that you were loved.*

"Help me!" The little boy screams.

Amelia closes her eyes and covers her ears and weeps softly. She
can hear little sniffles coming from Mili, but she can't look at her
right now, or anything else. *Am I ever getting out of here? How can I
destroy this demon? He's untouchable and mean.* She considers that
anyone who can stand to hear the high-pitched squeals from a
defenseless child as he begs for his life, and still be inclined to hurt
him, must mean the Beast is indestructible. *They say, "A man
without fear is a man without hope." What does he have to lose if he
doesn't care about anything?*

"I can't do this. If I'm going to die then so be it! I have had enough
of this crap!" Amelia yells, then begins to sob. Her legs are moving
at an unfamiliar speed, but she doesn't care anymore. *Why should I
sit and hide? No matter what I do, I know the monsters will find us.*

"Amelia! What are you doing?" Mili shouts while running behind
her.

"Don't follow me Mili! I can't keep you safe because I can't even
keep myself safe."

"Yes you can. You just have to have faith in yourself and believe
in your powers," Mili begs.

"Ha! Ha! My powers, that's a laugh. Do you really think I can outsmart Mortis? Or the Beasts for that matter! If you can see an aura around me, then surely they'll see it too. I'm doomed."

"No Amelia, I know you're upset, but we can do this. I believe in you whether you believe in yourself or not. Aaron believes in you too, don't forget about him."

Amelia stops in her tracks and descends in the dirt. Tear drops plummet to the ground, forming small puddles of mud.

"He's all I ever think about Mili. I just want to be with him. I don't want to fight or do anything except find him and get back to our lives. I…I don't know."

"Life isn't easy Amelia. No one ever said it was going to be easy, but at least you have a life to go back to. Once you find Aaron, and you will, it will have been worth it because you will appreciate each other more. You just can't give up."

Amelia knows Mili's right, but it's so hard to deal with everything. "I didn't think it was going to be easy, but this is ridiculous."

"What got into you by the way? Why would you walk directly into fire? Any one of them could have seen you." Mili smirks.

Amelia innocently looks into her eyes and confesses, "I was cold."

"Ha! Ha! You were cold. Geez, well next time give me a warning before you take off like that." She laughs.

Amelia offers a warm apologetic smile.

A tree branch creaks behind them, forcing Amelia to rise up and look around. She hadn't noticed before, but they're in a dark forest with giant watermelons everywhere. "Where are we?"

Mili glances around and sighs, "I know where we are. We have to get out of here and fast!"

"Why?"

"This is where Mortis brings Stylot. The fruits that hang from the trees and the ones on the ground are what he eats to enhance his powers. For some reason, his powers wane after a day, so the Beast created this forest to make sure he stays fortified."

Amelia gives her a curious look.

"It's like how Popeye has to eat his spinach in order to be strong…."

Bark! Rrruff!

"Oh great! I am so sick of that damn evil dog!" Amelia screams.

"Just keep running behind me Amelia!" Mili shouts.

Amelia runs close behind her but the barks are getting closer. She's afraid that this time he's going to catch her for sure. She desperately tries to block out his terrifying growls as they run. She scans her surroundings to get an idea of where they're going, but everything is gross and unfamiliar.

"Ahh!" Amelia screams. She staggers and trips over a giant lady bug. When she stands up, she sees Stylot coming towards her as Mortis trails him. For reasons Amelia can't explain, she is frozen and her legs are immobilized. She looks down and sees a black snake, which has cradled itself around her ankles and is holding her hostage. "Well this just gets better and better," she grunts.

She looks around for Mili, but she is nowhere in sight. *I hope she got away.*

The snake continues to wrap itself around her legs, paralyzing her with fear. Although she's afraid and can't move, she's determined to try and free herself. She bends over and takes her chances by touching the serpent. She wills her mind over the fear, and discovers it wasn't the snake, but the fear that had her paralyzed. Grateful she can move, she runs and hides behind a nearby bush.

Stylot slows when he sees her footprints—a perfect fixture in the thick mud. He sniffs around and starts to bark again.

She stares at her hands in awe of what they're capable of. With one touch that snake was history. *This is so amazing,* she thinks and then she realizes that the barking has stopped. But instead of feeling better, she has a bad feeling. She turns around and there's Stylot, staring right into her eyes.

Grrrr! Bark!

Once again, she is too frightened to move. *Do I get up and run? Or do I stay put?* The four-eyed creature is petrifying up close. She cocks her head and in a strange way, finds it cute—like a mutated Rottweiler. Saliva and fruit residue drips from his mouth. His snowy white canines are as sharp as knives.

"What do you see boy?" Mortis says. Mortis now stands in front of her and Stylot is looking to the side of her but…they can't see her!

How is it possible that I am invisible to Stylot? I know he can smell me.

"Mili if you're here come out right now. Step forth," Mortis says as he walks over to where Amelia's footprints are. Amelia looks, hopeful that Mili can't hear his undeniable command. Something rustles behind a nearby bush. Amelia starts to cry; she knows that no matter how hard Mili fights it, she must do what Mortis demands. Mili appears from the bushes with tears in her eyes.

"No! Mil…" Amelia shouts, but someone puts their hands over her mouth, tightly securing them to her lips. She fights, trying to get away, but someone holds her down and forces her to stay put. She's so scared she can't see straight.

"Come with me," Mortis says to Mili. "Let's go Stylot!" he yells.

Stylot finally trots away, whimpering. He glares back in Amelia's direction with no doubt in his four-eyed mind that someone is there, if only he could see her. The tears flutter down Amelia's face as she sits and watches her little gifted friend being taken away, back to that evil castle. The invisible force that's been holding her and keeping her quiet finally reveals itself cautiously.

"Carys?!" Amelia shouts when she reveals herself.

Carys smiles at Amelia like she's her best friend.

Amelia could never befriend a traitor. Her anger clouds her better judgment and she slaps Carys across the face.

"Ouch!" Carys hollers. She holds her face and sulks. "Did you have to hit me?"

"You had it coming! Do you understand what I've been through, and I'm still no closer to finding Aaron! Maybe this is a game to you, but this is my life you're playing with! I'm sorry that the Beast took your life, but I'm still alive and I'm going to stay alive!" Amelia shouts.

"You're right, I should have been there for you but I'm terrified of him. Whenever he's around I get scared and disappear."

"What do you mean disappear? And how are you able to touch me without vanishing?"

"I will answer all of your questions, but I have to get you out of here before Mortis and Stylot come back. Come on, we'll go back to Hues Pond to see what the sky looks like."

They race through the indefinite rotting smell and unworldly creatures until they make it back to the pond. Amelia never thought she'd be happy to see this place again, but this is the safest and warmest place she's come across since she stumbled upon Bram. They plop down by the water and look around, just in case they find anything unwelcome prowling around. The sky is orange and is slowly getting lighter as time goes on. Without speaking, Amelia scowls at Carys for her cowardly behavior.

"Look, again, I'm sorry for leaving you alone. Technically, you weren't alone because when the sky turned black I disappeared, but I was still there, watching you. I didn't make you disappear because I knew you would freak out and I didn't want the Beast to hear us," Carys explains.

"So what are you?"

"I'm sort of a jack of all trades. You could also say I'm a chameleon."

"Like a lizard?"

Carys smirks. "Not exactly. I can adapt to anything, but mostly, I make myself invisible. I can also see your weakness with one touch. When I first saw you, I touched your hair and saw that Aaron was your weakness. That's why I turned into him. I wanted to make you happy," she admits.

"Wow, now it all makes sense. I just wish Mili wasn't captured, I feel so guilty. You should have made her invisible too."

"I didn't want them to capture you again. If the Beast sees you, I don't even want to think about the outcome."

"Yeah, me neither. I don't know Carys, maybe I can just touch him and he'll vanish like everyone else."

"I don't think it will be that easy Amelia. Believe me, he will know when you're coming. Do you really think he's going to let you get close to him? You're probably the only thing that has the power to kill him, and he knows it."

"Oh right because of my purity?"

"That's part of it, but when he sees you, you will know right away why you have the power to kill him. You're the closest thing to him...you're *his* weakness. I'm sorry I didn't get a chance to tell you all of this before."

"I don't understand. How can I be close to him?"

"It wasn't until I touched your hand for the first time that I realized who you were. That's why I grabbed you and told you that I was taking you to the Crying Forest. I knew at that moment that if he ever laid eyes on you, he would destroy you instantly, before you even had a chance to think about hurting him. And I saw that you desperately needed to be with Aaron. But things have changed since you were able to use your powers. I'm glad you did, because it's easier to explain everything to you now," Carys says.

"So how come you can touch me but no one else can?"

"Long ago, when I finally agreed to accept his powers, he made me a guardian or a secret weapon. He gave me certain powers so that I could outsmart people as they passed through here. I was able to coerce them into doing whatever he wanted. That's why I can tell your weaknesses with one touch and I can disappear. But when Mili came through here, he realized that some people have powers of their own and could outsmart *us*, so he made me immune to anyone else's powers. The disadvantage for the Beast is that he can't make himself immune. When I realized he was never going to let me go, I decided to stop helping him and he's been looking for me ever since. As for Mortis, I haven't been near him so I don't know for certain if I'm immune to his powers."

"Yeah I guess his plan backfired. So how were the Gobblewits able to touch me?"

"They also made a deal with him. If they agreed to help him, he would grant them immunity to all powers as well."

Amelia shakes her head and takes a deep breath. "This is crazy. Is Mortis also immune?"

"No, after I decided to stop helping the Beast, he didn't want to give anyone else the opportunity to turn on him. All he gave Mortis was the power of manipulation, which is a great power in itself."

"So explain to me how I can be his weakness? What about that little boy who wandered over here? I'm sure he was pure, but the Beast killed him," Amelia mumbles. The thought of the event makes her shiver.

"He did it to gain more power. Virgins are at the top of the food chain around here and he doesn't want to give them a chance to be an enemy. But everyone else gets suckered into staying here by accepting his powers. Now there are times when he just wants to be malicious and kill someone for sport, such as that night the sky turned black," she says.

"Do you think he knows I'm here?"

"Yes, he knows now. I'm sure they've been picking Mili's brain at this point. I'd bet he's trying to figure out the best way to overpower you."

"Why is he so wary of me? I'm nobody, just someone who happens to be a virgin and has a strange power that makes monsters vanish."

"Amelia, you still don't get it do you?"

"Get what? Everyone says he's been waiting for me, but I think your powers are far more valuable than *mine*. He should be afraid of *you*," Amelia replies. Carys shakes her head no. Amelia sighs and asks, "What are you not telling me?"

"I shouldn't say. It would only make matters harder for you to deal with. Besides, I know Aaron is your main priority."

"What is it?!"

"You have to figure it out Amelia," she insists.

This is getting on my nerves. What the hell am I supposed to figure out? "All I know is that I'm in this horrible place called Bram and that there's a Beast who keeps souls," Amelia says. *What am I missing?* She ponders all the information she's been given from Mili and from Carys. *I'm the only one who can kill him and I'm his weakness. Mili told me I have to see. But what else is there?*

"The Beast, the Beast from Bram. He has unfinished business and he's been waiting for *me*. I've only heard of one beast in my lifetime and…huh! No! This can't be! Bram is short for Abraham!" Amelia screams. "Carys! Is the Beast my grandfather?"

Chapter Five

"Yes! That is why he's afraid of you. You have a pure heart and you have been untouched. Normally, that would be a great thing for him, but not someone who is a direct descendant. With all of those deadly combinations, that makes *you* more powerful than him. He has no choice but to get rid of you, especially if he wants to continue this tumultuous reign." She rolls her eyes and grits her teeth.

"I have a headache." She starts biting her nails. *All I wanted to do was find Aaron, and now I'm forced to fight a monster.* "Carys, I understand that you and Mili think I can defeat him, but I don't think I have the capabilities to stand up to that creature. How were you even able to look at him before?"

"He doesn't always look like the Beast. When he wants to make a deal to entice you, he transforms into his normal appearance."

"What does he normally look like? I've never seen a picture of him. My parents always said that it was best if I never laid eyes on such an evil soul. I guess the jokes on them."

"Well, he's actually a very handsome man. He was part of the reason why I decided to stay at first because I was drawn into his charisma and good looks. He has short black hair, olive toned skin, and he's very tall. A gal can get lost in his big amber eyes." She stared off in the distance, smiling, remembering better times with him.

Amelia stares at Carys and almost chokes on her own saliva.

"What is it? You've turned pale," Carys says.

"I think I've met him. When I first got here, a man offered to help me find Aaron, but he wouldn't give me his name. I told him I didn't want his help."

Carys gets up slowly, her eyes agape. "You met him? How are you still alive?"

"I don't know, but I knew he was evil and that I had to get away from him. Now it all makes since." She scratches a nagging itch along her forearm and then drives her fingernails through her scalp. The realization of meeting Abraham makes her skin crawl.

"What makes since?" Carys asks.

"After I told him no, I walked away—and I swear, I felt something hot on my back. But by the time I turned back around, he was gone. It's like he was never there."

"Oh no. This isn't good. Trust me, he was going to kill you, and that heat you felt was an attempt on your life. But things changed when he got too close. He knows who you are now and is going to send every creature imaginable after you," Carys whispers. "But Amelia, I have to say, you are the one. *You* can do this."

Part of Amelia has heard enough and just wants to run away to the Crying Forest. She knows they can get her out of there and she's positive that she can overthrow the army that's guarding it. *But...,* she wonders, *I would be forever convicted if I left everyone here to rot in this hell that my own grandfather created. If I ever hear anyone complain about their family again, I'm totally going to lose it, because mine has got theirs beat any day of the week.*

"Can you give me a few minutes alone? I need to think," Amelia says.

"Sure I'll just take a walk around the pond. Just call me when you're ready to talk."

Once Carys is gone, Amelia can't help but think about all the people in her life that she holds dear to her heart. *All the souls he has trapped here are like flies in a spider web.* As she slowly makes her decision, she can't help but weep for them, for Aaron. Her stomach churns at the thoughts of never seeing him again. She harbors thoughts that she prays will never come to pass. She gently rubs the pearl necklace he gave her, remembering the day he slipped it onto her neck and told her he loved her. At such a young age, she was given the gift of meeting the love of her life…her soul mate. This memory softens the realization that if one of them doesn't make it, or if they both die, it was meant for her to experience his love—and holding onto that love—and carrying it with her in this godforsaken place—that's enough to keep her going.

She recalls all those times Aaron denied her advances to make love, and then, the one time they get close, he received the news about his dying mother. *I am so glad we decided to wait,* she admits to herself with surprise, *because that one decision might be the key to saving our lives.* With her mind made up, she looks around for Carys, who has disappeared.

She cautiously walks towards a nearby tree, remaining on guard. *No matter where I go, I run into trouble.* "Carys! Are you here?" she calls out.

Someone taps her on the shoulder but she can't see anyone. Then suddenly, Carys appears right in front of her.

"Ha! Ha! Very funny," Amelia smirks.

Carys laughs but then her smile turns into a grimace.

"What is it?" Amelia asks.

"The sky is turning red. Remember, I told you that when it's red, all his guards are awake."

"Yeah but I'm not afraid of them anymore. I mean, they look scary, but I can kill them."

"Oh, well it must be nice to no longer live in fear," Carys jokes.

"Trust me, I'm scared out of my mind, but at least I know I have something going for me."

"Just be careful. They can overpower you in large numbers."

"I agree. So how can we defeat this Beast, aka my grandfather?"

Carys's face lights up. "So you'll help us?"

"Absolutely! I mean all I can do is try, right? Besides, if my own flesh and blood is responsible for all of this, I feel like it's my obligation to stop him. It was no accident that I came into this world, just like it's going to be no accident when I take him out."

"This is so great! I'm going to go see if the coast is clear. I have to make sure there are no guards coming. Stay put," Carys advises.

"Okay, I'll be right here."

Amelia watches Carys fade away into nothing, thinking, *She's pretty remarkable. Why couldn't I have gotten that gift when Leona was taking over my life?* She quietly sits under a tree to gather her thoughts. As Carys's invisible footsteps move away from her, she tries not to talk herself out of what she just promised. *I hope I didn't just commit to a death sentence. Either way, I have to give it my all.*

"How can I defeat him?" she whispers, biting her nails. *I still can't believe that the Beast is my grandfather. How is all this even possible?* Tears arise when she thinks about her dad being raised by him and how Abraham has managed to create an insane version of hell. After witnessing all of this, nothing surprises her anymore. *First, I'll rescue Mili with the advantage of Carys's help.* She hopes that Carys's powers alone can really take them far as she ponders her moves. "I got it!" Amelia shouts. "I know what to do!" She jumps up and runs to find Carys. "Carys! I know how to…no way…" *Is this an illusion or a favor from God?*

"Amelia! Are you here?" He shouts. He looks back and forth, searching for her.

Amelia rubs her eyes and stares at him as if this is the first time she's ever laid eyes on him. He's even more beautiful than before. *Is it possible that he was able to break free?* She wonders. She steps closer to him without caring about the consequences of her dangerous actions. She leaves the pond and heads right for him as he walks into a nearby garden, searching for someone…for her.

"Aaron? Is that you?" she asks the stranger whose back is to her. She hopes it's him because her heart can't take it.

He slowly turns around and runs his fingers through his curly, black locks. When their eyes meet, everything around them stops. She jumps into his arms and wraps her entire body around him, kissing every inch of his face. She stares into his green eyes again and passionately kisses his soft, delicious lips.

"It's really you! I thought I would never see you again," she cries.

"Don't cry. Everything is going to be okay now. We're together and that's all that matters," he whispers.

"Aaron, I was trying to get to you but so many horrible things have happened that I thought it was over. How did you escape? I was told that you were being held somewhere far away."

"I'll fill you in on all that later. Right now I just want to hold you and never let you go," he replies and swings her around. They embrace in another kiss and walk away hand in hand, entering deep into the garden.

"Why don't we sit down over by the water?" he suggests. She leans up against a tree and relaxes while he rubs her feet. Everything seems to have a different light. Suddenly, she's no longer bothered by anything. With him by her side, she knows they can escape and defeat the Beast.

"Oh no!" Amelia shouts.

"What is it?"

"Carys!" She jumps to her feet. "I have to find her. She's probably searching for me."

"No, it's too dangerous, why don't we stay here and go find her later. I mean we just found each other. I'm sure she can find you with her powers," he assures.

"I guess you're right. I have so much to tell you Aaron. First, let me start off by saying I love you so much. You know that right?"

"Of course, I love you too?" he replies while caressing her hair.

"I just can't believe you found me. I'm so happy you're here with me. We have a lot to do."

"How so?"

"Well, there is no easy way to tell you this but…" Aaron quickly kisses her on the lips, forcing his tongue into her mouth. She pulls away and asks, "How am I supposed to explain things with you kissing me like this?"

"I'm sorry; I just want to be with you. Amelia, I have something to ask you?"

"What is it? Is everything okay? You're acting a little weird."

"Yes I'm fine. I just missed you is all. What I want to ask you is…would it be alright if we made love? I don't want to wait any longer."

"Um, Aaron we decided that we wanted to wait, remember?"

"Yes, but don't you think this changes things. I mean, we're in another world now and I don't want to put it off any longer," he urges.

She studies his face and whispers, "I know Aaron but…"

"Please, let's just be together. I love you so much Amelia." He kisses both of her cheeks and covers her lips with his before she can respond. His lips feel so good that it's hard for her body to deny him of whatever he wants.

"Wait Aaron. My purity is the only reason that I'm still alive and I can't just let it go now. There are people who are counting on me to get them out of here," she explains.

"We can help them together, and I'm sure your purity is not the only reason why you're still alive," he declares.

"I know it must sound crazy, but I think it's true. With one touch I was able to kill some of the guards and who knows what else. I have to help them. Will you help me?"

He puts his head down with disappointment. She doesn't want to hurt him by denying his request, but she knows that putting her desires ahead of everyone else would be detrimental. Her answer had obviously upset him. *Maybe I should just give in.*

"Amelia! Where are you?" Carys shouts.

"Oh that's Carys! I want you to meet her." Amelia runs off.

"Amelia wait!" Aaron yells.

"It's okay Aaron. I'll be right back." She runs out of the garden and into the path.

"Carys! I'm over here!"

"You can't just take off like that. I thought you were captured again." Carys sighs and puts her hands on her hips.

"I'm sorry, but you'll never guess what happened."

"What's got you so excited?"

"Aaron's here! He found me! Isn't that great? He's over in the garden. Come on, I want you to meet him," Amelia says, pulling Carys's hand.

They move quickly but cautiously.

"Aaron, where are you?" She looks around the trees and over by the water. "That's weird. He was just here a second ago." She walks to the other side of the garden and around some bushes, praying that he didn't get captured, or worse.

"I'll go around to the front to see if he's there!" Carys shouts.

"Okay thanks!" Amelia hollers back. "Aaron! Where are you?"

"I'm over by the giant strawberries!" he finally shouts.

She runs over to him and jumps into his arms. "I still can't believe this has happened," she shrieks.

"Me neither, I can't wait to be with you."

Amelia sits next to a freakishly large strawberry and droops her head, dejected. He sits down and she faces him and takes his hand. "Aaron, I will make love to you, over and over again, but first I have to help the people here. The Beast has held them hostage for all these years. It's just not fair to them."

"I'm sorry Amelia, but I don't see him!" Carys shouts.

"Oh! We're over here Carys, I found him!" Amelia replies. She snuggles up next to him while Carys comes from behind a row of tall green bushes.

"Carys, I would like to introduce you to Aaron."

Carys takes one look at Aaron and stops in her tracks, shocked. She stares at Amelia, trying to convey her concern.

Amelia looks at Aaron and notices that he's very uncomfortable and doesn't look into her eyes. "Is everything okay? I feel like something is kind of weird," Amelia says.

"Oh no, everything is just fine. Carys, it's very nice to meet you," Aaron says.

Carys continues to stand at a small distance, dumbfounded.

"Carys!" Amelia grunts. *She's being really rude.*

"Oh! I'm sorry, its' very nice to meet you Aaron." Carys stays where she is.

What is going on with her? "I was just telling Aaron about the Beast and how he's been capturing souls for a long time. I thought of a great way to overpower him. You are going to love it. I don't know why we didn't think of it sooner," Amelia explains.

Carys finally takes her eyes off Aaron and forces herself to say, "What's your plan?"

"Well…I was thinking that we could outsmart him. It's definitely going to take both of us." While trying to explain her plan, she notices that Carys's mind is clearly elsewhere and wonders if she has a crush on Aaron. "So I was thinking that we could bury you in the garden," Amelia says sarcastically.

"That sounds great. Wait! What?"

"I was just checking to see if you were listening. Obviously you weren't. So would you like to tell me what's going on?" Amelia snaps.

Carys slowly walks over to Amelia and whispers, "I'm sorry Amelia, but are you okay with this? I mean, aren't you upset?"

"Upset about what? I'm the happiest I've been in a very long time. What I can't seem to figure out is *your* strange behavior."

Carys looks over at Aaron who has been quiet the entire time and says, "Aren't you going to tell her. She was so worried about you."

"Why don't you just stay out of this and mind your own business," Aaron barks.

Amelia turns to Aaron and stares at him, suspiciously. "Aaron, what is she talking about?"

"I don't know, but I want you to stay away from her. Let's go!" he yells. He grabs Amelia's hand.

"Wait a minute! Carys is my friend and she saved my life. I can't just leave her!"

Without listening to her protest, Aaron continues dragging her behind him like he's pulling a sled.

"Aaron! Will you let me go?" Amelia yells. *He's never treated me like this. What is he afraid of?* "Okay just stop!" Amelia shouts as she snatches her hand away. "What's going on?"

He turns to her and bows his head.

"Well? Are you going to tell me?" she demands, frustrated.
He looks into her eyes and opens his mouth, but nothing comes out.

"He's dead Amelia," Carys says with her arms crossed.

A sharp pain pierces Amelia's heart and her head feels heavy. She turns to Carys as her tears flow down her cheeks. "Carys, don't you ever say that to me again. He's not dead, he's as alive as I am."

"Amelia, I am so sorry, but I can't hear his heart beating. Touch his chest," she whispers with sadness.

Amelia looks into his beautiful green eyes and shakes her head in disbelief. With a trembling hand she slowly touches his chest. "No!" she screams. She turns and puts her hands over her face.

"Shh, Amelia please don't cry," Carys pleads.

Amelia is completely consumed with grief. Her worst fears have come true before her eyes and at this moment, nothing else matters to her. Everything she has told herself is moot and what she's done thus far is pointless. The only thing she knows to do is cry.

Carys puts her hand on Amelia's shoulder to comfort her, but Amelia is inconsolable. Aaron's death has cut her to the core. *There is nothing left to fight for.*

"This is your fault!" Amelia shouts through moans. She jumps up and pushes Carys out of her way. She walks out into the dangerous path, feeling she has nothing left to lose. "Why did you have to tell me that he's dead? I was so happy, and you took that away from me!" Amelia cries.

"I'm sorry, but I thought you should know the truth," Carys replies. She is following closely behind.

Aaron catches up to Amelia and grabs her arm. "I'm sorry. Please don't be mad."

"Aaron, I'm not mad at you, it's not your fault," she says and she kisses his hand. "Is this why you wanted to make love?"

He looks down and says, "Well..."

"It's okay; you don't have to answer me. I will make love to you Aaron. If you're dead, then I have no more reason to fight to stay alive. I want to be with you, now," Amelia declares.

"Amelia, please think this through. Do you really want to give up your powers?" Carys implores her. She turns to Aaron and yells, "Is that what you want for her?"

Aaron's face hardens and he grimaces at her. "Amelia can make her own decisions. Now leave us alone," he grunts. He takes Amelia's hand and leads her back into the garden.

Amelia looks back at a devastated Carys and sighs, remembering what she promised her. But she doesn't have the will any longer. *I just want to be with Aaron and if I have to stay here with him then so be it*. She sits down under a tree near the water and her eyes again fill with tears.

Aaron sits down next to her and takes her hand.

"Aaron I'm so sorry that you died. I tried desperately to get out of here so that I could find you," she sobs.

"Amelia, it's not your fault," he says and kisses her cheek. "I love you so much," he continues as he lays her down in the grass. He gets on top of her and kisses her fervently. While caressing her neck he looks into her eyes.

"I missed those green eyes more than you could ever know. I love you too," Amelia says as she kisses him again. She runs her fingers through his hair as he moves his lips to her neck. Suddenly, he sits up and smacks his teeth. "Aaron, what's wrong?"

"I can't do this." He stands up, angrily and looks away.

"Is this about Carys? Don't let her get to you. I want to be with you, in every way."

"It's not about that. I—I'm not Aaron."

Chapter Six

"Are you serious? You don't have to make excuses to save me from heartache. Aaron, I want to be with you whether you're dead or alive, as weird as that sounds."

"You're not listening to me! I'm someone else! My name is Langston Monroe."

Why is he doing this? What does he have to gain from breaking my heart any more than it's already been broken?

He takes her hand. "Amelia, I am beyond sorry for the pain I've caused you. I can see that you're a good person and you don't deserve this torture. They wanted me go along with this plan, but I can't do it. Why do you have to be so damn nice?" He punches a tree stump in frustration.

"Okay, so if you're not Aaron, then explain to me what you're doing and what you want from me?"

He paces and she can see that he's terrified of something. He sighs and clasps his hands together. "I've been here in Bram for quite a while and I've been working for Mortis," he says.

Amelia is shocked. *He really isn't Aaron. Aaron wouldn't know anything about Mortis.* She rises slowly and backs away from the impostor.

He strolls towards the water and transforms before her eyes.

"You're really not Aaron! Get away from me!" she screams. She runs towards the pond. "Carys! Help me!"

"Please Amelia! I'm sorry but you have to understand why I did it!" He runs to catch up to her. "They promised me that if I went along with this plan, then I would be rewarded."

Amelia faces him and glares into his fraudulent eyes. "Reward?
You did all this just for a reward? You were going to sleep with me!
You bastard!" She grits her teeth and kicks him in his shin, forcing
him to his knees; then she kicks him in the nose.

He groans in agony and rubs his face.

"How could you make me believe you were him? Why would you
do that?" She cries.

"I suppose I deserved that. But you have no idea how long I've
been here. I just want to get my family and leave."

"Your family?"

"Yes. You see, the Beast and Mortis told me that if I get you to
have sex with me and take away your purity, then I could be reunited
with my daughter, Milena. I know she's here because I can feel her. I
also think they've been keeping her away from me so that they can
use me." He wipes his bloody nose on his shirt, which leaves a red
smudge; he rubs his shin.

"So the Beast knows that I'm here? Carys told me that he knew,
but I want to be certain."

He nods.

Amelia paces, trying to figure out what she's going to do. "That
son of a..."

"Amelia! It's Carys, are you okay?" She yells from afar.

"Yes, I'm over here by the bushes!"

Carys appears and pauses with her mouth open.

"What did I miss?" Carys asks, stepping closer.

"Well um, Langston, would you like to reintroduce yourself, or
shall I do the honors?" Amelia sneers.

He slowly rises to his feet and looks down with shame. "My name
is Langston Monroe and I was working for the Beast. I must admit,
you almost blew my cover."

Carys moves slowly towards Amelia while maintaining her gaze
on the good-looking stranger. "I knew something wasn't right about
you but I had no idea," she declares.

"Yes, well neither did I. Apparently, he made a deal with the Beast
to seduce me into giving up my purity so that my powers would go
away."

Langston's face hardens and he rolls his eyes.

Amelia has no empathy for him, but she chastises herself for
almost sleeping with a complete stranger. *I'm such an idiot. Why
couldn't I figure out he wasn't really Aaron? What happened to all
of my instincts? Carys took one look at him and knew that something*

wasn't right. On the bright side, she's thankful that he had an ounce of morals left in him, before she submitted to the calamity and ruined everything.

"Wait a minute, how did you know what Aaron looks like?" Carys asks him.

"I didn't know. Once I agreed to go along with the plan, they transformed me into the Aaron you knew," he replies while pointing to Amelia.

Carys shakes her head at him. "You should have known better than to make a deal with them," she snaps.

"Look I'm sorry, but I was desperate to find my baby girl. And you have no right to judge me. You're here just like I am. What deal did you make with him?"

"This isn't about me! At least I wasn't about to seduce an innocent girl," she roars and jabs her finger in his face.

"Guys please! Let's just figure out what to do next," Amelia interrupts.

Carys takes Amelia's hand and looks at her in shock. "Amelia, you are not to blame yourself for this moron's actions. I can feel your suffering and you shouldn't do that to yourself."

"I know, but it doesn't hurt any less."

"You know, I think you should look at the big picture here."

"What's that?"

"Aaron is still alive. Don't you see? He was never here, so that means he's still waiting for you. And, another great thing is that you still have your powers. You didn't sleep with this fool so that means that we can go back to figuring out our next plan."

"You know what Carys? You're right. Aaron *is* still waiting for me and I know he loves me. We all have to get out of here."

"So what should we do? Please help me find my daughter," Langston pleads.

"I bet once we rescue Mili, she'll be able to tell us where to find her," Amelia says.

"Mili? That's my daughter! Have you seen her?" he cries.

"Mili is your daughter?" Amelia is shocked.

"Yes! Mili is short for Milena. Her mother shot her in the chest just as I showed up to get her. But I was too late. Then, her mother turned the gun on me. I've been searching for her this whole time, for years, but the Beast got a hold of me and has been lying to me ever since."

"We should have known. They must have asked her what Aaron looked like. She's the only one who's seen him. Langston, Mili is an exceptional little girl. She helped me escape from the castle with her powers. You're very lucky to have her as a daughter. She's been looking for you too."

"Thank you. You know you're pretty exceptional yourself. Aaron is a lucky guy."

She smiles, thinking about how Aaron saved her from a lot of abuse. "No, I'm the lucky one. Anyway, I think we should all work together and do it with haste. If he knows I'm here, then we have to be very careful and we can't afford to make any mistakes. First thing we need to do is rescue Mili. Now Langston, Carys can make us invisible with one touch and I can kill them with one touch. Do you have any powers of your own?"

"I don't think so. I think once I went back on the plan, my powers went away."

"One way to test the theory is for you to try to touch my hand."

"Be careful," Carys urges.

Amelia walks closer to him and holds out her arm. He proceeds to touch her with caution.

"Ahh!" he shouts, drawing back. "Amazing! It felt like I was lowering my hand over an open flame."

"Okay then. If I touch you, you'll vanish, so steer clear of me," Amelia advises. He warily nods his head. "Carys it's your turn. See if you can make him invisible."

Amelia is ready to get this battle started. *To think that my grandfather tried to get a stranger to seduce me can only mean that he's pretty desperate and afraid, which is good news.* Now she knows without a doubt that she has the power to kill him. Without realizing it, her friends have vanished into thin air. She smiles. "Yes! This is great!"

Langston and Carys slowly reappear with huge grins on their faces. But their delight is short-lived when a dark overcast spreads across the sky, meaning that the Beast is awake. They nod in unison and start walking towards a dark path. She's nervous and worried that the beast and his minions are torturing Mili and forcing her to tell them where the three are.

They probably don't know about our invisibility. "Carys, you get in between me and Langston so that we can all be invisible at once?" They stroll in the darkness until they're out of the pond and immersed inside the gloomy road. As they embark on the long journey towards the castle, they run into a huge nest of large bees.

"That was close," Amelia says while swatting away the last of the angry insects. "Carys, remember when I almost died after falling into that hole? I swear that bee was just waiting to put an end to my crazy life."

"Yeah, that was something. Until I turned into that giant wasp and ripped its little heart out," Carys reminisces.

Amelia stops and releases Carys's hand where they all reappear. "*You* were the giant wasp? You can turn into wasps too? What else are you keeping from me?"

"I told you I could adapt. Have you forgotten how we met? Besides, why would I tell you everything?"

"Why wouldn't you?"

"Because, I didn't think it was relevant. But now you know, I can turn into giant insects—big deal. Besides, it takes a lot of concentration and resolve for me to do that. It's not like turning invisible, which takes no effort at all. He only gave me that power in case a giant thing tried to eat me," she explains.

"You mean a giant thing like him?" Amelia yells. "Carys, you could have turned into a massive locust and ate his beastly eyes out!"

"Gross! Those annoyingly loud bugs? Never! That's why I didn't want to tell you. I knew you would say something like that and make me feel like a coward. Well you know what, fine. I'll be that. I'm scared to go near him!"

"Look, I'm sorry for going off like that, but I just feel like maybe you could've stopped him. You've turned into Aaron before, which means you can do anything you want. You could've done some major damage and ended this. He should be afraid *you*."

Carys sulks with her arms crossed and says, "And by the way, Locusts eat plants not eyes."

"Whatever!" Amelia grabs her arm and they become invisible again.

"Way to go Carys," Langston utters.

"You shut up before I eat *your* eyes out!" she yells.

Amelia looks over and notices that only Langston is visible.

"Carys! Please grab his arm. That's not cool."

"Fine, but he had better stay on my good side or I will purposely shove him into the nearest bat cave!" Amelia watches as he slowly fades again.

"Let's just not talk until we get to the castle," Amelia sighs.

"Fine with me," they both reply instantly.

After quite a bit of walking, they finally make it to the outer surroundings of the castle. Amelia starts to perspire. She had no idea of the amount of horror and anxiousness that has stayed with her as they walk up the gloomy hill. Her heart is racing and her legs start to wobble. She recollects how scared she felt when Keno and Suko carried her paralyzed body into the darkness. Then, the way she lost control of her mind only heightens her anxiety, forcing her to stop. *I can't go any further?*

"Amelia! What are you doing?" Carys whispers.

"I—I can't go inside the castle guys. I'm sorry, but its bringing back some terrifying memories that I can't shake."

"I understand, why don't you get rid of the two guards at the gate and Langston and I will find Mili."

The way they threw me in that cell, I can't go in. Amelia ponders.

"Amelia? Hello?" Carys says.

Amelia snaps out of her daze and replies, "Yeah, sure I'll just wait out here."

The three of them silently approach the guards and stop. One of the guards looks from side to side but can't see them.

"Okay Amelia, now is the time," Carys whispers.

With limbs trembling, they step closer. Amelia pats herself on the back for getting this close to the beetles because she really wants to scream at the top of her lungs. Carys slowly lets go of her arm and Amelia appears. Both guards jump back in astonishment.

"It's her! Get her!" They scream. As they reach for her, Amelia holds out both of her shaky hands. Within seconds, the guards vanish. She takes a long, deep breath and sits down on the stone-lined steps.

"Okay guys, hurry up. I'm not sure how long I'll be able to sit here," Amelia warns.

Without reappearing, their footsteps go inside the gate. As the gate slams shut, Amelia springs up. *If anything happens to them…no, think positive.* They're just innocent bystanders who happened to wander through and it wouldn't be fair for them to lose their souls so that *he* can live. Amelia doesn't have the mental capabilities of being alone and she's finding it difficult to keep it together. The more she sits there in fear, the more worried she becomes.

"Ow! Amelia!" Carys screams. Without thinking, Amelia rushes inside the castle and follows the echoes of the howling screams.

"Carys! Where are you?"

"We're around the corner to your left! Follow the torches on the wall!"

I can't believe I'm back inside this damn castle. I distinctly remember telling them that I had no intentions of coming back inside. "I don't see anything! How could you two do this to me? I didn't want to come back inside this dungeon and the moment you run into trouble, I'm forced back in!" Amelia yells.

"Well, we're sorry! Think of it as therapy!" Carys shouts.

"Thanks Doctor Carys! What would I do without you?" Amelia hollers as she rushes to find them.

"Hurry Amelia!" They scream.

She runs towards the end of the passageway and stops, realizing that none of this looks familiar. *Is this another way out?* Although she can't see them, she can tell they're standing near her because she can hear them breathing. She looks up ahead into the dim hallway and stifles a scream.

"Carys? Is that what I think it is?" Amelia whispers.

"I'm afraid so," she replies.

At the end of the long hallway, lies a giant tarantula, guarding the back door.

It's black fuzzy hairs and slime infested fangs send Amelia into a paralyzing state of shock. "Go ahead Langston, you're a guy. Take care of it," Amelia whispers.

"You can't be serious. That thing is three times my size."

"It's just a little spider."

"A little spider? Look, I'm not going near that thing. If it takes away my man points then so be it!" he gripes.

Carys and Amelia bursts out laughing.

"I was just kidding. You can keep your man points." Amelia laughs. "Carys, you're going to have to make me invisible so that I can sneak up on it."

"I don't think that's going to work. I think it senses our presence, it doesn't have to see us," she explains.

"What? So how do we get out of here? We can't just leave. Let's just try," Amelia sighs.

The three skulk towards the huge spider; it jumps back as it climbs down from the door and creeps towards them.

"See, I told you," Carys says.

The arachnids crawls in their direction and makes a startling screech, they brace themselves.

"That didn't go well. Since it knows we're here, there is no reason why we need to stay invisible. We're going to have to do it the hard way," Amelia declares.

They reappear.

"I don't like this," Langston utters while shaking his head.

"What do you mean the hard way?" Carys asks.

"Langston, I really need your assistance. You're going to have to be brave," Amelia whispers.

"Oh hell, what do I have to do?"

"I need you both to run in the direction of the spider. That way, it will be caught off guard and won't know which one of you to grab first. Carys, you need to be invisible when you're running and head straight for the back door."

"So what will *you* do?" Langston asks.

"Once I see that it's busy with you two, I'll run up and kill it." The tarantula starts crawling closer to them, forcing them backwards.

"Guys, on the count of three," Amelia murmurs. "One, two, three!" she shouts.

They run towards the giant monster. Amelia can only see Langston, but knows Carys is aiming for the door. A rush of adrenaline ignites inside Amelia as she readies to kill it. Langston rises in the air and is engulfed within the legs. Amelia listens for Carys to make sure she's safe. The back door bursts open and the spider scurries in that direction with Langston still in its grasp.

"Okay, I think its busy now!" Langston screams, agitated. Amelia runs at full speed and leaps up just in time for it to spit silk into her eyes. She falls down and desperately tries to remove the last remains of the web. It's sharp fangs are hanging right over her as she holds out her hand to touch one measly hair, but it quickly moves back and spits more silk into her eyes.

"My eyes! I can't see!" she yells, panicked, as she tries to remove the stickiness. She scratches her eyes and face to get it out before it kills them all.

"Ahh! Help!" Langston screams.

"Hold on Langston!" Amelia shouts. She can finally see.
Wham!

Amelia looks up and sees Langston, falling face first in her direction. She rolls over, being careful not to touch him. His face is dripping with sweat and his clothes are disheveled; he's out of breath and panting. "Don't ever ask me do that to me again," he says.

Amelia scoots backwards towards the wall. Just then, a giant black wasp with red-orange wings battles against the giant creature. Her wings aren't the same color as they were when she fought that bee, but Amelia knows it's Carys. The tarantula appears to be winning as it clutches their friend in its grasp.

"You can do this Carys!" Amelia encourages.

"That's Carys?" Langston whispers.

Amelia nods as Carys breaks free from the monster's legs and grabs a hold of its body with her hooked claws. With precision, she stings her victim and flies away. The tarantula lets out an ear screeching sound and falls down, paralyzed. As the tarantula takes its last breath, Carys flies out of the castle. Langston and Amelia stare at each other, relieved. Amelia gets up, walks past the tarantula, and heads out of the door.

She whirls around and sees Langston still on the floor. "Are you coming?"

He rises sluggishly and follows behind, into a cloudy mist. It's so foggy that it's almost impossible to see where they're going. There are monstrous roars coming from the north—and the sound of rushing water falling in the distance.

"Carys! Are you here?" Amelia croaks, trying to keep her voice leveled. She's afraid to keep walking.

"I'm right here." Carys runs up to them.

"Thank you so much, I thought we were going to die," Amelia says.

"No worries. I didn't have time to think, and I guess I just reacted when I saw that you couldn't see."

"So what kind of wasp were you?" Langston inquires.

Amelia smiles when she notices how intrigued Langston is.

"I was a tarantula hawk. They're giant wasps who prey on tarantulas," Carys says.

"That was really brave of you. I wish I had your powers. I'm grateful that you were able to save our lives." Langston smiles.

Carys returns a smile and turns to walk away.

Bang!

"Huh! What was that? I hope we can find Mili in time. I have a feeling we might get caught up in another disaster," Langston declares.

"I also have a strange feeling in the pit of my stomach," Amelia replies.

Carys disappears and walks ahead of them.

Amelia wonders if being invisible has become Carys's comfort zone and wishes she had that power. "Carys, do you see anything?" Amelia asks.

"No, not yet. But I do *hear* something."

"What is it?"

"Do you remember when I told you that there's someone else here and that they're still alive?"

"Yes, you said that you could hear their heartbeat."

"Yeah, well, I swear the more we walk in this direction, the louder it is to me."

"Really?" Amelia is eager to meet another one of the Beast's victims. *The more people we can actually save the better.* She knows they're supposed to be looking for Mili, but this person who still lives takes precedence.

Suddenly, Carys stops and doesn't make a sound.

"Carys? I don't hear you walking, what's wrong?" Amelia asks.

"It's here, right here. I can hear the heartbeat, but I can't see anyone."

Amelia and Langston cautiously walk deeper into the mist and stop abruptly, almost stumbling over something. "Found him!" Amelia yells.

An unconscious man covered in slime lies right in front of them. Amelia looks closer and realizes that it's slime from Suko and Keno; she knows this poor person couldn't move if he tried.

"Carys, we have to help him. Turn him over so that we can see his face."

They watch as the prisoner's body turns face up. His face is covered with dirt and goo. Carys reappears and moves the slime away so that they can see his face clearly. Amelia kneels down to get a closer look. Immediately, the tears stream down her face and her heart starts to race.

"Amelia what's wrong?" Carys inquires.

"He's my dad!" she cries.

Chapter Seven

I knew there was a reason why he didn't wake up from his coma. He's been here this whole time, trapped just like everyone else. I can't believe this has happened and I don't know how to help him, but I'm sure as hell going to try.

"Your dad? Cash? All this time it was your dad's heart that I've been hearing?" Carys asks.

Amelia nods as tears leak from her eyes. She gets closer to his ear and whispers, "Dad? It's me. Can you hear me?" *This feels like déjà vu I remember the night he was shot.* "Dad, you have to get up before…"

Wham! They all know what that sound means. While still trying to keep her composure, Amelia says, "Langston, can you pick him up for me? I can't touch him."

"Of course Amelia, you didn't have to ask." He squats down and hauls Cash over his shoulder like a duffel bag. "Let's get out of here," Langston grunts.

Amelia rises up and folds her arms across her chest. She suddenly feels cold. "Carys?" she whispers.

"I know Amelia; give me your arm and that bastard will never see us," Carys assures.

Boom!

Their invisible bodies shake with fear as sounds of thunder follow them back into the castle. As the uproars get louder and more apparent, they speed walk through the darkness until they see an opening. Amelia had assumed there was only one way in and one way out, but they find themselves in another section of the castle.

They exit the side entrance and surprisingly, there are no guards waiting. Amelia was sure the Beast would've stopped them by now and wonders, *Does he want us to think we're getting away?* She inhales the worst smell imaginable and almost projectile vomits from the effect.

"Why don't we go back to that garden? We need to lie him down somewhere," Carys says.

"Yeah that sounds like a good idea," Amelia replies. Knowing that her grandfather is the creator of this hell, it doesn't surprise her that he kept her father here like a prisoner. *All those times I called to check on him, he was never going to wake up…ever.* She sniffs and wipes her nose at the thought. She is certain that Abraham would've kept him alive for all eternity just to make them suffer…to make Cash suffer. The abhorrent words from the suicide note cross her mind. It read: *Don't worry, I'll see you again*

Abraham knew exactly what he wanted to do, Amelia concludes. *He could no longer control Cash in life, so he had to control him in the afterlife.*

"Oh no!" Carys screams.

"What is it now?" Amelia asks, jolted from her thoughts.

A large shadow engulfs them, causing them to look up at a giant…Dinosaur?

"What the hell is that?" Langston yells.

"I think it's a T-Rex!" Amelia shouts. *Crap! I don't know whether to laugh or cry.*

"Wow! Your grandfather's pulling out all the stops," Langston says.

"What do we do now?" Carys bellows.

"Let's just keep walking, I mean it can't see us. Right?" Amelia replies.

They move as swiftly as possible with her father in tow. They try to jog past the giant creature—then all of a sudden—enormous balls of slime descend all around them. They stop and look up. Keno and Suko are soaring above them. They start to panic and run. The dinosaur stomps down right in front of them, almost smashing Langston and Cash into nothing.

"I think it can see us!" Amelia yells.

"You think!" Langston shouts. He pulls away and runs in circles, trying to evade the onslaught.

"Ahh! The slime got on my leg!" he yells.

Thump!

Amelia turns back and sees Cash on the ground. She and Carys run towards them.

"Langston, are you okay?" She is concerned but knows not to touch him.

"Yes, I'm fine, but my right leg feels numb."

The slime is still coming down in all directions. Carys pulls the slime off his leg and disappears with Cash.

"You won't get away!" Suko screams from above as he gravitates down.

"Run Langston!" Amelia yells while sprinting towards Suko.

"Amelia no! They'll kill you!" he shouts.

"Get out of here!" she yells back. Langston tries to balance on his left leg and disappears. She can hear his foot dragging on the ground as Suko and Keno close in on her. Luckily, they can't see Carys and Langston, although she's certain the Dinosaur can. Keno spits slime onto Amelia's legs, forcing her to fall. She lies down and puts her hands over her face, pretending to cry. "Go ahead! Just kill me, I'm ready to die," she says as they get closer.

Plunk!

She peeks through her fingers and moves back when she sees that Suko was just smashed by the T-Rex.

"No!" Keno screams. "You idiot! You killed my brother!" he shouts and flies up towards the dinosaur.

Amelia realizes they've forgotten all about her, so she quickly scoots as fast as she can in the direction of Langston's footprints. She starts to panic because she's not getting that far. The T-Rex lunges for Keno, but Keno spits huge amounts of paralyzing slime into its eyes.

"Grrr! Rahh!" The dinosaur roars as it stumbles.

"I have to get out of here!" Amelia says. She tries to lift herself up, but her legs are paralyzed. As a dark shadow covers, her she looks up and notices the dinosaur is about to fall right on top of her. "Ahh!" she screams.

Keno realizes she's about to be smashed and flies away. Amelia puts her hands over her head and anticipates the worst possible death. Her nerves are in overdrive as she falls back, hoping to pass out before it happens.

Suddenly, someone grabs her and carries her away just as the creature falls to the ground, creating a massive division between them and the monster.

"Thank you Langston. I don't know what I would have done," she says without looking up.

"You're welcome, baby," he replies. *I know that voice.* Amelia looks up. "Dad!" she cries and wraps her arms tighter around his neck as he carries her. She rests her head on his chest, hoping to never lose him again.

"Yes, how are you feeling?" he asks and kisses her forehead.

"I'm fine. How are you?"

"I've been better." He sets her down by the water in the garden. "I'm so sorry Amelia, the way I've acted all those years," he whimpers.

"Dad, don't do that to yourself."

"No, let me get this out. You and Alexandria are everything that I could've ever dreamed of and I love you both very much. I need you to believe that, and know that I tried so hard to come back to you. I heard your beautiful voice, begging me to open my eyes and willing me to come back to you and Alex. But, I just couldn't," he explains.

"I know Dad, I know," Amelia replies as she hugs him. She quickly pulls away when she realizes that she's been touching him this entire time.

"Hey, how am I able to touch you?"

"I don't know, maybe because I'm your father. Carys told me I couldn't touch you, but when that damn thing was about to fall on you, I didn't care if I died. I just wanted to get you away from it," he admits.

"Well, I'm glad you did. I can't tell you how many times I almost died in this place. I was lucky to meet Carys. She's saved my life more times than I can count." Amelia looks around curiously. "Where are they by the way?"

"They went over to Hues Pond to keep an eye on the sky," he replies. He looks into her eyes and frowns. "So, is that Langston a nice guy?"

"Um, let's just say we didn't hit it off at first, but his integrity was good enough to keep him around. He's a good guy. He's been here looking for his daughter Mili. She's just a little girl who's been trapped here like all of them—and you. The Beast is definitely a force to be reckoned with," Amelia says.

Cash puts his head down with shame. "You know who he is, don't you?"

"Yes, I found out not too long ago. Dad, what's wrong with him? Why would he do this?" Amelia cries.

Cash shakes his head and shrugs his shoulders. "For as long as I can remember that man has been as hateful as the devil. I don't understand him at all. When Mom died, he just changed. Overnight, he became—a beast. He wanted to make my life miserable because he was miserable. And for a while, I let him. I did whatever he wanted whether I wanted to or not. My feelings didn't matter."

"It's ironic that you didn't take *your* own life with the way he treated you," Amelia laments.

He looks at her and softly touches her chin. "I wouldn't have had you. You were meant to be born Amelia. Trust me, there were times when I very much thought about ending my life. When I met your mother, my world changed for the better. My father kept a dark cloud over my life from the time I was a child until I turned eighteen. But when I saw her, she was a ray of sunshine," he says with a smile.

Amelia notices the way his face lights up when he talks about her mother.

"Anyway, when Dad committed suicide in front of me, I wanted to die. All I could think about was ending my life; it sounded like the right thing to do. I had every intention of going into the bathroom and slitting my wrists. But then I saw her picture and I realized that I didn't want to die without ever seeing her face again. And when she called me for the first time since we were torn apart by that bastard, I knew that there was something better for me than what I had. Hearing her voice gave me a reason to live. She made me realize that maybe I *don't* have to be alone."

"I'm so sorry Dad. It seems like you've had to endure so much as a child, and even when he died, he still haunted you."

"He haunted me every night. I didn't know a person could hate their own flesh and blood as much as he hated me." He looks over at her and grabs her hand. "I'm so sorry you were somehow dragged into all this, baby. I would take your place a hundred times over rather than to have you spend another second here."

"It's not your fault Dad. I knew he had a hold on you all those years. I'm just glad that your heart still beats because that means we have a chance of getting out."

"How *did* you get here?" He inquires.

Amelia rolls her eyes and takes a deep breath, annoyed that she has to relive the worst day of her life. "Leona shot me," she grunts.

"What?" he screams and jumps to his feet.

"Dad, calm down, it's okay."

"No the hell it isn't! That witch!" he shouts. He paces like a caged tiger.

"It's fine. There's nothing that can be done now."

Cash stares off into space with an angry glare.

"Dad!" Amelia shouts.

He turns around and faces her with blood shot eyes.

Amelia looks away to keep from breaking down again. "She's dead. The police shot her in the head; she can't hurt us anymore. We're free," Amelia confesses, hoping to brighten his mood.

"No! She needs to pay for what she did!" he roars.

"I'm sure she is. I can't imagine her going anywhere except hell. She should have a first class ticket straight into the fiery pit."

He smirks at her theory. "Yeah, I hope so."

"Um, there's another reason why I came here. I'm in love."

Cash frowns at her with a confused look.

"What do you mean you're in love?"

"Just hear me out before you get all parental on me," Amelia pleads.

He crosses his arms and stands in front of her, scowling.

"His name is Aaron and he is the most beautiful guy I have ever seen. I had a dream about him once, and I swear he somehow came to life. We met and had an instant connection. Ever since then, we fell deeper in love as time went on."

"Uh huh," he replies with a frown.

I guess this is a normal reaction from a father. "He was what I needed. Leona kidnapped me and made my life a living hell. When I met Aaron, it made things bearable. He loved me unconditionally and protected me as long as he could. When she and Eli beat him within an inch of his life and shot me, I knew I had to find him before it was too late."

"They beat him? What exactly has Leona been doing?"

"It's a long story, Dad. But for the sake of time, I'll just say, she orchestrated that fight you and Mom had; she made me promise to never contact you and Mom ever again, and lastly, she abused me to no end, until Aaron came along."

"I am so sorry, baby. Alexandria tried to warn me about Leona, but she's my sister you know. I just didn't think she was that dangerous, and now all this has happened. I don't know why I'm surprised. If my own father can create a hell, what makes me think my sister can't do something just as outrageous? I'll never forgive myself for not being there to protect you. I guess I'm glad you were able to meet a nice young man. But I'm not over the moon about these strong feelings you have for him. You're basically risking your life in this underworld to find him when only God knows where he is," Cash says.

"You would do the same for Mom. I can't explain it Dad, but I know he's still alive and he's waiting for me. I have to find him."

"I know Amelia, but…" His face goes blank as he begins to stare at someone.

Amelia looks behind her but doesn't see anyone. She's a little glad he's preoccupied because she knows he wants to talk her out of finding Aaron, and that's a losing battle on his end. As if in a trance, Cash slowly heads towards the dangerous path with his mouth wide open.

Amelia stands and surprisingly, her legs are no longer paralyzed. She follows behind him with worry. "Dad, where are you going? It's dangerous to…Mom?" she screams.

Cash runs up to his wife and hugs her tight. "Alexandria!" he cries.

Amelia remains cautious and stays behind as they embrace. Then, she moves slowly towards her mother, looks into her blue eyes and asks, "What are you doing here?" She desperately wants to hug her, but can't risk killing her.

"I heard what happened to you and I couldn't take it any longer. I didn't want to live without my family. So I took my own life," she cries.

"No! Mom, why would you do that?"

She shakes her head and says, "I'm sorry."

"Alexandria, Amelia and I are still alive. Our hearts are still beating. Why baby?" He says as he holds her.

Amelia's legs give out from the shock. She feels helpless and devastated. *I can't take this. Now my mother is here and she's dead.* Amelia starts to wail. *Who the hell could've seen this one coming? I sure didn't.*

"What's going on here?" Carys asks, confused.

Amelia stifles her sobs and says, "She's my mother, Alexandria."

Carys looks at Alexandria and then walks over to Amelia. She kneels down to comfort her.

"You don't have to say it Carys, I know she's dead. She told us that she took her own life because she thought Dad and I were dead."

"I'm so sorry Amelia. How much more can you take?" Carys says. She caresses her hair and hugs her.

"I don't know Carys, but I think my body has had enough. I can't take much more."

"I'm never leaving you Alex, not ever," Cash says while holding her.

"Are you going to stay here with her?" Amelia asks.

"Yes. I can't live without her and I want to be with her for eternity," he admits while touching her face. He's completely entranced with her, as if nothing else exists around them.

"Why don't we head over to the pond so that we can make sure it's safe to be over here?" Carys suggests. She takes Amelia's hand and helps her up. With shaky limbs, Amelia walks to the pond and sits down under a tree while Alexandria and Cash walk towards the water. The sky is cyan blue and slowly changing.

Amelia is numb inside and exhausted from all the drama. *What do I do now? My mother is dead and my father is alive but wants to stay here. I can't live without my family. What is the point of fighting to stay alive if I don't have them or Aaron to share my life with?* She wants to find him, but contemplates if she should accept the fact that she probably won't. She glances at her parents as they look into each other's eyes without a care in the world and knows she could never ask her dad to leave her mother. *It would be criminal.*

It's time she makes a decision. "I'm sorry Navid and Aaron," she whispers through tears. She notices that no one is paying any attention to her. She quickly walks into the pond and immerses herself beneath the colorful water. *If I end my life, then maybe Aaron will die too and come here looking for me. Then just maybe, we'll be together again.*

She holds her breath as long as she can, to savor every moment of life she has left. She starts to meditate and think about Aaron. She's walking into the forest with the long green vines. *He's there; he's behind the gate.* She can see him. His head is low and his curls are covering his face. He wants to give up, but can't. *Aaron, I love you so much. Come look for me.* He looks perfect to her. But then something happens—he slowly starts to fade away from her. She's choking on bubbles and can feel the water invading her lungs. Everything is getting dark. As she feels her life slipping away, she hears someone say, "Go get him." Suddenly, she can see him again. His head shoots up with happiness. He can feel her. His green eyes are as vibrant as ever and his beautiful face beckons for her touch. With a dimple bearing smile he whispers, "Lisette..." *He's alive! He knows I'm alive!*

With great strength she swims to the top of the pond, gagging and choking on the water.

"Amelia!" Cash screams. Carys rushes over and sees Amelia choking and jumps in the pond after her. Cash, worried, quickly follows behind her.

"Ugh! Ugh!" Amelia coughs. She vomits a river of water until the contents in her stomach are gone. Cash pats her on the back and forces more water out of her lungs. Carys holds her upright as Langston stands by a nearby tree with a worried glare. He feels useless because he can't touch her. Cash picks Amelia up and carries her out of her water and sets her on the grass.

"What were you doing?" he asks as he moves her hair from her face.

"I…I'm sorry Dad. I just wanted to get it over with," Amelia pants. She looks at her friends' and her dad's worried faces and immediately regrets her actions.

Alexandria walks over and says, "I'm so glad you're alright. I thought we were going to lose you."

Amelia remains silent while thinking about her decision to end her life. She knows her mother would've been the first person in the water if she had almost drowned. *My mother was always a worrywart; she never took anything lightly where I was concerned. Unless her spirit has somehow turned cold, this person has to be an imposter.*

"Yeah, I can see how worried you were?" Amelia utters, sarcastically.

"What's that supposed to mean?" Alexandria snaps.

Amelia stands with wobbly legs. Carys holds her up when she almost falls back down. "I don't know, Mom, you didn't seem too worried when I almost drowned."

"Amelia, that's not fair. I'm sure your mother was very worried about you," Cash says.

Amelia looks at him and recognizes the happiness he feels and the delight in his eyes. She hates how devastated he would be if he finds that this imposter isn't her mother. *Maybe I'm wrong. My instincts haven't exactly been up to par lately.*

"I've been worried about you since the day you were born my precious angel," Alexandria says.

"When was I born?"

"Amelia!" Cash snaps.

"Let her answer dad," Amelia whispers. She looks at him and then smiles at Alexandria. With a devious stare, Alexandria slowly fades away just as a man appears in her place. A huge grin forms on his face. Amelia shakes her head. "That was pretty clever…Mortis."

Chapter Eight

It's not going to be easy getting rid of him. He may even be harder than the Beast because I don't know anything about him, except that he can make us do whatever he wants. She knows that this may be her toughest challenge yet.

Mortis smiles callously and with confidence because he knows that he has the upper hand, but he'd be a fool to think Amelia's going to make it easy for him. She can't show her vulnerability. He glares at her with his cold black eyes and quickly looks away as if he'd somehow become entranced by her gaze.

If only it were that easy, she muses, aware of his stare. His masculine build, light brown curls, and bearded face remind her of the Greek hero Ulysses from Homer's epic poem *The Odyssey.* Ironically, Ulysses was supposed to be a cunning trickster. Mortis definitely fits the bill.

"Oh don't look so disappointed. I enjoyed playing your weak-minded mother," he laughs at her. His mannerisms resemble a drill sergeant as he paces back and forth, enjoying his victory.

What could he be contemplating?

Amelia's frightened friend slowly starts to fade, wanting desperately to escape this madness, but Amelia knows it's not going to work this time. She grabs Carys's hand and holds on tight, hoping Carys won't give Mortis a reason to overpower her, but it's too late. She's gone.

"Carys! Please grace us with your presence and reappear. You don't want to miss out on the festivities now do you?" he says, coyly.

Carys resurfaces and squeezes Amelia's hand tighter, realizing that she's not immune to his powers. Amelia can feel her anger and humiliation. She's spent so many years outsmarting them with every move and has used the Beast's powers against him. But unfortunately, all good things come to an end. Her brilliant antics have finally caught up with her, at least for now. Her sweaty hand begins to tremble and it breaks Amelia's heart. When Carys starts to cry it infuriates Amelia more.

"Mortis, why are you doing this?" Amelia demands. "It's not like you're going to get a prize by hurting us. You do realize that this isn't your creation."

Mortis stops pacing and stands right in front of Amelia and stares at her. The smile on his face gets bigger and bigger until it turns into a hysterical laugh. He's unquestionably in his element and his arrogance enrages her. He tilts his head to the right as if he feels sorry for her and says, "Sweet Amelia, if you haven't figured it out yet—this is what I enjoy. This is my prize. We've been waiting a long time to meet you and I must say the pleasure is all mine. You are an extraordinary creature and it is an honor to finally meet you."

"I'm happy to meet you too," she replies as she holds out her hand. He steps away from her powerful reach and smacks his teeth.

"Surely you didn't think I'd fall for that, did you? I think I'm a little insulted."

"You're insulted! You just told me your prize is making us suffer. The Beast has convinced you that this is right and you believed him. Obviously, your brain is made of mashed potatoes so I thought I would take my chances. I don't know anyone who would waste their time doing someone else's dirty work. You don't even know us!" The more Amelia talks the angrier she gets. She grits her teeth and scowls at him.

He rolls his eyes and walks away. "So, you thought you were free?" he whispers to Cash. "We wanted you to think you got away. And that little reunion with your daughter was so touching," he sneers.

"You leave him alone Mortis! You don't get to talk to him!" Amelia shouts, standing directly behind him.

Mortis grins and slowly backs away from her, taunting them. "Let's not forget who's in charge here Amelia. Let me give you a hint—it's not you."

"That's it! I've heard enough!" Amelia hollers. She crouches down.

"No Amelia!" Cash shouts.

Fearlessly, she steps closer to Mortis. He backs away with a mischievous look and grabs Cash by the throat and proceeds to choke him.

"Get away from him! Mortis, with one touch I will end your disgusting, miserable life."

"That may be true, but your father is going with me!" he shouts, laughing.

"Let him go!" Amelia demands.

Carys disappears and tries to break Cash free. Her invisible footprints appear in the dirt and traces of her hands make an imprint on Mortis's arm.

"Carys, get away from him!" Amelia yells as Mortis raises his arm.

With one punch, Carys lets out a lurid scream and lands in a bush. She reappears and moans in pain.

"Are you okay?" Amelia asks her, without taking her eyes off of Mortis.

"Yes," Carys groans.

Langston rushes to her side and helps her up.

Bark! Bark! Bark!

Uh oh. Amelia takes a step back in fear of what's coming.

"Ha! Ha! Over here Stylot, come here boy!" Mortis yells.

Amelia stays very still and glares at Mortis, who has loosened his grip on Cash's neck. It aggravates her that he's enjoying every bit of this, especially now that his dog is coming. But at this very moment, she no longer gives a damn—she has nothing to lose. As Stylot trots towards them, Amelia looks at Mortis with a devilish grin. She walks behind a bush and kneels down to hide.

"What are you doing? Get back here!" he commands.

While following his authority, she stands up and walks back to the front just in time to finish her plan. She's calm and at ease but Mortis has a confused look on his face.

"Get her boy!"

Amelia smirks and runs towards Stylot just as he lunges for her.

"Wait! No Stylot!" Mortis hollers.

Before Mortis can object, Amelia quickly touches Stylot and pushes him to the ground. He immediately begins to whimper and whine as he lies in fear. Amelia stares at her hands in shock. *Why didn't he disappear? Am I losing my powers?*

Mortis realizes what just happened and starts to laugh hysterically. Stylot remains on the ground and appears to be afraid to move.

"Ha! Ha! I guess you're not as powerful as you thought," he chortles. He pushes Cash towards her and walks closer to Stylot.

Amelia hugs her dad, thankful that Mortis didn't kill him. She knows they need to run, so she grabs his hand and slowly steps backwards. In the midst of her worry, something strange happens. She can see it in Stylot's eyes and feels it in her heart.

"Come on boy. Kill them!" Mortis demands.

The frightening growls start to rise within in his chest, becoming louder and fiercer with every breath. Cash's hands are shaking and she can feel him tugging her arm to move further away. But he doesn't understand the complexity of the situation. *I have control,* she knows.

Stylot slowly rises to his feet and snarls, displaying his sharp white teeth. Large drops of saliva splats to the ground. He's at least a foot and a half taller than he was and has a huskier build. His eyes have reduced from four to a normal two. Another growl shakes them to their core, but she's not afraid. Stylot looks into Amelia's eyes and waits for permission. Somehow he knows what she wants and turns to Mortis.

Mortis's expression changes. The laughter he once embraced is now replaced with terror. He realizes what's going on and backs away with his hands up. Stylot looks at Amelia. She walks closer and rubs his soft fur.

"Get him boy," she whispers.

Grrr! Ruff! Ruff! Stylot leaps up five feet in the air just as Mortis sprints away. Stylot chases after him with rage.

"Stop it! Stop it I command!" Mortis yells, but Stylot won't stop.

"Bye Mortis!" Amelia yells, waving.

Cash smirks as they watch Mortis run for his life.

"That was close. How is it even possible for Stylot to change like that?" Langston inquires.

"I don't know. I was trying to kill him. It was going to be him or me," Amelia says. She searches her hands for an explanation. "Maybe it's because he's an innocent and pure creature, like me. I don't think Stylot's powers were that strong to begin with because Mili told me that they had to keep feeding him fruit to keep his powers up."

"But either way, shouldn't he still have to follow Mortis's commands. Even *you* have to do whatever he says," Langston whispers.

"When I touched him, I could immediately tell that something was different about him. I knew what he was feeling and he knew what I was feeling. I must be his new master somehow, which means he can only follow *my* command. My touch gave us a connection and in the process, it made him good. Luckily for us, he's on our side now."

Cash squeezes Amelia tight. He pulls away and shakes his head. "Please don't ever do that again. You could have gotten hurt provoking Mortis like that."

"I'm sorry. I just couldn't take it anymore. He was torturing us. I don't have the patience for that anymore. Leona has ruined it for everyone. The torture and extreme pain she put me through—I'll never endure that again. I'd rather die than watch someone laugh in my face while putting me through hell. When he grabbed you like that, I just lost it," she explains.

Cash smiles and kisses her forehead. She knows it's hard for him to hear the horror she's been through, but he needs to know so that he can understand her actions. He walks over to the pond and sadly stares at the water.

"Is he okay?" Carys asks.

"Yes, he will be. I know that look, he really misses Mom."

"Are *you* okay? I know you also thought that idiot was your mother."

Amelia glances at her father and then back at Carys. "Honestly, I'm thrilled that it turned out to be another trick. If she's not here, then that means she's still alive and well. That's all I can hope for. I know he'll be with her again because I'm going to make sure of it."

"What do you mean?"

"He has been through way more than I have and if I can give him another chance at life, then that's what I'll do. Mom is waiting for him."

"She's waiting for you too Amelia, we're going to get you both out of here, somehow," she sighs.

Amelia takes a deep breath and nods at Carys with a smile. Carys strolls over to where Langston is sitting just as Amelia goes to comfort her dad. She puts her hand on his shoulder. "You okay dad?"

"Yes, I'm okay," he bemoans.

She hates seeing the hurt in his eyes and doesn't know what else to say. He has the same look on his face that she had when she didn't think she was going to make it out of here. Sadly, she still doesn't know if they will. And it didn't help that he got a glimpse of being with her mother again, even if it was just a ploy. *I have to find a way to make sure he gets out of here…that we all do.*

Ruff! Ruff! Stylot rushes back and plops down next to her feet. Cash backs away from the huge animal in fear.

"It's okay, Dad. He's on our side now." She rubs Stylot's ears and pets the top of his head. "You didn't want to keep working for that nasty Beast did you?" Amelia whispers.

Stylot groans and turns over, beckoning her to rub his warm belly.

"You are an amazing and unexpected gift Stylot, even if it was on accident," she giggles. "Did Mortis get away?"

He flips over, puts his head down, and his tail between his legs.

"It's okay, we'll get him."

"This is so weird," Langston says while staring at Stylot.

"Tell me about it, but at least we have another ally. The more the merrier," Amelia declares.

Carys walks over and slowly pets his head. "So what now?"

Amelia looks up at the purple sky. "First of all, we have to find Mili before they bring out my entire family. If Navid comes walking through here, I'm going to lose my mind."

"How do we find her? She's not at the castle," Langston gripes. He looks away and sighs.

"We'll find her. I promise," Amelia confirms. *I just wish I knew where to start.* She bites her lower lip and thinks about the next plan. *It's hard to figure out the layout of this place when everywhere you go something jumps out and grabs you. There has to be more to this world than what we've seen.* "Carys can't make us all invisible anymore because they would see Stylot and know that we're near. There really is nowhere to hide."

"If only we knew which places were safer to travel? We need more eyes out there," Langston contemplates.

Amelia looks down and then it hits her. "Hey! We do have eyes!"

"We do?" Carys asks.

"Stylot," she says.

They all stare at him curiously as he licks his paws without a care in the world. Amelia kneels down and whispers, "Hey boy, can you help us find Mili?" He jumps up and barks and starts trotting towards a forest.

"Let's go guys," Amelia says.

He takes them down a long dark trail where the chocolate sky shades the dead land. It's so cold and damp that they can see their own breath. The rotten smell of decay is potent in the air and there's an eerie sound coming from every dark corner. Amelia can't stop herself from shaking. Cash puts his arms around her as they stroll in silence behind Stylot. The thought of the Beast putting Mili somewhere here is unbelievable.

"I hope we can find her because I can't go another moment without my baby girl. It's been way to long already," Langston sighs.

"We'll find her, don't worry. Stylot can find anyone. Ouch!" Amelia screams.

"What's wrong?" Carys asks.

"Something's on my leg." She feels a large welt on her calf where white bumps begin to form around it.

"It looks like a spider bite," Langston declares.

"Guys, I need to sit down for a second. I feel lightheaded." Everything starts to spin. Amelia falls back and begins to vomit.

"Amelia! What the hell is wrong with her?" Cash yells.

She's trying to gain control of her body, but the vomit keeps expelling out of her. Cash picks her up and starts to carry away from the dark place while the others follow behind.

"There it is! What kind of bug is that? It looks like a black widow spider, but it has wings," Langston observes.

"What! Oh no! Get her to the pond now!" Carys screams.

Everything is a blur. Cash frantically rushes to the pond. Amelia knows her cowardly grandfather must be behind this, and realizes he won't let them get far. She tries to take a deep breath but finds it difficult and her eyes are too heavy to open.

"She's dying! Throw her in the water now!" Carys shouts.

Ugh! Ugh! "What, what happened?" Amelia croaks, still coughing.

"You almost died when you got bit by the Beast," Carys replies.

"The Beast? No, she was bit by a spider with wings," Langston interrupts.

"It was him. I've seen him turn into things you couldn't even imagine. I've seen him in that form before. The venom from the spider will kill anyone almost instantly. When people refused him, he would come up with all kinds of ways to kill them when he was desperate for another soul," she explains.

"He did this?" Cash roars. He looks up at the sky and screams, "You sick bastard! Why don't you come after me! You leave her the hell alone. Do you hear me? You're nothing but a joke!" Shaking with anger, he rushes over to Amelia and helps her out of the water.

"Dad, please calm down. This is what he wants, he's probably laughing." Without saying another word, Cash sits down next to her. He runs his fingers through his hair and then chunks a rock into the water.

"Hey, why did you guys throw me into the water?" Amelia asks. She is still shivering and rubs her leg. The bite mark is gone and so are the bumps.

"I think the water has healing powers," Carys answers.

"Have you always known that?" Amelia asks.

"No, it was a lucky guess. Do you remember when we found your father and he had a long scratch over his eye? Well, when he jumped into the pond to save you from drowning, the scar he had just disappeared. I thought it might have been just a coincidence until now. It seemed like it was worth a shot and you appear to be fine."

"Well I'll be damned, it *is* gone," Cash says, rubbing his face. He turns to Amelia and whispers, "Are you alright?"

"Yes I'm fine now, just a minor setback. Are *you* okay?"

"Yeah, I'm alright. I'd like to apologize to you all for losing my temper like that. And, I want to apologize for my father. The devil made this creature of a man and I can't believe that this world is the resolution of a possessed soul. That thing is not your grandfather, baby, he's a demon and he will be stopped. He's going to pay for this," Cash insists. He looks to the sky and yells, "Do you hear me! You will pay for this!"

A rumble shakes the ground where they sit, followed by another overhead. "What was that noise?" Carys screams.

"It sounded like thunder!" Amelia says. Her legs are shaking and she's scared of what is to follow. The rumbling sounds start up again.

They slowly move away from the water as the thunder continues to roar. All of a sudden, a huge bolt of lightning crashes into the pond, forcing them backwards.

"Ahhhh!" they scream.

Chapter Nine

Underneath a thick layer of smoke lies a single smile. Cash, Carys, and Langston find themselves engrossed in the aftereffects of an explosion. But as much pain as she's in, Amelia is glad to cough, to heave, and to be alive. *The Beast is going to have to try harder,* she smiles. She promises herself that every time she makes it out of a catastrophe; she will celebrate and be grateful.

"That was crazy!" Amelia whispers. She sits up and holds her stomach while wincing from a pulled muscle in her calf. "Crap! He ruined the pond."

"Is that all you have to say? We could have been fried to a crisp," Carys grunts while rubbing her throat.

"Ha! Ha! I'm sorry guys but—we sure pissed him off," Amelia giggles and falls back down. Langston and Carys snicker while Cash covers his mouth to stifle a laugh.

"This is a disaster," Cash says.

"Hey Amelia, how about a swim?" Langston jokes while still chuckling. They all stare at the smoking, baron pond and laugh.

"Oh man, I needed that," Cash snickers while holding his stomach.

"By the way, Dad, you are no longer allowed to address the Beast," Amelia advises with a smile. "I know you want him to pay for what he's done, but I think it's better if we don't tell him about it."

Cash nods while still laughing.

"Besides, on a more serious note, I've got a pretty good plan in mind. I just have to figure out the best way to go about it."

They all stop giggling and stare at her with curiosity. Amelia's almost positive that the Beast won't see this one coming. She knows now that it's their only chance of getting out.

"Well, what are you thinking?" Carys probes.

With tremendous effort, she stands up. "You'll know soon enough. I was going to tell you before, but we kept getting interrupted. Either way, I think we should focus on finding Mili right now."

"You're right. Come on guys let's go," Langston urges as he jumps up and dusts off his clothes.

Stylot trots from around a tree and patiently waits for Amelia's next command. She assumes that he ran for cover before the blow because he doesn't appear to be hurt. She pets his head and looks into his eyes. "Stylot, we need you to take us to Mili," she whispers. He perks up and trots far enough down a path and waits for them to catch up.

I'm not eager to go back into that dark and scary place, Amelia thinks, *but if Mili's in there it's worth the trip*.

Cash takes Amelia's hand and checks around for small sneaky insects or bugs. Carys walks on the other side of her, guarding her against anything creepy, and Langston is cautiously walking behind them.

"You're doing good Stylot, find Mili, boy," Amelia says. She's amazed at how focused he is. He sniffs the ground and stops when something seems off, but never loses sight of his purpose. Amelia's still not sure why he survived her wrath, but is so glad he did. The Beast has been trying everything he can to bring her down but his plans haven't worked—yet, so she's not going to underestimate his ability to come back harder than before. Especially since his efforts were trumped by a greater good. She can't help but wonder why he won't face her and contemplates if he's just trying to figure out just how powerful *she* is.

Bark! Bark!

"Is she here? Where?" Amelia asks. She glances to her left and right but can't see anything except dark winding trees and fog. She looks down and squirms when slimy creatures cover every inch of the ground. She can't help but wonder if the Beast is one of them. She treks forward and jogs after Stylot with her dad and friends trailing behind.

Stylot stops in a murky spot. Amelia catches up to him and halts— then she almost plummets into an abyss.

"Is she in there?" Amelia says.

Bark! Bark! He wags his tell and begins to whimper as he stares down into the dark pit. Amelia faces the others as they're walking closer and folds her arms over her chest. It's not going to be easy having to deliver the news that Mili is in the hole and that she may or may not be okay.

"Is, is she in there?" Langston inquires.

Amelia tearfully nods yes and steps aside, being careful not to touch him. She wants to grab his hand and tell him that it's going to be alright, but she honestly doesn't know if it will be. Carys and Cash walk over and look down to see if they can see anything. "We have to go get her! Come on let's go. Let's go!" Langston shouts.

"You have to calm down. We have to be careful. For all we know, it could be another trick," Amelia warns.

"What do you mean? You said that dog can find anyone!" Langston yells.

"He can, but it doesn't hurt to be sure."

Cash steps closer and puts his hand on Langston's shoulder. "Try to pull yourself together, man. If she's in there we'll get her out."

Langston takes a deep breath and fights back the tears. He proceeds to walk over to a tree and carelessly leans against it, with little regard to the many worms that have quickly intertwined their bodies around his feet. Amelia notices that Carys has disappeared without saying a word.

"Where's Carys? Where did she go?" Amelia asks, panicked.

Cash shrugs his shoulders and tries to squint through the haze to find her while Langston stays put next to the tree. "Carys!" Amelia walks away to see where her friend could've gone when a giant bee buzzes towards her. She ducks just as it flies into the hole. "You could have warned me!" Amelia yells.

With a bewildered expression, Cash points in the bee's direction and asks, "Was that?"

"Yes, it was her," Amelia replies.

He shakes his head. "I will never be able to understand what kinds of things lurk in these parts. You have some very weird friends," he joshes.

"Weird, yet very helpful," Amelia counters.

He smiles and goes to check on Langston. It won't do Langston any good for them to feel sorry for him, but she hopes there will be a happy ending. He's been searching for his little girl for so long only to reach one dead end after another. *Please be in there Mili. Give poor Langston a break.*

The bee flies out of the hole with haste and lands behind a tree. Carys comes from behind it with a worried look on her face. They patiently wait to hear the news. "What did you see? Is Mili…" Amelia can't find the right words to say in front of Langston.

"I think she's okay, but her body is very still. I couldn't tell if she was conscious. Let's just get her out," Carys replies.

Langston gets closer to the hole and waits in anticipation, wishing he could jump in after her.

"She's okay, she has to be. Hey why don't you and dad head over to that tree right there and unravel some vines. We can use those to lower Carys down," Amelia suggests.

He nods his head but his body is paralyzed; he won't move.

"Langston, you have to focus. Mili will need to you to keep yourself together."

"I think I should go in and get her," he offers.

Amelia shakes her head no and motions for Cash to help her out.

"Hey man," Cash says, "It's better if Carys goes because you're too upset, and what good will that do? Not to mention, they need us men out here to pull Carys out; she's much lighter than you are."

"Dad's right. Listen, I want you to know that I would love to get her out myself, but I can't touch her, so Carys is the best option. And there is no way we can pull *you* and Mili out."

"Yeah, I guess that makes more sense, and I know that you would get her if you could. I really appreciate how much you've helped my daughter and me, considering how we first met. I'm not proud of trying to seduce you."

"What!" Cash roars.

Langston quickly clears his throat. "Um, I'm going to go get those vines." He swiftly walks away.

With a furious glare, Cash grits his teeth. "What the hell is he talking about?"

"It's a long story. W-why don't you help Langston with the vines, Dad?" Amelia advises.

Cash stares at her for a long moment and slowly walks away.

Why did Langston have to open his big mouth? Now I have more explaining to do.

After wrapping the vines around a tall and sturdy tree, they hand the other end to Carys. She wraps them around her waist and readies to be lowered down.

"Wait!" Langston shouts. Carys turns around and looks at him. He takes her hand and smiles. "I want to thank you for doing this. You don't even know Mili, but nevertheless, I'm grateful." He caresses her wavy brown hair. She smiles and winks her eye. As much as they've been through, it was only natural for them to make a connection.

"Alright playboy, let the girl go so she can save your kid," Cash snaps.

"Dad! Don't be so rude," Amelia whispers. He frowns at her and rolls his eyes. She knows he's not going to let this go so she decides to explain. "He made a deal with the Beast that if he pretended to be Aaron and take away my innocence, then they would give him his daughter. But the good news is he couldn't go through with it. So technically you have no reason to be mad at him."

"Uh huh!" Cash grunts. "But what if he really was Aaron? You were going to have sex with him?"

"Of course not!" Amelia lies. She knows her father will never understand her undying love for Aaron and her obsession for his touch. *If I make it out of all this alive, I don't want to spend the rest of my life in a convent against my will.* She chooses not to tell him how she really feels.

Even if Cash's glare tells her that he knows she's lying. She finds it annoying, yet comical, that no matter how convincing she is, her parents are the only ones who can see right through her lies. As he stares at her for the truth, she turns to Stylot and hugs his neck.

"Alright guys, lower me down," Carys says.

"Be careful," Amelia whispers.

As they lower Carys into darkness, Amelia's hearts starts to race and her palms sweat. She hopes there's no creature down below waiting to attack her friend while she's in human form. *I hate waiting.* She crosses her arms and sulks at the idea of waiting, whether it's for a favorite cup of coffee or for a doctor to give her news. *Even if the news is great, the waiting part sucks. They say good things come to those who wait, and that may be true, but the horror and stress your body suffers in the process is an imperative detail that can't be ignored.*

She bites her bottom lip and sighs, hoping they can get them out before the Beast tries to stop them again. *Mili has been such an important figure to him all this time and we'd be fools to think that he's going to just stand around and let us take away his eyes.*

"Okay I got her! Bring us up!" Carys hollers from below.

"Hurry Dad! We don't have much time," Amelia says, nervously.

He and Langston begin to pull aggressively.

Ruff! Ruff! Stylot takes off running towards a set of bushes.

"No Stylot! Come back!" Amelia screams while running after him. She looks around and can't find anything, but knows that Stylot sees something.

Grrr! Ruff!

"Come on boy, let's get back." She sprints back to the hole just as they're pulling Carys and Mili out. A low sound of something breaking catches Amelia's attention. "Watch out!" Amelia shouts. She pushes Carys and Mili out of the way before a giant tree almost crushes them. The tree lands directly onto the dark hole. "Oh my God! Are you guys alright," Amelia pants.

"Yes, I'm fine but we need to check Mili; she hasn't woken up yet," Carys replies.

Mili landed in the grass a few yards away. She's completely still with a peaceful look on her face.

Langston rushes to her side and kneels down. "My baby," he cries as he cradles her in his arms. He gently touches her face and kisses her cheek.

Amelia tears up, realizing that he's finally reunited with his daughter, but in the afterlife. *At least they'll have each other for all eternity, if she wakes up.*

They sit in silence, waiting for Mili to come around. Stylot trots back and forth and finally rests next to Amelia.

"Mili please wake up honey. You have to be okay," Langston whispers in her ear. He rocks back and forth while holding her limp body and stares off into space. "Guys, do you think that they hurt her because they knew we were close to finding her?" he asks, worried.

Amelia and Carys look at each other without saying a word. They're very concerned, but can't risk Langston catching on for fear of him having a meltdown.

"Of course not, she's too valuable for them to do that," Amelia lies, hoping to ease his mind. *Crap! I expect nothing less from the Beast than to silence Mili forever. If he wants to hurt us, then it only makes sense for him to do this. Not to mention that Langston went back on his plan he made with them.* But, she can only hope that the Beast wasn't clever enough to figure that out. Especially since he and his army aren't the smartest things in the world.

"Then why is it taking so long? She should be waking up by now," he cries.

Carys walks over to him and rubs his back without saying a word.

Are there ever comforting words to say in tragic situations?
Amelia wonders. *The ones that I've heard in my short lifetime suck
and never made me feel better. If Mili doesn't wake up, am I
supposed to say she's in a better place? Or should I say everything is
going to be okay? Because the truth is that it's not going to be okay
and who the hell wants to hear that their loved ones are in a better
place? I think I'll say nothing.* Amelia cuddles up next to Stylot and
hides her face to keep from showing her tears.

It's going to take a miracle for Langston to keep it together. He
continues to hold Mili and sniffle while Carys wipes a few runaway
tears.

Amelia sits up and wipes her face. She notices that Stylot's starts
to wag his tail. She looks at him curiously, but Mili creeps back into
her mind and she remembers how she helped her escape the castle.
Although we were both frightened, Mili was happy she wasn't alone.
While deep in thought, Stylot's tail wags so hard it hits Amelia in the
leg.

"Ouch! What is it boy?" Amelia whispers, rubbing her thigh. He
barks in Langston's direction so loud it startles him and Carys. They
look up and stare at Amelia with confusion. Suddenly, Mili's tiny
fingers move and then her eyes open. Langston is so overcome with
grief that he doesn't even notice the change.

"Daddy?" her tiny voice croaks.

He looks down and squeezes her. His entire body brightens and
comes to life. "She's okay! Milena, my sweet baby, you're alright!"
Tears glide down his face. "I thought I lost you. I love you," he cries.

Her eyes well up as she wraps her arms around his neck. "I love
you too, Dad."

Amelia rubs Stylot's ears. "Is that what you were trying to tell me?
You knew she was coming around didn't you?"

Bark! Bark!

Amelia kisses his fur. She stands up and walks closer to Mili. "If I
could hug you I would. We were so worried."

"I was worried about you, too. The Beast is so angry with you."
She stands up.

"You don't say? And here I thought we were getting along,"
Amelia jokes.

Mili's smile fades. "Amelia, I saw you when you tried to kill
yourself. Please don't do that again."

"It was a moment of weakness, and I promise I won't do that
again. This may sound strange, but I saw Aaron. He said Lisette and
I somehow knew that he was okay."

"I know. I saw him, too. He's hanging in there and waiting to see
you again."

*I have to be with him again. I'm ready to get the hell out of this
place.* "Guys, now that we have Mili, I think we should regroup and
head back to the pond. I have a plan!"

Langston happily grabs Mili's hand without a care in the world
and Carys takes his other hand. She has a giddy smile on her face.
They both glance into each other's eyes and grin shyly. Mili realizes
what's going on and rolls her eyes. Cash takes Amelia's hand and
leads the way back to the pond, or the spot where it used to be.

Once they get there, the sky is a forest green, which gives them a
little time before all hell breaks loose. They don't know how long
they'll be safe because the sky can turn black at any given moment.
When Amelia thinks about what has already happened, it makes her
second guess every choice she makes. She's eager to tell them her
plan, but wonders if it's a good one. Their lives and souls are at stake
and she won't take any of that for granted, especially because she's
still not quite sure if she can beat him. Everyone looks at her with
hope in their eyes. But she's afraid…for them. So she decides to go
another route and inform them of her very recent decision, however
unpopular.

"So what should we do?" Carys asks.

"I think it's time we get to the Crying Forest while we still have a
chance. At least they can help us get out of here."

"I thought you wanted to try and destroy him?" Mili says.

"I do, but he's a coward and won't come near us. Surely you don't
think I'm going to go searching for *him*. Honestly, I don't care to
ever see him again. Now I'm no fool, I do have a plan B, which is
my original plan but hopefully I won't have to implement it. I'm
hoping we can just get away from here," Amelia explains.

"I would rather we get rid of him. He's horrible, Amelia. He'll
continue to trap people if we don't do something," Mili cries.

Langston pats her hand and tries to comfort her.

"I know Mili, but I believe if we don't try to get out of here, we
may never leave. I won't forgive myself if anything happens to any
of you. I just want us all to be safe and I think we should just leave
instead of trying to fight a battle we can't win."

"You have the power to win Amelia! You just have to stop convincing yourself otherwise!" Mili yells.

"I've made my decision. If we stay and fight, he'll kill every last one of you. Is that what you want?" *I knew they wouldn't understand, but I'm tired of having their lives in my hands.*

Mili wipes away her tears and puts her hands on her hips. "You're being a coward…just like him."

"That's enough!" Cash shouts.

Langston frowns and scowls at him.

Cash's face hardens. He gives Amelia a hug and she starts to cry on his shoulder. The right decision isn't as evident as it used to be. Everything is weighing on her and her choices and it's not fair. Giving up isn't something she likes doing, *But what choice do I have? It may be selfish, but I want my Dad to live and go back to my mother. And I desperately want to find Aaron. I won't return to my life without him. I need to be in his arms again.*

"It's okay baby. We will find this Crying Forest and get out of hell," Cash proclaims.

With watery eyes Amelia nods and takes his hand. Carys and the others follow behind with somber looks and unresolved emotions.

Chapter Ten

Stylot trots in front of them, leading the way to the Crying Forest. Amelia can't concentrate enough to pull herself together. All she can think about is Aaron and how much they need each other. She contemplates which one of them loves each other more and concludes that their love is endless on both parts. It's not often people share the same amount of love for each other. Some people never know how their partner feels about them until it's too late. Others often wonder if their partner's love grows stronger or weaker as time goes on. *My parents' love for each other seems to get stronger by the day…and so does Aaron's and mine.*

Their love is the impetus for her current decision to escape Bram. *Would Aaron be proud of me for fleeing? Or, would he want me to stay and fight the Beast?* Tears pool her eyes; in the back of her mind, she knows what he would want her to do. But the thought of her never seeing his face again angers her. *If I fight the Beast, there's a good chance that I won't win.* But Aaron always told her to fight and never give up, because he would never give up.

He was so brave and selfless with the way he fought for me and stood up to Leona and Eli. He didn't care about the consequences and just did what was right no matter the cost. But now the cost may very well be their lives. *If I must die today, then my life will have been well spent, especially if it means saving someone else.*

The last time Aaron kissed her was when they almost made love. Unbeknownst to them, that may have been their goodbye.

Remembering that moment, Amelia is so devastated and overwhelmed that she can no longer walk and crumples to the ground. She draws her knees to her chest and cries so hard Stylot begins to wail. Cash sits next to her and holds her tight. She can tell he has no idea what to do, so he starts to hum a song that he wrote for her when she was a little girl. For some reason, that song is the only thing that ever made her feel better.

By the time he's done humming, her heart has slowed down and she's calm. She wipes her swollen eyes and takes a much needed deep breath. "Thank you, Dad. I know this is weird to say, but I'm glad you're here."

"Me too, baby. I'm just sorry that you're hurting. Why are you crying?"

She stands up and faces everyone. "I've decided to fight him. I freaked out before because I didn't want you guys to get hurt. But I realize that as long as you are willing to fight with me, then just maybe we can be the victors. If we're not, then at least our deaths won't have been for nothing—and I can live with that. I'm tired of living in fear and I refuse to do it any longer, no matter what comes my way."

"Are you sure, sweetie? You don't have to do anything you don't want to," Cash whispers.

"I know Dad, but Mili was right. I *was* being a coward and putting my own selfish needs ahead of everything else. It wasn't right."

Mili walks over to her and grins. "I knew you would come to your senses, and, I'm sorry for what I said."

"Don't be, I needed to hear it."

"You still didn't tell me why you were crying," Cash whispers.

"I—I just miss Aaron, and I realized that there's a chance I won't see him again. He is the love of my life, Dad." He nods his head without probing, which she totally appreciates.

"Well, I hate to be a thorn in your side, but we're at the Crying Forest," Carys says.

Amelia turns around and looks at her, surprised. "What do you mean? I don't see anything?"

"Look behind you. Do you see how the leaves are all vibrant and glowing, and the trees are twisted in a disorderly fashion? Behind those magnificent branches lies the forest. Everything inside is magical. It's the heart of Bram."

"How do you know so much? If you've been inside, why haven't you asked them to get you out of here?" Cash asks.

"You'll see. Just move that tree branch," Carys replies.

Cash steps closer; he carefully removes the branches. He runs back to where Amelia's standing and grabs her hand. They all warily look at each other, but nothing happens. Then suddenly, the leaves begin to wiggle and the ground vibrates under their feet.

Click! A huge wooden door covered with greenery swings open. Thousands of black birds rush out as if they've been locked away for an eternity. Amelia covers her head with her arms and squats, and the others follow suit. The birds continue to soar out, having no mercy for innocent bystanders.

Once the coast is clear, Amelia glances at them for silent approvals to move forward. They all slowly walk inside the door together, invisible. The moment they set foot onto the olive green grass, the wooden door swings shut, startling them. The smell of fresh roses and rain flows through the air. It's intoxicating scent makes them drowsy, but they trudge deeper into the forest and stop in their tracks when they see about fifty beetle guards no more than thirty feet away. Mortis is standing in front of them with his hand up. Amelia knows what happens when he drops his hand so she crouches down and gets in position.

"What's happening?" Cash inquires, bracing himself for battle.

"Well, Dad, when Mortis drops his hand, it will give the guards permission to come and destroy us. He can only see Stylot right now, so we have to make it count."

"Let's not give him a chance to make a command," Carys whispers.

"I'm ready if you are," Amelia replies.

"What do we do?" Mili asks.

"When Carys, Dad, and I take off to fight, I need you and Langston to go and hide behind the bushes at the door. There are huge branches and sticks in case you need to fight. They're not smart creatures, so just use your survival instincts and aim for the eyes. But Mili, I really need you use your ability to search for any surprises. Langston can do most of the fighting if needed." Amelia turns to Stylot. "I need you to aim right for Mortis so that he'll be too busy to command anything."

He growls in response and looks straight ahead.

On the count of three, they run straight for the guards. Mortis's facial expression oozes fear as he can hear noises but can only see Stylot from a distance. This advantage wills Amelia to run faster before he commands them to stop. Within the blink of an eye, an invisible Amelia kills eight guards as she, Carys, and her dad runs through ten more. The beetles disappear almost instantly without making a sound. Some of the guards are noticing a change, but are too ignorant to put it together.

Mortis turns to look at his disappearing army and yells, "Hey!"

"Now Stylot!" Amelia screams.

Stylot rushes from a distance towards Mortis who takes off running. He hides behind some trees, but Stylot is right on his trail this time. Luckily, there is nothing this dog can't find.

As Amelia continues to run through and kill the guards, a loud rush of thunder makes them all stop and look at the sky. Amelia ignores her will to stop and focuses on getting rid of as many beetles as she can. To help out, Cash makes the most of being invisible by grabbing their torches to burn them alive. The squeals sound like wild pigs waiting to be slaughtered.

"Carys! I need to see your lovely face!" Mortis screams while running from Stylot.

I guess he finally figured it out.

He glances in their direction in time to see more beetles parish forever.

Carys reappears at his request, which forces Cash and Amelia to appear as well.

This sucks, she thinks.

They back away with their hands up as the few guards that are left closes in on them. Cash nervously holds Amelia's hand so tight it goes numb. While trapped, they ponder their next move. Carys looks at Amelia and smiles, almost laughing. Amelia frowns in confusion until she starts to fade away. The guards stop and look around to see what has happened, but they didn't have to look for long. Amelia races towards them and kills ten more.

Cash watches in amazement as the last of the guards slowly disappear before his eyes. There were so many of them that it seemed like an impossible task. But Amelia has made it look easy. Carys and Amelia reappear and high five each other. Stylot is still battling Mortis across the forest as he runs around like a mad man.

"Ahhh!" he screams.

"I can't believe we defeated them all," Amelia giggles.

"Yeah that was something else. I'm so proud of you Amelia, you are so brave," Cash says. "Carys, I want to thank you too. I don't know where any of us would be if it weren't for you and your gifts."

"Aww, it was nothing."

Amelia strides over to the bushes to tell Langston and Mili that the coast is clear, but they're gone. Her hearts drops into her stomach. "Mili! Langston! Where are you guys!" she hollers while walking towards the door. As she gets closer, Langston stands up and motions for them to be quiet. Cash and Carys look on in confusion. Amelia steps closer and realizes that Mili is in a trance and searching for something. She has a troubling look on her face.

After a few seconds, she snaps out of it and starts to cry. "I'm so sorry Amelia, but I couldn't see him in time and now it's too late." She puts her hand over her mouth and cries as Langston tries to comfort her.

"It's too late for what?" Amelia asks, worried.

Mili continues to sob, but, with shaky hands, points her little finger right past them.

Without asking any further questions, Amelia realizes that this is the moment she's been waiting for. The hairs on the back of her neck are standing at full attention as her fight or flight instincts kick in. She purposely turns around and takes a deep breath. The smell of fresh rain slowly fades from her nostrils and the forest gets darker.

"What is it baby?" Cash probes. She takes his hand and turns him around so that he can see for himself. Carys follows suit to see what all the fuss is about. When she and Cash turn around, they quickly glance at Amelia for confirmation of what their eyes are seeing.

"It's the Beast," Amelia whispers as she walks towards him. Cash frantically reaches for her hand to pull her back but she can't stop herself from moving forward, nor does she want to. They are all scared beyond words and have no clue on what to do, but that's okay. They have every right to be afraid and so should Amelia, but she's more furious than afraid of him for all the crap he's put them through.

As her shaky legs get closer to the Beast, he slowly fades away and Abraham appears in his place. She's confounded by how much her father looks like him. His olive toned skin, black silky hair, and tall frame is a replica of Cash. She grits her teeth at her grandfather when she thinks about the hell Cash has been through, and the hell she and her mother have been through because of him.

Amelia stops about ten feet away. "So you finally decided to show up?" she asks. His eyes have turned as black as night and the smug look on his face angers her more. "So, Abraham, What's in a name?"

He takes one step forward and smiles without responding. Stylot rushes to Amelia's side and growls at him. Abraham tilts his head and stares at the ferocious creature that looks totally different from what he created. Amelia pets Stylot's fur.

"Ha! Ha! I would expect nothing less from you, sweet Amelia," Abraham finally says. His deep voice is alarming, and his kind mannerisms can easily be mistaken for good. If she didn't know any better, she would assume he's a moral person. *No one would ever suspect that he's a demon.* As she stands in front of him without fear, she must keep in mind of his true self. The moment she lets her guard down, he'll kill her. Without looking back, she hears footsteps getting closer and closer. A warm hand grabs hers and holds on tight.

"Dad, you should've stayed with the others," Amelia whispers.

"Yes, he should have! His presence makes me sick!" Abraham roars as he takes a step closer. Cash and Amelia step back. *Why does he hate Dad so much? I guess this is a good time to ask.* "What the hell is your problem Abraham? And why would you leave your own son a suicide note, blaming him for your dumb decision! You caused a lot of heartache for me and my mother you demented waste of space!" Amelia yells.

"Amelia!" Cash yells.

She realizes his voice is coming from a distance. She has unknowingly walked right up to Abraham. A normal person would run or move further away, but at this point, she's right where she wants to be. She reaches out her hand so fast that Abraham roars and takes a few steps back. Her hands are glowing in the dim atmosphere and she can feel the hotness of her own flesh. She realizes she must have burned him without fully touching a single hair on his body.

Does my anger make me more powerful?

Cash runs up to her and grabs her arm, forcing her to move backwards. He gets directly in front of her and walks closer to his father.

"Just let us go! Haven't we been through enough?" Cash pleads.

"Shut up you worthless thing! I never wanted you in the first place, but Grace insisted that we have a child! I've known since the moment you were born that you were a big mistake!" Abraham roars.

"You bastard!" Amelia cries. The look on Cash's face is the worst she's ever seen. Tears and anger consume him. Abraham laughs at his misery as if he's watching a comedy show.

"Look at you, crying like a little girl. You are not my son!" Abraham shouts. He draws back his hands and throws live snakes onto Cash. Amelia quickly kills them before they have a chance to strike. Abraham scowls at Amelia. She glares at him, hoping he knows he's met his match. He grits his teeth and forms a ball of fire in his hand when Amelia steps closer and shakes her head. She holds up her glowing hands with an unspoken warning that whatever he does will come with a price. Abraham's face hardens as the fireball in his hand disappears. With revenge on her mind, Amelia runs past Cash and lunges for Abraham. He transforms into the Beast and punches her down. Amelia shakes off the dizziness and rises up to try again.

The Beast stands firm and waits for her next move, but Mortis appears from behind him and walks forth. He's planted at a safe distance from Amelia's reach and looks at her friends, who are all scared as they watch from afar.

"Langston, Mili, and Carys go jump inside the hole you pulled Mili out of. I have something in store for you three. I took the liberty of removing that tree just for you." He turns to Amelia and Cash and whispers, "Stay put. I want your dad to watch you suffer and then we'll gladly finish him off once your malicious blue eyes close forever. And believe me you will suffer for stealing my dog."

Bark! Bark!

Mortis jumps back in fear of getting ripped to pieces.

Amelia tries not to let her tears fall, but the thought of her friends in harm is devastating. This is exactly what she didn't want to happen. She can hear their softs cries as they follow his command. The loud crash of the wooden door opening makes her jump. Stylot growls fiercely and walks closer to Mortis, but Amelia can't bear to see him hurt so she carefully pets his head and whispers, "Go." He whimpers at her request. Knowing he can hear her thoughts, she tells him to follow the others and keep them safe. Stylot licks her hand and backs away. He runs out the forest door.

Cash composes himself and tries not to be emotional. The Beast roars in their faces so loud and hard that it forces them to fall backwards. There is no comparison to the eerie sounds of a soulless monster. Amelia wants to fight him and make him disappear, but with Mortis around, there is no point in trying when he'll just stop her. As the Beast gets closer to Cash and her, she can't help but be thankful that he's there to hold her hand—even if this is the end.

He looks at her with tears in his eyes. "Are you ready, baby?" he asks.

Trying her best to keep it together, she nods yes and turns to face their killer head on. Suddenly, something strange happens. Cash is on Amelia's left and is holding her hand, but she can feel someone holding her right hand. *Could it be Carys? How can she be here if Mortis told her to jump in that hole?*

"Carys?" Amelia whispers without moving her lips.

"Yes?" she whispers.

Amelia can tell she wants to laugh but tries her best to stay silent and invisible. "I thought?"

"He told me to jump in the hole, but he didn't say for how long so I flew out," she whispers with the tiniest giggle.

Amelia grins, relieved. She takes a deep breath and thanks her lucky stars that it won't be her last. "You are awesome. Hey, I think now would be a good time to tell you my original plan on how to defeat him."

"I'm way ahead of you, I sensed what you were thinking before, but I didn't want to say it out loud in case he could hear us. I got a little help from Mili and now I know exactly what to do," Carys admits. "You know Amelia, your plan is brilliant and I can't believe I didn't think of it before."

"Well, I know you were afraid to go near him so I understand. Besides, we needed Mili's powers to help us out."

The Beast turns into Abraham again and Mortis crouches down to get ready. "Which one do you want boss?" Mortis asks with a grin.

"You take my cowardly son and I'll take miss magic hands," he growls.

As they lunge for them, Stylot appears and bites a chunk out of Mortis's leg.

"Ahh!" Mortis hollers. He hobbles over to the magic trees and whispers something to them. Abraham grows about twelve feet tall and throws a huge lightning bolt at Stylot, but misses.

Bark! Bark! Stylot goes after Abraham, but he kicks him so hard that he flies through the air and lands across the forest. He begins to wail in pain and has trouble getting to his feet.

"No! Stylot!" Amelia shouts as she tries to run towards him, but Cash grabs her hand and refuses to let her go. "You're going to pay for that!" Amelia yells to Abraham.

He laughs so loud the ground shakes and with one hand, he flings Cash against a tree and knocks him out. Cash sinks to the ground unconscious. Amelia runs over to him, but he won't open his eyes. She cries and silently prays for him to be okay. With Stylot whimpering across the forest and her father's head in her hands, she can't help but feel helpless. Abraham returns to his normal size. He strides to where Amelia and Cash are. She assumes he's about to finish them off.

He holds up his hand and screams, "I'll see you two in hell!"

Amelia holds up her arm, hoping to block the blinding lightning bolt that thrives in his hand. If he throws that onto them they'll be done forever. She looks down with tears in her eyes and focuses on Cash because pleading for her life will be a waste of time. Abraham draws back and gets ready to kill them when a small voice stops him in his cold-hearted tracks. Cash's eyes finally open, he smiles at Amelia with relief that they're somehow still alive.

"Abraham! Please stop this! Enough!" A woman says. She has mesmerizing brown eyes and flowing black hair that drapes down to her waist. Her all-white gown barely hides her slender frame as she glows with every step she takes. Abraham stops what he's doing and stands there with tears in his eyes. Amelia knew the woman would be the only person to stop this madness as Abraham walks closer to her. He pays no attention to Cash and Amelia who are following close behind. Cash is also drawn to her and wants to greet her, but Amelia grabs his hand and pulls him back. He stares at her with confusion.

"Just enjoy the view dad," Amelia whispers. Cash smiles at her and stays put as Abraham walks closer to the love of his life.

"Grace? Is it really you?" he cries. He reaches out his hand to touch her but she steps back with caution.

"Yes, it is me. What you have created is shameful and a disgrace. You are not the man I married," she murmurs. The look on her face is full of disappointment.

Abraham puts his head down. "I'm sorry. I just wanted to be with you forever and you left me!" He sobs.

"That's no excuse for what you've done to our son and all of these innocent lives." Her melodic voice gives Amelia chills.

"Please forgive me," Abraham whispers. He turns to Cash and says, "I'm sorry, son. I did love you once upon a time. Forgive me?"

Cash treads over to him and gives him a hug. He looks into his eyes and says, "I'm sorry too…for what needs to be done." He looks at Amelia as he holds his father and yells, "Now baby!"

With all the power she can muster, Amelia grabs Abraham with both hands.

"No!" Abraham shouts as his body begins to burn. He falls backwards and moans in pain as Amelia's never ending touch burns him alive. She is perplexed that he didn't disappear like the others, but is glad it's working. She also wonders why he would go through so much trouble of making Carys and the Gobblewits immune to everything, but not do so for himself. She concludes that he didn't expect to cross paths with her. *An arrogant overstep on his part.* As his body slowly disintegrates, the ground starts to shake and everything around her comes back to life. Mili and Langston finally arrive to witness the dying Beast lying on the ground. Stylot gathers enough strength and kneels down next to her feet as she continues to kill the Beast. A brighter atmosphere emerges while the creation known as Bram is slowly starting to diminish for good.

The ground rumbles again, harder than before, and the trees start to tilt. Amelia figures since he's dying, they can get out of there together before the world crumbles to hell. She stands up and instantly realizes it was a mistake. The moment she let go, everything went into reverse and started to die. Abraham's color returns and he's slowly regaining his powers. As he sits up to fight her, she pushes his weak body down and grabs his arms with both hands, not wanting to make that mistake again. The moment he starts to burn, everything comes to life just like before. His body begins to morph into the many creatures he's transformed into over the years as she sits and waits for his final destination.

Something crashes and startles them. "What's happening?" Mili yells.

"Bram is about to be destroyed. You guys have to get out of here, now!" Amelia cries.

More trees fall and the loud crashes of destruction inform them all that the end is coming very soon. Abraham opens his mouth and lets out the many souls he's trapped for so long. As they fly out of his body, they look over and smile. His body is practically glowing with the bright souls that continue to leap out. With tears in her eyes, Amelia realizes that it's time to say goodbye to her friends forever.

The land around them proceeds to fall into darkness. They're surrounded by billows of fire and smoke. "It's time for you all to go. You've been here long enough and it was my pleasure to have met each and every one of you. I love you all." Amelia looks into each of their eyes.

"No!" Mili cries. "We can't leave you." She kneels down to Amelia's eye level.

"You have to, it's the only way. I will never forget you, Milena. You were meant to do great things, go and shine in Heaven." Amelia looks at Langston and says, "You take care of her and never let her go this time. I'll miss you."

Tears run down his face as he nods and takes his daughter's hand.

Carys transforms from Grace into her original self. Filled with sadness, she walks over to Amelia and sits down.

"Well done. It worked," Amelia says to her with tears.

With a distraught look, Carys smiles and wraps her arms around Amelia's neck. "I have to give you something," Carys says as she touches Amelia's face. Amelia feels a warm, tickling jolt of electricity for a brief moment. Carys's smile fades as they hear another piece of Bram destroyed. "How do I say goodbye to my best friend?"

"You don't," Amelia whispers through tears. Saying goodbye to Carys is so painful Amelia can hardly stand it. Both continue to cry as Carys continues to squeeze her neck. Langston walks over and picks Carys up. As she watches them turn and walk into the beautiful light, Amelia can't help but cry and thank God that their souls are finally free. She wonders what Carys wanted to give her but realizes it doesn't matter now.

Cash is crying so hard it hurts her to look at him.

Boom! Another tree has fallen and another piece of this place has crumbled to hell. Abraham is almost completely burned, but she won't let go until there is nothing left but ashes in the wind. Because when there is nothing left…she will die as well.

"Dad, you know it's time."

"Don't you dare ask me to leave you, I would rather die," he croaks.

She sighs. She knew he was going to be stubborn and hard to convince. "Dad, everything is about to crumble, you have to go. Mom needs you. She's sitting in jail and may never get out unless you wake up and clear her name. Please dad, this is hard enough as it is."

"Amelia, please, you're my baby. If I left you here, I would never forgive myself if something happened to you. Please let me stay with you."

She forcefully shakes her head no and cries, "I can't leave until he is finally dead." Another strong boom makes her heart pound. She looks over and sees a huge roaring fire. "Please, Dad, before it's too late! Go and be with mom!"

He reaches over and hugs her tight as they both sob. Finally, he kisses her cheek and rises. "I love you, baby…forever." He gets up and runs towards the wooden door. As he opens the door to walk out, he turns to face her and shouts, "I'll see you soon!" He blows her a tearful kiss and walks out.

She breaks down and cries so hard her stomach starts to hurt. Saying goodbye to her father was the hardest thing she's ever had to do. When she came to Bram, she had a plan. A plan she had every intention on keeping, for obvious reasons. But things change and there is nothing that could've been done about it. *They always say if you want to hear God laugh, just tell him your plans.* It's not until this moment that she finally understands what that means, except she doesn't think he's laughing because none of this is funny.

She has to admit she wouldn't wish this on her worst enemy. If someone told her a year ago she would be fighting tooth and nail to not only save her life, but the life of others, she would have thought they were crazy. *I'm not anyone special, just an ordinary girl who was thrown an unconventional purpose. I just couldn't look at Dad and allow him to suffer another day. He deserves to be happy and if that means I have to sacrifice my life, then so be it. To know that he will go on and be free means I'll get at least one more chance to see him before my demise. Who knows, maybe one day I'll see him and Mom on the other side in a much more heavenly place.* Either way she's made her decision and she's not backing down. Putting his needs before her own is worth it to her, and as devastating as things are, at least she knows Aaron would be proud of her, and that is something that she can cherish always.

She finds it unfair how love rips the rug right out from under you with no regard to the consequences thereafter. Because of love, she has fallen into a tailspin of battles and emotions that no one person can handle alone, yet here she is. She's overjoyed in knowing that Cash can finally be happy, but distraught that her plan to rescue Aaron has backfired. Her last thoughts on the matter are: *Love is the most beautiful, joyous, and exceptional thing, and everyone should experience it in life. But it is also the most biased and selfish bastard I've ever had the pleasure of knowing.*

As the last of the world is crumbling around her, Stylot snuggles under her arm and hides his eyes. Now that Abraham is dust in the wind, Amelia covers her face and buries it in Stylot's side while holding onto him as tight as possible, knowing that the creation formerly known as Bram no longer exists. And soon—neither will they.

BOOK 2
"Zerios"

Chapter Eleven

With her face pressed into Stylot's side, Amelia softly weeps. She misses Cash and her friends. It's been minutes since they parted ways, yet it feels like days. Relief doesn't begin to describe how she feels about the death of Abraham. *Now my dad can live a better life and Carys, Langston, and Mili can shine in their own glory.* She hopes to see them again and realizes it may be sooner than she thinks as time runs out for her. But strangely, she can't help but wonder why she hasn't perished yet. Warm grass rests under her feet and calming clean air still soars in her lungs. *What did I miss? What's going on?*

Ruff! Ruff!

His bark startles her into opening her eyes. She quickly closes them because the bright sun shines down on them as if angry. The heat is smoldering and exhausting, but it doesn't seem to bother Stylot as much as it does her. He happily wags his tail. She opens her eyes again, which takes more effort than it should with all the light, but she manages. She stands up and stretches. Her body retaliates. Every muscle and joint in her body aches.

Bark! Stylot jumps up and runs around in circles as if he's thankful to be alive. With shaky hands, Amelia reluctantly puts her hand on her chest. Thump Thump! Thump Thump! Her heart is still beating, stronger than it ever did before. "I'm alive!" she yells with excitement. She hugs Stylot's neck. "We're alive boy, isn't that great!"

Bark! Bark! He licks her face.

Amelia is elated that she made it out of Bram alive, especially because she expected to die. She doesn't understand it, but certainly won't question her luck. As she takes in her surroundings, she shudders to think what odd beings could be lurking in this place. Having spent all that time in Bram, she's given up on the idea that she'll come across anything normal. But at least this world has life, which is a relieving change. The tall green grass sways effortlessly in the wind and the blue sky is a nice touch to a perfect picture. From afar she spots a small pond that's almost hidden under a large tree.

"Come on Stylot, let's get you some water," she suggests. He jogs beside her and sniffs the ground. Her bodyguard is surprisingly not in any pain. She didn't think he would be able to walk after what the Beast did to him.

Grrr! Ruff!

"What is it boy? What do you see?" With her heart racing she looks around, hoping it's just his imagination. He gets on his hind legs and whimpers loudly. She rubs his back and takes a step forward. *The last thing I need is something popping out at us.* She hasn't had an opportunity to see if she still has powers. She walks closer to the pond when a giant black snake slowly rises up and hisses at them. Its large frame is terrifying as it casts a dark shadow over their vulnerable bodies. Amelia stops breathing and freezes. Frenzied, she loses control and takes off running, knowing that's the last thing she should do. Her rationale is that the snake was never going to let them live.

Stylot howls while following close behind. As she runs to safety, she realizes the snake was a massive king cobra. Visions of its expanding head and forked tongue motivate her to run faster. What baffles her most is that she could've sworn it looked right into her eyes. *It had every opportunity to strike and it didn't.* Not even when they ran like idiots.

They rest in a field of six feet tall purple and yellow wildflowers that give off the tiniest aroma of perfume. With Stylot leading the way out of the field, they stumble upon two enormous pyramids that weren't visible before. It's almost as if they appeared the moment she set eyes in their direction. *If I didn't know any better, I'd swear I'm in Africa.* The pyramids look like the ones from in her school's history books—but more magnificent. As the sun shines off the reddish brown stones, she ponders their purpose. There is nothing in their vicinity. A statue of a lion's head rests atop the one on the right. *Where am I?*

As she treks closer to the one on the right, Aaron comes into her mind. It pains her that he's still waiting for her and she has no idea if he's still okay. *Mili would come in handy right about now.* She was supposed to die in Bram and that very fact upsets her. Aaron would've been waiting and waiting and she would've never shown up. *I wish he was here.* She still doesn't understand why he was put in Beryl in the first place. For the umpteenth time she wonders, *Who put him there and why? He didn't deserve to be taken away from his family and me.* Just like she didn't deserve to be enchanted and obsessed with his soul just for it to be ripped from her grasp. *It's just not fair.* Through it all, she believes he's still alive, but the heartbreaking reality is…he's not there with her. She's knows she's closer to getting to him, but the question remains, *will* she get to him?

An unexpected rush of nausea brings her back to reality and makes her question her current actions. The queasiness is getting worse the closer they get to the pyramid door, but strangely, she can't stop walking until she gets inside. It's as if she's being summoned. They enter the dark, cryptic dwelling. Immediately, Amelia runs to a dark corner and heaves like she never has before. Her wobbly legs are still strong enough to keep her upright as she glances at the hieroglyphics on the wall. The all too familiar scent of death and musk releases a fire inside of her, leading her to believe that something isn't right about all this.

She composes herself enough to stomach the smell and head towards a dark hallway. Stylot is reluctant to follow her and she can't deny her wariness, but she has to keep going. The extended hallway becomes shorter and narrower with not much room to move around. She ends up on all fours crawling through different mazes that lead to dead ends. Although each entrance takes them to another level, they keep finding themselves disappointed by the outcome. Amelia's not afraid of the dark, but Stylot keeps whining and it breaks her concentration. "Just follow behind me, boy; you'll be okay," she whispers. Her inner voice is telling her to stop but something is willing her to continue. *I hope we're not inadvertently burying ourselves alive.* When they reach the ninth level, a light guides them out of the small space where they enter into a large well-lit area. Amelia crawls out relieved and Stylot jumps out and licks his large paws.

We must be in the center of the entire pyramid. She can tell by the pointy ceiling that they've finally reached their unplanned destination. She wipes the sweat from her brow and swallows hard to rid her mouth of the puke that refuses to die down. She's incredibly nauseous, but the image in front of them is much more disturbing than her desire to upchuck. There are people dressed in forest green cloaks walking around like cattle, chanting something unknown to her.

They're in a lost state of mind, like they don't belong to themselves. They're eating orange berries and drinking red juice and can't get enough of it. A mysterious woman dressed in all black sits at the very top of a steep flight of stairs. The woman stares down at the people as if she's taking inventory. Her mannerisms are unfazed by the disturbing view and she actually seems a little bored, like she'd rather be elsewhere. Amelia can't imagine her having a prior engagement, considering the horror of this scene.

Bark! Bark! Amelia jumps as Stylot growls at the people. He steps forward without a care in the world, as if he's forgotten *they're* the intruders. In a normal situation, Amelia could brush this off as him being a typical animal, but Stylot is different. He knows what she's thinking and he understands her perfectly. He growls again, baring his sharp canines.

"Stylot!" Amelia whispers while clutching his back fur. *I should have taken his leash from Mortis, but I guess that would have been overkill since I took his dog.* She huffs under her breath and looks up at all the eyes gazing at them. The chanting has stopped. Every eye in the room is hooked on them and the silence frightens her. Their golden eyes are difficult to ignore and she anticipates the significance. Running away at this moment would be a wasted effort so she stands firm and waits for the woman in charge to come down from her throne to approach them.

While gawking in their direction, the woman walks down gracefully. Amelia watches her in awe, knowing she would have easily fallen all the way down and landed on her face. The irritating sound of her high heels echoes off the stone steps as she marches to the bottom. Two bulky men, dressed in black, pause at the foot of the steps and follow behind her with curious yet stern looks on their faces. *Why does she need bodyguards? It's not like we're armed. Then again, Stylot isn't a normal size dog by any means.* The woman stops about five feet away.

Seeing her up close is intimidating as she's much taller than Amelia thought. Her full red lips are flawless and her dirty blond hair is in a perfect bun. The black framed glasses she wears remind Amelia of her English teacher, Mrs. Brook.

As they make eye contact, the woman smiles courteously and walks a little closer. "I'm Lily," she whispers and holds out her hand.

Amelia looks down at it nervously without moving. She tilts her head to the side and smiles again.

Lily appears to be annoyed by Amelia's rudeness.

Amelia glances at Stylot and takes a deep breath. *If I touch her and she disappears her guards will have us for lunch. Also, I have no idea what these weird people are capable of.* "Hello, I'm Amelia and this is Stylot." As Amelia holds out her hand, she secretly pinches Stylot. He lets out a loud wail and glares at her with confusion. Amelia quickly pets his back to calm him down. She wants to cry for hurting him, but at least it took Lily's mind off of her shaking hands. "I'm sorry boy," Amelia whispers in his ear.

"Is he alright?" Lily asks. The look on her face appears to be concern for her safety opposed to Stylot's. She backs away and turns to look at her bodyguards.

"That's a very big animal. Are you sure he's okay?" A guard probes with a frown.

"Oh yes, he's fine. I think he's a little confused is all. He doesn't like being indoors." Amelia obsessively pets his fur while they stare at him. While pretending to be nonchalant, she uses this opportunity to look around for an exit just in case they get ambushed by this freak show. Across the room, she sees two guards leaning up against a wall with blank stares. An elongated table with two giant bowls of red juice surrounded by orange berries sits directly in front of them. Although she can't see a door, she knows they must be guarding an exit. She squints and notices a hint of sunlight passing through the cracks from where they stand. *There must be a door there.*

"Oh where are my manners, this is Horus and this is Jordan," Lily informs her.

"It's nice to meet you all. Forgive me for intruding, but I couldn't stop myself from entering this place and I have no idea where I am."

Lily turns and walks passed Horus and Jordan. "Please, come and have a seat," she says without turning around.

Amelia feels compelled to follow her even though she knows she probably shouldn't. Stylot stays put and sits on his back legs without taking his eyes off Amelia. She can tell he's waiting for them to give him a reason to annihilate them. She's so thankful for his protection and his unconditional loyalty to her. His massive build alone is keeping everyone at a safe distance. She can practically smell the fear in the room and is positive he can too.

Lily sits down "Where did you come from?" she asks. She motions for Horus and Jordan to give them a little privacy. Once they walk away, Amelia sits down.

"To make a long story short, I just came from a place called Bram. I managed to destroy it indefinitely and escaped unharmed. I'm looking for my fiancée before time runs out for us both," Amelia explains. Lily shifts in her chair and crosses her legs, which makes Amelia wonder how much Lily already knows.

"It was you? *You* killed the Beast?" Lily says, shocked. She quickly cranes around in fear that someone might have heard her. She removes her glasses and rubs her eyes.

"You knew him?"

Lily crosses her arms and looks down. "No, I didn't know him. I just—I don't understand how *you* could have killed him. You're just an ordinary girl."

Well she's a big fat liar. Does she think I didn't notice how quick her demeanor changed. She's clearly disturbed that he's dead. Of course, it could be just my imagination. Maybe I'll test my theory. Amelia leans forward and looks into Lily's gold eyes. "Yes. I, an ordinary girl killed that disgusting excuse for a soul."

Lily stomps her high heels on the gray stone floor and gets up slowly. Her guards walk towards them, but Stylot growls exceptionally loud to remind them of his presence. Lily stops them and gives a silent warning that she's fine. She looks back at Amelia and smiles as she sits back down. Amelia glances at Stylot and nods for him to remain calm. He looks away and stares at the guards, patiently waiting for any sudden movements. The chanting has started up again as the people in green walk around, still drinking the red juice.

I guess it wasn't my imagination after all. "Who are you?" Amelia asks.

Lily takes a sip of the red juice and answers, "Lily, I told you that." She takes another sip and stares at the other guards planted across the room.

"Did I upset you?"

Lily shakes her head no without saying another word.

Damn, she's going to be hard to crack.

Lily pours herself another cup of juice. "Would you like something to drink?"

"No thanks, I'm on a diet. Gotta stay healthy," Amelia jokes.

"Oh what's the point? Aren't you dead anyway?" Lily gives a half smile and hands Amelia the cup anyway.

Amelia takes the cup and peeks inside. *It doesn't look like fruit juice and it doesn't smell like it either.* She holds it up to her nose and sniffs to be certain. *This is blood. What the hell have I gotten myself into?*

From the corner of her eye, Amelia notices one person in green stop and look at her with apprehension. He's not moving or chanting like the others and appears to be waiting to see if she's going to take a sip. She does a double take at his brown eyes and wonders why they're not golden.

Lily turns to see what Amelia's looking at but the person puts his head down and moves his mouth to chant.

Amelia forces herself to look away and sets the cup back on the table. "Actually, you're wrong, I am alive."

Lily leans forward and snickers, "That's impossible."

"I have no reason to lie to you. My heart is still beating."

Lily giggles and rolls her eyes.

Amelia scowls and bites her lip to avoid an argument.

Stylot stretches and walks over to Amelia. He plops down next to her chair and quietly groans at Lily.

Her eyes are big with horror, but she controls her fear enough to stay seated. She glances at the cup on the table and sulks with annoyance. "Have some berries…they're organic," she grunts while pushing the bowl near Amelia's grasp.

With a warm smile Amelia pushes them back. "No thanks, I'm allergic," Amelia says, looking around. "So what is this place, and why are you living in this pyramid?"

"Why should I answer any of your queries? You have insulted me by refusing my delicious punch and vibrant berries."

"I didn't mean to insult you but I've been poisoned before so you can understand my hesitance."

"You can trust me, I wouldn't harm you," she assures as she moves the cup closer to her.

"I'm sure I can." *If I were born yesterday.* Amelia stands up and crosses her arms. "So have you been here long?" She's trying to shift the conversation to a lighter note because she can no longer stand the smell of blood and feels nauseous again.

"Yes, I've been here for quite a long time; this is my home." Lily gets to her feet. She paces while pondering something. For a moment

Amelia fears Lily's thoughts. Lily looks at the guards and motions for them to come over.

"Stylot, I think we've overstayed our welcome." Amelia steps back with her hands up as Lily's guards saunters towards them.

Stylot leaps in front of Amelia and roars at them, but they seem unfazed. Jordan rushes in Amelia's direction as Horus jumps on Stylot's back.

"Get off of him!" Amelia screams. She runs to the other side of the room to get away from Jordan when she realizes she can use her powers. She halts and turns to face him.

"Ahh! He bit me!" Horus screams while holding his leg.

Lily furiously runs over to Amelia and grabs her from behind. She proceeds to choke her while griping something about the Beast.

"Let me go!" Amelia gags while trying to pull the cold hard hands off her neck.

Lily squeezes tighter and Stylot rushes over and jumps on her back. They both fall to the floor where Amelia inhales for as much air as her lungs will allow. Jordan stands over her and proceeds to kick her. She jumps up and grabs his throat. For a split second, Amelia stops and wonders why nothing happened. He pushes her down and kicks her in the stomach. She holds her abdomen and breathes through the pain. "What do you want!" she mumbles.

"We just wanted you to drink the juice, but you had to be difficult!" Jordan yells while grabbing her hair.

Amelia touches his arm to see if there's an ounce of powers left but it's gone. Tears pool her eyes as she realizes she has nothing going for her. *How can I get out of this with no powers?* She turns to her side and sees Stylot's teeth tightly gripped around Lily's neck. The woman is so frightened she can't even scream.

Jordan pulls Amelia's hair even harder and grabs her neck. His golden eyes are filled with hatred and rage as he grits his teeth. *He's about to kill me.*

"No!" Amelia cries.

Chapter Twelve

"Please don't do this!" Amelia gasps. Her eyes are bulging and her air supply is closing off. It's only a matter of time before she passes out—or dies. An image of the Beast enters her mind and every evil thing he's ever done. All it took was her. She had to end his reign and that very thing reminds her of who she is and how strong she's become.

Jordan squeezes his fingers tighter around her neck as he straddles his legs over her body. Powers or no powers she has to get out of this. Mr. Wilkers taught her how to get out of this type of hold, in a much gentler manner of course. *I have to make him proud and survive this.* She angrily rams her knee in the center of Jordan's spine. When he leans back in pain she kicks the back of his head.

"Ahh! You blue eyed witch!" He holds the back of his head with both hands and jams his eyes shut. Amelia turns to her side and inhales. She instinctively jumps up and rubs her neck. Jordan grits his teeth and knits his brow as he attempts to stand. She takes a few steps back and kicks him in the face and punches him in the sternum. As he falls back to the floor, puffing for air, she jumps on his stomach. While in the fetal position, he gawks at her and pants, "I, I will get you for this."

Her throat is on fire and her head is throbbing, but she manages to crouch down and pin his arm behind his back. "Thanks for the heads up." She pulls hard.

"Ouch! Please, it hurts," he begs as he tries to get his arm out of her death grip. She yanks harder until she hears it breaking. His earsplitting screams are music to her ears as she dislocates his shoulder. She slowly rises up and stares down at Lily.

"Grrr!" Stylot still has his teeth around her neck, patiently waiting for permission to kill.

"Not yet boy, I have a few more questions first." Amelia kneels down and tilts her head at Lily, whose golden eyes are still as lively as ever. It's clear that Lily is terrified, but Amelia would be remiss if she didn't recognize how eerily tough Lily is. Her face hardens as she suffers the pain of Stylot's wrath. Amelia nods at Stylot to let her go as she returns to the table to sit.

The people in green are still in a mindless state as if nothing ever happened. Amelia notices that Horus is trying to stand.

He looks at Amelia and slumps back down when he sees her "I dare you" look. He glares at her while holding what's left of his leg. Stylot slowly removes his jaw from Lily's throat and trots back to where Amelia is sitting. Lily flashes her eyes at Jordan and shakes her head.

"Some bodyguards you turned out to be," she grunts while caressing her throat. "I could have died you morons!"

"Oh what's the point? Aren't you dead anyway?" Amelia snaps.

Lily smacks her teeth and carefully lifts her sore body off the floor. She limps back to her chair, glides down, and tries to fix her not so perfect bun. Her evil stare gives Amelia chills but at least now her kindness won't be taken for weakness. Lily touches her throat again and frowns at Amelia with angst.

"Look, I'm in just as much pain as you're in right now, so from my standpoint, we're even." Amelia desperately hopes to get some answers, although Lily is wearing a "screw you" look on her face. Amelia still has to press her to find out what's going on. Staring at the floor to avoid Lily's gaze, Amelia asks, "Can you please tell me where I am?"

Lily studies her fingernails and glances over at Horus as if Amelia never said a word.

Amelia's patience is running out. Every second she loses here is another second away from Aaron, and she can't afford to lose many more. She gives Stylot a nod and he growls.

Lily relents. "You're in Felinity. I created this world for my family and me to live for eternity. You see, I chose not to go to Heaven because I was told that this would be a better option."

"What idiot told you that?"

"The Beast, aka Abraham," Lily says.

The way she says his name sickens Amelia. There is so much adoration in her voice.

"He helped me create this so that we could all be in charge of whoever crosses over. We are supposed to invite them to live in paradise with us."

"Ha! Ha! So how's that working out for you?"

"Look! I don't expect you to understand any of this. You're just some freak who happened to pass through. By the way, you said you're looking for your fiancée, well how is *that* working for you?"

Amelia's smile fades. The question went straight to her heart. "Honestly, not so great, but I have no intention of giving up on him. He's my soul mate and I won't live without him." A single tear falls on her lap, reminding her that she stills has a fighting chance.

The mindless people offer her a minor distraction from her thoughts as the chanting gets louder and louder. When Lily glares into Amelia's eyes, Amelia can't help but notice something oddly familiar about her.

"If you don't mind me asking, what happened to him?" Lily asks.

"I'd rather not get into it. Just tell me how I can get out of here."

Lily smirks and scoots further back into her chair. "You're not getting out of here. Sorry." She grins.

"What do you mean? Do I need to show you again that you're not in charge of me?"

Lily flashes a nasty look down at Stylot and uncrosses her legs. "All I'm saying is that there is no way out of here. You mine as well drink the juice so that you can be accounted for. That's the best advice I can give you."

"What are you talking about? I know that's not juice," Amelia whispers. *What does she mean there's no way out? There's always a way out. Of course she's not going to tell me the truth. Ugh!*

"How did you…well I guess it's no secret now. It is blood, but Abraham told me to drink it so that the real ruler can find me. Also, whoever passes through here must drink it as well to be a part of Felinity. He told me that if people don't drink the jui…I mean blood, the ruler will think they're food and eat them. The blood also keeps us strong," she explains.

I can't believe she's serious. Abraham sure pulled a number on her, but why? Why would he feel like he needs to help her? What's so special about her? "Why couldn't you just stay in his world with him?"

She laughs. "Well geez, I'm glad I didn't." She smirks while taking a sip of the blood.

It's too bad I'm going to do the same thing to this world. But for now, I'll let her enjoy her "paradise". "Who's blood is it?" Amelia asks. She puts her hand over her mouth and silently counts to ten to keep the contents in her stomach at bay.

"Why it's the Beast's blood silly. He gave us enough to last for forever and ever. The ruler will smell the familiar scent of the blood and come running to paradise. So, would you like a cup?"

"Absolutely not! I think Abraham has brainwashed you into thinking this pyramid is a good thing, but it's really crock of crap."

"Ha! Ha! The crock of crap will be when the ruler shows up and eats you and your dog for breakfast, lunch, and dinner." She laughs.

Jordan gets off the floor and limps over to the table across the room. His face is an obvious indication that he's writhing in pain. With his one working arm, he pours himself a cup of blood from the bowl on the left, whereas the others drink from the one on the right. *Is there a difference?* He chugs two full cups in a row. Lily smirks at Amelia's look of disgust and takes another sip from her cup.

"So, why are these people dressed in green and acting like zombies? Did the blood do that?"

"Unfortunately, there are some individuals who have a reaction to the blood and in turn they end up like that. They have to be strong minded and willing to live their life with us. However, I've noticed that the most innocent and pure individuals don't react well to it at all. A few of them have died. As for the attire, my favorite color is green so I figured why not. It's also easier if I dress them all in the same color to differentiate them from everyone else."

Amelia clears her throat and looks away. *I guess now is not a good time to tell her that I'm a virgin. She would take great pleasure in making me guzzle it down if she knew I could end up a damn zombie for eternity.* It's pretty clear that no one has ever made Lily work this hard and fight this much for answers. *How can people be so naïve that they could be persuaded to drink blood of all things? There has to be more to it than that.* "Level with me Lily, how do you get them to drink it?" Amelia asks as the knots turn in her stomach.

"You'd be surprised how far a little coaxing will take you. Most of them just need to be told the right thing, and the ones that refuse, well, we force them," she confesses.

She's no different than the Beast. "Why would you trick people into staying in this place with you? The Beast did the exact same thing and it's wrong. How can you take joy off of someone else's misery?" As Amelia says the words, she perspires and breathes deep to slow her racing heart. Because what she really wants to do is rip Lily's head off. *I'm so tired of these creatures thinking they can do whatever they want to people and expect no consequences.*

"Like I said before, I don't expect you to understand. It pays off in the end because I have my kingdom and I can rule endlessly. When the other ruler gets here, we can finally be together forever and take over the underworld. It's been such a long and exhausting wait and I know they will be here soon, I can feel it."

Geez, her head is so far in the clouds she can probably sniff the rain before it forms. Amelia shakes her head.

Lily's euphoric outlook on future plans is almost as sickening as watching the poor people walk around in a daze for all eternity. *If I live to destroy this pyramid, they will be free from all this and their souls will finally reach its final destination.* As Amelia scans the large room, she assumes there must be at least ninety people dressed in green. "Hey, are these all the people who have entered the pyramid?"

Lily rolls her eyes. "Yes. All of the people in here have drank the blood. But I know there are people all over this creation."

Amelia realizes that something's not adding up. *All of these people are zombies, but they can't all possibly be pure. There's a whole other world outside of the dwelling. If Lily won't let people leave, there must be a reason why. I started getting nauseous the closer I came to the pyramids. I wonder if it was the blood forcing me to enter. Is this how she traps people? The blood beckons them to find her and once they arrive, she makes them drink so that they can follow her every command. Why not go out and see what's out there? That must be it! She can't leave the pyramid.*

Amelia stands up and walks over to the small hole that she and Stylot crawled out of. A giant beetle pops out and almost lands on her feet. She jumps back and watches it scurry across the room. One of the guards by the wall picks it up and starts to eat it, although it's little legs are still moving. Amelia wonders what kinds of creatures she passed in order to get here. *Oh gosh! Did we crawl over dead bodies?*

"Oh no!" Amelia yells. Vomit shoots out of her mouth so fast and strong she ends up on the ground, hoping and praying for an end. Stylot jumps up and guards her as they all stare. She looks over at the horrified look on Lily's face; she seems more disturbed that there's vomit on her perfectly shiny floor. Amelia wipes her mouth and smirks. Luckily, Stylot is there to hinder Lily's plans since Amelia's at her most vulnerable. She finally gets up and walks back to her chair while holding her stomach.

"You know, if you drink the blood, it will make you feel better," Lily says with a smile.

Before Amelia can respond, Jordan burps loudly and drinks a third cup of blood. Something is certainly different about the bowl on the left. His immediate ability to stand up straighter and roll his neck informs her that he's slowly healing. His arm that was dislocated is no longer restricted. With that same arm, he turns around and waves at Amelia wickedly as if she needed to be educated of what she already knew.

She can't deny the fact that this terrifies her. *All that hard work was for nothing since they're automatically healed again.*

With a huge smile on his face, Jordan grabs two more cups and gives them to Horus.

Lily is clearly amused that the ball is back in her court. "The blood has healing powers. So you see it's not so bad. Just drink some."

Amelia glares into her golden eyes and scowls. "For the last time, I'm not drinking that damn blood! And, I know you're lying to me! You trap people here because *you* can't leave! Is this what you call ruling a kingdom? Lying and scheming to make people think that disgusting blood is the greatest thing of all, just so they can be your puppets for all eternity? I would rather die than to be in your shoes. The sad thing about it all is that you actually believe the Beast helped you. He told you this is a good thing and you bought it!" Amelia shouts.

"Look, you annoying brat! I have heard just about enough of your insults. The Beast saved my life and built this place for me until the ruler comes. When they get here, I will be free and can take as many people under my wing as I see fit. He was my friend and you killed him!" She cries. She tearfully looks up and says, "And I will kill you."

Amelia brushes off her idle threats and asks, "Why are there two pyramids? If this one is so great then what is the other one for?"

Lily looks up from crying and stares. Horus stands to his feet and walks over to Lily's chair without a single ounce of pain. Stylot gets in front of Amelia and growls. Jordan grabs Horus's arm and scoots further away.

"Well? Are you going to answer me?" Amelia demands.

"That pyramid is not to be entered. If you go inside you'll die. That's all I'm going to say about that. Not that it matters anyway, because you will never leave this one!"

"Like I told you before, you are not going to tell me what I can and can't do. I don't know why you continue to underestimate my powers to overcome you."

Lily laughs aloud. "Look around you Amelia. Do you honestly think you have a fighting chance? You are surrounded by strong guards, and at least a hundred people who will do whatever I tell them to. You're lucky you're not already dead. I wanted to answer your questions because you're different than most intruders. I can't put my finger on it, but I feel drawn to you. But just know that that stunt you and your dog pulled earlier will never happen again. All I have to do is tell them to attack and they will eat you within minutes." She leans forward in her chair and whispers, "By the way, I don't appreciate you talking about the Beast in that manner. He was all I had. He looked after me for a very long time when I was lost. My mother killed me a long time ago and he took me in as his own."

Well that explains her loyalty to him. I do understand what it's like to not have anyone except a demon to look after you. "I'm sorry your mother killed you, but you have to realize that not everyone is going to see things the way you see them. He was horrible and did awful things to people for years on end. I was the only one who could save them," Amelia explains.

Lily shakes her and looks away. She doesn't believe Amelia.

I have to find a soft spot in this girl so that just maybe I can get out. "Why would your mother want to kill you?" *Poor Mili went through a similar situation. I still can't wrap my brain around it.*

Lily looks down, twists her fingers, and smiles. "She had to get rid of me. She loved me so much that she chose to keep me away from danger. Abraham told me that if I wait in this pyramid, she will find me so that we can live together for eternity."

"I'm confused, what could she have saved you from?"

"Well, I was the product of an unconventional situation. She was raped by her father's brother and later found out she was pregnant. She chose to get an abortion when she was fifteen years old. Her father killed his brother for what he did and kept her secret from everyone so that she could have a normal life. When he died and came here, he found me all alone with nothing. He told me that my mother loved me very much and would come for me one day, that's why he helped me create this world. Once it became successful, he went on to create his own."

"I'm so sorry. You never even had a chance. But what I can't seem to understand is…why would Abraham help you? No offense but what makes you so special?"

"Family takes care of family?" She says with a grin.

Aw hell! Amelia can feel her ears getting hot and her palms starting to sweat. Her whole body is starting to shake with rage. She slowly stands up and turns around to face nothing more than a brick wall, one that she could easily run through with all the fury soaring through her. She turns back around and asks, "The Beast is your family?"

Lily tilts her head and furrows her brow. She stands up. "Yes, he's my grandfather," she says as she walks a little closer, studying Amelia's face.

Amelia steps back and looks over at the guards by the wall. She wonders if she can take them. *Play time is over.* This disgusting bit of news changes everything and she doesn't want to be a part of it.

"Are you okay? You're acting strange," Lily probes with a frown.

Amelia straightens her face and smiles. "Oh yes, I'm fine. If the Beast is your grandfather, then what's your mother's name?" *Please don't say Leona, anyone but her.*

"Her name is Leona…"

Well I'll be damned!

Chapter Thirteen

Well this disaster just gets better and freakin better. Amelia runs her fingers through her hair and sighs. She thinks about the vow she made to God. When she said if ever given the chance, she would get Leona back for what she's done. *I have got to stop making promises I'm not sure I can keep—but I plan to take full advantage of this opportunity—I just need to get to her.* Aaron is still her main priority.

"Hello!" Lily shouts. She glowers at Amelia and knits her brow.

Amelia snaps out of her reverie. "Yeah, what's up?"

"What's up? Look, I'm no fool. I know you're hiding something. I can feel it!" She puts her hands on her hips and taps her heels on the floor, waiting for an explanation.

"I'm not hiding anything! I'm just…"

Lily grabs Amelia's arm. "Don't lie to me! Who are you really?"

Amelia's saddened that Lily can touch her and *not* vanish. It doesn't seem right. *Where are my powers?* Amelia snatches her arm away, walks over to the table, and stares around the room. Stylot follows behind and looks up at her, waiting for her next request. She looks into his eyes, *Follow my lead.* He immediately perks up and guards her as she cases the room.

"I'm going to give you one more chance to tell me what you're hiding!" Lily grunts.

With her back turned to her, Amelia shakes her head and slowly turns around. "Abraham was my grandfather too. Your mother is my aunt," Amelia whispers.

Lily snickers and inches closer. Stylot's growl rises in intensity, compelling her to stop in her tracks as he positions himself between the two. Horus and Jordan walk closer to her and stare at Amelia with malevolence. She is amused by their eagerness to abolish her.

"No way, that would make us cousins? I don't believe you," Lily whispers. Lily scrunches up her face and bites her bottom lip.

"Suit yourself. I don't have time to argue with you about the logistics. But just so you know, your mother and I have unfinished business."

"You will not touch my mother!"

"Do you really think your mother wants anything to do with you? You're a constant reminder of a horrific event that changed her life forever. That's why she got rid of you. And I'm going to get rid of her! I'm going to kill her just like I killed Abraham! They don't deserve to live for eternity. Her soul *will* perish," Amelia says.

Lily bristles with anger and jumps over Stylot. She and Amelia tumble and Amelia punches her in the nose. Lily grabs her hair and yanks hard. Stylot fearlessly walks towards them with saliva dripping from his mouth. A lurid growl explodes from his monstrous frame, scaring Lily. Lily has Amelia's hair in one hand and her throat in the other. "Tell your dog to move!" she shouts. She's standing directly behind her.

"Never!" Amelia croaks as Lily squeezes her throat tighter. Amelia stomps Lily on the foot and pulls Lily's arms so hard it breaks.

"Ahhh! My arm!" she screams.

Horus grabs Amelia from behind. She fights back to get out of his hold when Stylot jumps on both of them. Amelia lands directly under Stylot and rolls over just as Stylot tears Horus's head off his body. She wipes the splattering blood from her face and sees Horus's head land over by the steps. She glances back at Stylot in shock; she's momentarily forgotten just how powerful he is.

"No!" Jordan shouts as he heads towards Stylot. Realizing that Horus cannot be saved, Lily stops Jordan and redirects his attention to fetch more blood. Jordan frantically sprints to the table and grabs some of the blood while Lily limps behind him. She gulps down as much blood as possible and snaps her arm back in place. Amelia runs passed them and head towards the guards when Lily trips her and pulls her up by her hair again.

Grrr! Ruff! Stylot crouches down, readying himself to bite Lily when Amelia notices the huge guards by the wall looking in their direction. They glance at Lily, waiting for her permission to attack.

"No Stylot! It's okay, I'm fine." He sits on his hind legs and begins to whine. His loud cries force the zombies to stop and look at the chaos.

Lily pushes Amelia down where she crawls over to him and hugs his neck, wondering if this is it. Lily stands over them and grimaces with bitterness. Amelia can practically hear her mind working, searching for an appropriate resolution to satisfy her need for revenge. She diligently walks back and forth while clicking her heels on the hard, shiny floor. Finally, the clicking stops.

Amelia looks up at her with tear-filled eyes, hoping there's an ounce of compassion. But instead, Lily leans over and spits in her face.

"Gross! Did you really just spit on me!" Amelia screams. Amelia rises up and slaps Lily so hard she falls backwards. Jordan rushes over just as Stylot rams him into the table and bites his hand.

"Help!" He cries as he hurdles towards the steps. Stylot stays put while keeping a close watch on him. Lily attempts to get up when Amelia kicks her in the face and runs into the crowd.

"Guards! Get them!" Lily hollers as Amelia and Stylot race through the green mass. The golden eyed giants move away from the wall and walk in their direction. Thankfully, they're no longer guarding the exit, which is just what Amelia wanted. It's their only chance to escape. She sprints her way through as fast as possible while Stylot follows close behind. The guards continue to walk at a steady pace almost as if they know they'll catch them. Amelia and Stylot make it halfway through the crowd when suddenly the people begin to close in on them. They are completely surrounded with nowhere to run.

Amelia can see Lily halfway up the stairs with her right hand raised. She assumes that's Lily's signal to command them to do what she wants. The people look up at her with understanding. Their eyes are filled with so much emptiness it's hard to watch. Amelia looks down and anticipates the worst as they continue to move in on her and Stylot. Stylot stands directly in front of Amelia, but it's the ones from behind that are the most frightening. She turns around and leans up against him, terrified of the unknown. She feels like vomiting again as her whole body shakes, but she refuses to give in, again.

"Bring me the blood!" Lily demands as she gravitates down the steps. Jordan runs to the large table in front of the guards and takes the blood from the right bowl. He hands it to her.

Great, I'll be a damn zombie in no time.
The circle around them is getting tighter and tighter.
Grrrr! Ruff! Ruff!
Amelia pets his fur to calm him down, knowing that it's no use in trying to scare the people away. They clearly don't belong to themselves anymore and probably can't understand human emotion.

"We won't go down without a fight, right boy?" Amelia whispers. Stylot barks in agreement.

One of the giant guards makes his way through the crowd and grabs Amelia. He holds her so tight she can feel her arms going numb. "Let me go!" She squirms to break free but it's no use. Her fervent will to stay strong is only making her tired and him happy. Without much success on her end, she plays the last card she has. "Stylot!" she hollers, hoping he'll scare some of them away. On cue, he jumps about eight feet in the air and roars loudly. Everyone scoots back. Amelia body slams the guard and makes a run through the tiny hole from the crowd but Lily greets her as she comes out. She pushes her back into the maze with the cup of blood in hand.

Dammit! I was so close.

As Stylot battles the other guard and tears off his arm, Lily pushes Amelia further into the crowd and kicks her in the leg.

Amelia kicks her back and punches her in the stomach, but Lily presses forward, seeming unfazed. Jordan gets a fist full of Amelia's hair and forces her to her knees. He holds her head back. "You *will* drink this blood…cousin!" Lily laughs.

"No I won't. You are so gonna pay for this!" Amelia shrieks. Lily smirks and holds the cup to Amelia's mouth. Amelia gets out of Jordan's strong grip and knocks the cup of blood all over Lily's clothes.

"Huh! Ugh! You troll!" Lily roars. The guard shakes off the effects of being slammed to the floor and brings Lily another cup.

Grrr! Stylot forces his way through the crowd, baring his teeth.

"Get back dog or I will snap her neck!" Lily screams with both of her hands on Amelia's face.

Stylot stands firm without moving, waiting for Amelia's command.

"Kill!" Amelia shouts. She punches Lily in the chest just as Stylot charges Jordan.

"Oh that's it!" Lily huffs. She throws Amelia to the floor and straddles her in order to hold her arms down. Lily motions for two zombies to come closer. Before Amelia can get up, two of them forcefully grab her arms while two more pin her legs down. Lily stands up and holds out her hand for the cup of blood. Amelia wiggles and twists her body to try and free herself, but she's trapped and defenseless. She looks over and sees Stylot still busy with Jordan, which is good because she wouldn't want him to see her like this. She starts to cry. Everything is happening in slow motion and it's frightening. She's so afraid of what the blood will do to her.

The noise is slowly fading from her ears and the sound of Lily's laughter and clacking heels is all that's left. As she leans over Amelia's immobile body with the cup in her hand, a victorious grin forms across her face. Her golden eyes light up with so much happiness because her future is getting brighter by the second. All Amelia can hope for is that Stylot somehow escapes because *her* future is about to become nonexistent. Lily looks into Amelia's eyes and smiles deviously, reminding her that she's won.

She's definitely her mother's daughter, in every sense of the word, Amelia thinks.

Lily leans closer while steadily holding the blood-filled cup to Amelia's mouth. As Amelia turns her head and tightly seals her lips, something strange happens. Her hands are suddenly free and she can move her legs. A horrified look forms across Lily's face as she slowly stands up with confusion. A soft-handed person takes Amelia's hand and pulls her off the floor. Whoever it is they're practically dragging her through the massive crowd, but all she can see is the back of their green cloak. Amelia looks back and sees Lily fighting her way through the mass to catch her, but the zombies have reverted back to a chanting state of mind, blocking her from Amelia's reach.

"Bring her back here!" Lily shouts while trying to get closer.
Bark! Bark!
The mindless beings stop their chanting and scoot away from the intense growls. The brave person stops and turns around to look at Amelia.

It's the brown-eyed man. I knew he wasn't like the others, Amelia observes.

He pulls down his green hood and unveils his pale skin and messy brown hair. Amelia smiles graciously. The silence around them becomes overwhelming and terrifying. Lily and her guards stare at them furiously as Stylot dares them to move an inch.

"What is your name?" Amelia asks.

"*Je m'appelle* Dumont," he answers with a smile.

"Ha! Ha! He can't even speak English. Sorry Amelia, I guess you'll never know what he's saying!" Lily giggles.

Amelia rolls her eyes. *"Combien de temps avez-vous été ici?"* Amelia asks.

His face lights up when he realizes Amelia can speak French. Amelia wonders if everything in life is one big coincidence or is this truly her fate. She never understood why her mother and grandmother insisted that she learn French. She understands that French is part of her heritage, but she honestly thought she would never really have a use for it. But now, she's elated because they were somehow preparing her for this moment. This man has just saved her life and she hopes he can tell her how to escape. Amelia looks back and smiles at Lily.

"E-eight years," he laments.

"That's quite a while," Amelia replies.

He nods but she can tell he doesn't understand her.

"C'est un bon moment," she says. "Thank you for what you did."

"Uhhh…welcome." He takes her hand and says, "Time—to—go." He looks around and points to the wall where the sunlight barely passes through. He puts his hands on her shoulders and looks into her eyes. "Door."

"I know, I figured."

"J'ai les distraira donc vous pouvez vous en sortir," he says.

"Distract them? No, you come with me. Please," Amelia whispers. She'd feel horrible if he stayed here to die while she breaks free. It just doesn't seem right. She shakes her head no. *"Viens avec moi?"* she asks again, hoping he'll say yes.

"No. Je suis prêt à être enfin libre." Tears fill his eyes as he assures her that he's ready for his soul to be set free. She can definitely understand that and is thankful he outsmarted that dimwit and never drank the blood. "When out, destroy," he whispers.

"How do I destroy the pyramid?" He looks puzzled and frowns with anxiety.

"Comment pour le détruire?" she inquires again.

He hands her a gold ball with a lion's head engraved on the front. She looks up confused. "What is this?"

He stares at her.

"Sorry, um…*Qu'est-ce que c'est?"*

"Power," he answers. He points to the top of the stairs, indicating he must have taken it from Lily. Before she can respond, the giant guard bravely rushes past Stylot and decides to take his chances.

Ruff! Ruff! Stylot runs after him as Lily runs closely behind him.

Dumont kisses Amelia's cheek and rams his entire body into the guard before he has a chance to touch her. Amelia slips the gold ball into her pocket and runs towards Lily as she sprints towards her. They both fall and battle it out until Amelia draws back and punches Lily in the mouth. She gets up and runs towards the large table, but Lily grabs her and pulls her back down. Amelia slams Lily's head against the floor and picks up the bowl of blood. As Lily stands to her feet Amelia throws the entire bowl of red liquid all over her, blinding her.

"I can't see!" She cries, rubbing her eyes.

Amelia looks back and sees Dumont losing his battle against the guard as Stylot tries to tear off the guard's leg. A bloody mass of fragments is scattered in the corner. Amelia realizes it's Jordan's remains.

"Go!" Dumont shouts while falling to the ground. With tears in her eyes, Amelia waves goodbye and jumps on the table.

"Stylot! Let's go!" she screams as her foot lands directly into the other bowl of blood. It falls to the floor and shatters, sending the zombies into a blood thirsty frenzy.

Stylot stops what he's doing and runs after Amelia as she finally makes her way to the wall.

"Get them!" Lily grumbles to her robots. Their eyes buck up and they start to run in Amelia's direction, almost as if they're battery operated. Amelia looks at Stylot and nods a silent warning for him to follow her. She takes a deep breath and runs as fast as she can, praying and hoping she's not being fooled. *What idiot purposely runs directly into a brick wall?* Before she has time to react, the sunlight hits her and Stylot in the face. They both fall out of the pyramid and land in the grass. She jumps up and touches her arms and legs to make sure she's still herself and not imagining things. Stylot jumps up and runs around happily. She puts her hand on her chest and hums along to the extraordinary sound of her heartbeat. *I guess Navid listened; he's keeping me alive on his end.*

She walks further out into the grassy area and admires the gigantic dwelling Abraham created for his granddaughter. *It's too bad that such a beautiful site is full of so much evil. I kinda feel sorry for Lily... sort of.* If Leona was planning on coming to be with her daughter, she is sadly mistaken. She will sniff the blood and find her way to her child, but all Amelia's going to leave her is…nothing.

She takes out the golden symbol and throws it directly towards the pyramid. She stares and waits for it to crumble but nothing happens.

At least I was right about my theory. Lily can't leave the pyramid, nor can the people inside. She turns to walk away when the ground starts to shake.

"Stylot, come over here boy!" Amelia hollers and glares at the pyramid. Suddenly, a loud crash followed by a crack awakens the entire area. Birds fly out of the way and the wind picks up speed, implying that a terrible change is coming. Stylot trots over to her and gawks at the pyramid.

"Let's go!" she commands.

They both sprint away to escape the magnitude of an impending explosion. "Help!" Amelia yells as the shockwaves casts their bodies through the air. "Ahh!" Her screams are nothing more than echoes in the wind. She's powerless to stop herself from slamming into a giant Redwood.

Aaron's beautiful face is staring back at her. The liveliness of his green eyes are enchanting. *I'll never tire of looking at him, the most beautiful man in the world.* He kisses her zealously while running his fingers through her hair. She opens her eyes as he slowly kisses her cheek. Her entire body is hot and anxious for more. Unexpectedly, he's no longer within her reach. She's staring right at him but can't get to him. He's distant and appears to be troubled. He's not alone.

Someone is with him, but she doesn't know who, nor can she see them, she just knows. Everything slowly fades away. She rubs her eyes and squints to see him again. It brings her to tears when she sees him sitting under an oak tree. He's surrounded by orange trees and bushes adorned with black berries. The water is crystal blue and the green grass looks good enough for Heaven. But through all of it, Aaron is despondent and could care less about his environment. He slowly lifts his head and says, "Lisette, wherever you are—I love you."

"Aaron! Aaron can you hear me! I'm right here!" she cries. "Please! Answer me! I love you too!" She attempts to run to him but the more she runs, the further away he gets. Everything turns into darkness. "No! Aaron, come back to me! Please," she moans, falling to the ground. She rubs her wet eyes and wails. "He needs me," she sobs. A single drop of water falls on her face. Aside from her own tears, she doesn't understand where it's coming from. She looks up at an impeccable blue sky with white puffy clouds. The sound of someone crying wills her to open her eyes. Stylot whimpers continuously as he licks her face.

"Stylot? What happened?" she asks. She sits up and rubs her head.

Bark! Bark! He jumps up and runs behind a tree then back around to her and licks her face again.

"Aww, were you worried about me boy? I'm okay now." She inhales and wipes her face. That heartbreaking dream about Aaron has confused her, but she knows there's a reason she had it. She needed to see him and know that he's still okay, and that he still loves her very much. "I will find you, love," she whispers.

She looks around and realizes they're in a forest. The tall redwood trees are endless and there are bushes and shrubs everywhere. She tries to stand, but her wobbly legs threaten to give out. She rocks back and forth, being careful not to fall back down. *I must have hit my head harder than I realized.* She steadies herself and moves forward. She reaches the edge of the forest and stares out at the vacant land, where the pyramid used to be. The one on the left is still standing majestically, completely untouched. She turns back around and reenters the forest with a big smile on her face. *I can't believe I destroyed it. Now all of those souls can finally meet their desired ends, the way life is supposed to be before my errant grandfather roamed the afterlife and decided to ruin their final resting place. When Leona shows up, I'll be waiting for her.*

With a grin, she takes off running deep into the forest to see what amazing things lie ahead. Fear is something she's no longer familiar with. Whenever she allows herself to give in and be afraid, something or someone gives her courage. And for some reason, the people around her become courageous as well, keeping her alive. Nothing can stop her now because she knows she's destined to find Aaron. That's the only thing that makes sense in all this craziness. *Maybe I'm invincible.* If she is, she can certainly live with that, but if not, she can only hope that their souls will meet and be free from evil. Dead or alive, they'll find each other. They have to.

Chapter Fourteen

"Come on Stylot!" Amelia gasps while racing him through the forest. She's intrigued to see what Felinity has to offer now that the pyramid is kaput. Of course anything is better than Bram. She grimaces at the thought of the gross toxic wasteland her grandfather created and is so thrilled that it's finally gone. Stylot brushes past her with ease as if she's not running at all. *Ugh! That'll teach me to challenge him.* She wishes she could run as fast as he can, better yet she wishes she was as big as he is. "I wish I could turn into a monstrous dog," she says through a laugh. She picks up speed and feels as free and light as a bird. Stylot is a few strides ahead of her as she closes in on him. She smiles wickedly while looking into his eyes, running right past him. *Wow, I'm really fast.*

She notices Stylot has slowed down and has a terrified look on his face. *What's that about?* "Come on!" she puffs, still running. He barks at her and trots, but at a much slower pace. The magical forest and all it's enchantment is inviting her in. She slows down, feeling tired and heavy. *I feel detached from my body, like something's wrong with me.* She looks down and freezes. "WHAT THE HELL! OH MY GOD!" she shouts. She turns around and looks at Stylot. He stops a few feet away from her and sits on his hind legs. *Are my eyes playing tricks on me?.* She jumps up and down and turns in circles with horror. "I…I have paws," she whispers while staring at her feet.

"*Yes, you do Amelia. I don't understand,*" Stylot replies.

His gleaming eyes are fixated on her. He walks a little closer and gawks at her shiny black fur, her short tail, and her giant paws. *We're the same.* She feels like she's looking into a mirror. She starts to cry and buries her paws over her head. *How on earth did this happen? Is this some weird curse Lily put on me before I escaped?* "I'm a freakin dog," she sobs. She starts to choke and cough loudly with exasperation. Even her cough sounds like a bark.

"*Are you alright?*" he asks while nudging her side with his nose.

"I can understand you. How can this be?"

"*Maybe because we're both dogs,*" he answers. He walks behind her. His tongue wags in sync with his tail as he stares at her. He slowly sniffs the back of her legs and groans.

Amelia slowly turns around and faces him. "Stylot, I swear on all that is holy, if you even think of coming near me again, I'm going to crush you."

His black eyes bug out and he scoots away from her. He whimpers and puts his head down in shame.

Great, now I feel bad. She walks over and rubs her head against his mane to ensure all is good. *He just needs to know that I'm not about to be his bitch.* "Listen, I don't mean to take out my anger on you, but this is very overwhelming."

"*I get it, and, I'm sorry. It was a momentary lapse in judgment, and it won't happen again.*" He perks up and holds his head high and chest out.

"No worries. Just be my protector, that's all I need," she sighs and walks over to a nearby bush.

"*You got it boss. But just so you know, you're one hot canine,*" he groans as he sticks his tongue out.

"Stylot! Enough! Please, keep your impure thoughts to a minimum!"

He nods and lifts his leg to pee, eyeing her with a devilish manner. His eyes motion for her to look down to check out his male parts.

She quickly turns around and walks behind the bush. *This is not happening to me.* She squats down and pees in the privacy of her own surroundings. She can't afford to pee in front of him with his mind so clouded with lust. *So this is what's it's like, being free and open to the outside world. Dogs really do have it easy. They can do whatever they want without the shameful guilt of being watched. I kind of like it. I just wish I could figure out what prompted this miraculous change.* Whatever the reason, she's decided she can't stay like this for long, realizing that Stylot won't be able to control his actions much longer. She looks up and sees him sniffing around the bush where she just urinated. "Holy cow." *Okay, let me think about this for a second. I was running with Stylot and somehow I changed, but why? How?* She shakes her head and wanders over to a small pond. The blue water looks so clean and crisp. She laps it up and marvels at the taste.

"I wish I could be myself again," she mutters sadly. *Oh no!* An overwhelming feeling of nausea invades her body and she becomes taller and less hairy. She falls to the ground and stares at her hands and feet. "Oh thank God!" She laughs as she hugs herself. "This is amazing." *So whatever I wish to be is my command?* She stares at her hands. *Is this just a coincidence?* Then it dawns on her. "Carys!" She remembers when they said their goodbyes Carys told her she was giving her something. *Wow! That's why I have no powers, she gave me hers.* She jumps up. "Carys wherever you are, thank you!"

Stylot appears from behind the bushes and stops abruptly.

She smiles and runs over to hug him. "Sorry boy, I know you had big plans for us, but I think this is for the best." She rubs his fur and hops up. She walks alongside the tall trees, hoping he'll follow her. *Bark! Bark!* She pauses and whirls around. An unnaturally large possum hisses at him and slowly moves forward. Green slime falls out of its mouth as it closes in on him. "I wish I was a large fox," Amelia whispers. Suddenly, she's back on all fours again. Without giving the enemy a chance to react, she pounces over and with her teeth, tears its head halfway off it's body. Lurid squeals fill the air as it slowly dies.

She squeezes her eyes shut and focuses hard on yet another anomalous transformation. She ponders the things people take for granted and declares that there is no greater feeling than being back in your own skin. She shakes off the eccentric sensation of the aftermath and trudges forward on her journey. *I have to find some way out of this world and I hate the fact that it's probably, like Bram, not going to be easy.* She thought she'd be in Heaven by now, but evidently there are bigger plans in store for her. "Come Stylot, we have a lot of ground to cover and not much time." He eagerly jogs on the side of her, relieved. While walking in silence, Stylot glances at her and takes off running down a grassy lane. She sprints behind him, laughing at his unexpected behavior. *He's never been this playful.*

"I'll show you!" she giggles. With less concentration than before, she finds herself flying high above the trees, soaring elegantly. Her yellow wings are beautifully spread beneath the azure sky. The warm breeze is in her favor as it permits her to glide carefully over the earth. She can see everything and it's breathtaking. She peers down and spots a black ferocious creature running like the wind. *He probably thinks I'm still behind him.* Since precision is not her strong suit, she cautiously alights down in his direction to keep from killing herself. She barely misses his head as she bounces off the grass and lands behind a bush. Stylot staggers to the side to keep from crushing her.

She quickly transforms back to herself and caresses her pulsating arm. Although the view was indescribable, her landing was pretty intense and quite painful. She pulls the leaves out of her hair and brushes off her clothes. *Note to self, never transform into a bird again on purpose.* Amazingly, she's always fully dressed when she changes back, which she appreciates given her newfound revelation about her protector. *Hey, where's Stylot?* She steps from behind the bush and yells, "Stylot where are you?" *Where could he be? Oh jeez, I hope he's not hurt.* She searches for him, feeling lost and disoriented without him. *I don't know what I would do without him. Is he mad at me?* As she peeks behind every bush and tree stump she starts to get worried. *It's not like him to just disappear on me.* She starts to panic. *What if there was another possum lurking?*

"Stylot!" she screams, hoping he'll pop out unharmed. She speed walks through the forest and frantically searches for him. Eventually, she finds herself in a large prairie field that reeks of animal musk. The smell reminds her of the animals at the zoo. They were so extraordinary and exotic in their own way, but their stench was revolting. Bile rises in her throat like an ocean tide; she gulps it back down and continues looking for Stylot. Her eyes begin to well up with tears and her nose runs. She can't ignore the terrible feeling that something is wrong. "Stylot!" she cries, running towards a distant tree. "Stylot are you here?"

Grrr! Bark! Bark!

She stops and turns around to see where the growls are coming from. But he doesn't appear. She looks forward and makes her way towards the tree, praying that the sounds get louder.

Ruff! Ruff!

"Stylot!" Amelia shouts. She can tell he's near. A gust of wind unexpectedly knocks her over. She leaps up and fights her way through the powerful breeze and grabs a hold of the tree. She is thankful that it's well rooted as she finds herself hanging on for dear life. Her feet are no longer planted on the ground and are swaying in midair. "What's going on?" she whispers, frightened. Another strong gust of wind practically forces her arm away from the tree, leaving her terrified. "Aahh! Help!" She feels as though she's in the eye of some weird storm. With determined concentration, she finally gets her other arm safely around a tree limb.

The sun is hiding behind thick stratus clouds and every living thing has run for cover. One wrong move and Amelia could be thrown into the madness and die a painful death. She uses all her strength and pulls herself closer to the tree, hugging it tightly. "Oh please let Stylot be okay," she prays as she squeezes her eyes shut. Her head is buried between her arms and the tree as the piercing wind worsens. Heavy rain beats down her like a drum. She is hanging onto life by a thread and she can't help but cry with worry for him. *I hope he's somewhere safe.* With her eyes still closed, she imagines being in Aaron's arms, embracing his every touch and kiss.

The happiness in his face is what she misses the most. Every time he looked into her eyes his face lit up with undying and unconditional love. She was nothing when she met him, just a shallow casing of a person, radiating hatred for her aunt. She wanted nothing except revenge and yearned to find a way to kill her, to kill herself, until he showed up. Suddenly, her life wasn't so horrible or unbearable, but worth sticking around for. Worth growing to love him and living for him because he lived for her. When she was helpless and frightened from abuse, he was her foundation…her protector. And now that her father will soon be reunited with her mother, that's all the motivation she needs to live as long as she possibly can. *I just need to find Stylot and get out of this place.* Crack! Her eyes shoot open and she looks around. A tree branch descends from the strong wood and falls into the grass. The sun peers out of the clouds and shines as bright as ever, imploring the land to come back to life. "Thank God that's over," she mumbles. She peels herself away from the tree completely drenched, and apprehensively puts one foot in front of the other.

She envisions something terrible, which makes her cry. *What if he was captured?* She mindlessly starts running through the tall weeds searching desperately for him. Ssssss. *Oh no! I know that sound.* She halts, almost falling forward and looks around. The giant king cobra slowly rises in the grass. *Not again! What does it want?*

It slithers closer to her, awkwardly moving from side to side. Amelia holds her breath. Her hands are planted by her sides. She keeps a watchful eye on its forked tongue, which protrudes every three seconds. They stand face to face for what seems like hours. She's afraid to move or do anything except stand there, frozen.

Finally, she breaks out of the trance and her mood slowly changes. She's not afraid anymore. For some reason, she feels connected to it and is baffled because it should've killed her by now. While still looking into its eyes, she gradually exhales and turns to walk away. *If it's going to kill me, it'll have to do it with my back turned.*

She walks further into the tall grass and finds herself headed towards a cobble-stoned bridge. Just for kicks she turns to see if the snake is still there and from what she can tell it's gone.

She walks over the bridge and admires the sapphire water beneath. The bridge leads her to a tall wooden door with an arrangement of large magnolias that form an arch. With shaky hands she turns the gold knob and pushes it open. She takes a swift step to the side, remembering that the last time she opened a door a million black birds flew out and almost beheaded her. After waiting for a spell, she inhales and gathers the nerve to walk through. She's immediately taken aback by the majestic new world that unfolds before her eyes. Even the air is different. The mouthwatering scent of fresh green apples and pine flows in the atmosphere. It's intoxicating fragrance summons her to continue walking further into the foreign masterpiece. She tucks her hair behind her ears and straightens her clothes. A feeling of unworthiness overcomes her as she trespasses on some forbidden creation that's built on innocence and sacred ground. From the horrific things she's witnessed thus far, she fears her eyes are diseased with enough sin to last a lifetime. A large tree filled with every type of fruit imaginable is planted right in the center of the land.

The mahogany dirt is smooth and feels like powder between her fingers; the sky is red-violet. Far beyond the fruit tree are hills and hills of emerald beauty. To get a closer look at the tree, she strolls forward until she is standing inches away, admiring the sweet and decadent scents it has to offer. Slam! She jumps back and sees a little person dressed in brown pants and a blue shirt running out of a small dwelling made out of leaves. He's heading right in her direction. She steps back with an apologetic look, but he seems to have his mind set on one thing. Without acknowledging her presence, he floats in midair and flies all the way to the top of the tree. He quickly snatches a kiwi fruit and shoves it into his mouth. He grabs another and noshes on it while moaning in the process. Once he gets his fill, he carefully gravitates all the way back to the ground.

Amelia's immobile and afraid to speak. *What if these little people are like the Gobblewits?* Her insides churn when she recollects their preposterous plans to burn her alive and feast on her flesh. The very thought makes the blood drain from her face and steals the strength from her legs. The little person walks back into his house and closes the door where a small amount of leaves drift to the ground.

She's dumbfounded. *Did he see me or am I invisible?* She shakes off her irrational thoughts of her relevance and reaches out to grab some grapes. "Oh! Well that explains a lot. I can't see my hands," she says. *When could I have possibly disappeared without knowing it?* She concentrates hard on making herself reappear, but then stops when thoughts of her safety pop into her mind. *It may be safer to stay like this until I find Stylot. Carys disappeared all the time when she was afraid, maybe this is a natural reaction from her powers.*

There's a row of houses to her left that are made out of an assortment of materials. Some homes are made of bricks, some are made from dirt, and others are made from black rock. She walks around a corner and comes across a family of little people gathering water from a well. They look up and sniff the air but remain silent. Her footprints are the only indication that she's present and she wonders if they know she's there. The red-haired woman smiles in her direction; then she looks down and continues filling up her bucket. The little boy runs around in the grass and kicks an orange ball to his Yorkshire terrier. Her husband takes the heavy bucket of water and sets it into a pocket that's bridled on their pony. There's a ton of fruit in the other bucket that they must have picked from the tree. They gather their belongings and slowly lead the pony away.

"Come on Gabriel! Time to go, son!" the woman yells. The little boy picks up his ball and runs towards his parents. Their little dog runs behind him. *Bark! Bark!* He jumps up and down with a stick in his mouth, his tail wagging, begging his owner to oblige him. A big smile forms across the man's face as he tosses the stick down the path. The cute puppy sprints in that direction but ends up tripping and rolling over a few times. They laugh aloud and pick it up. This makes Amelia think of Stylot. *Where is he? This is so unnerving.* More people come out of their homes and make a beeline for the tree to gather fruit to their hearts' desire. *The tree must be their livelihood, maybe their only means of survival.*

She walks around senselessly until she stops at the threshold of another piece of land. The only thing separating the two areas is an assemblage of bushes and tree branches. She's reluctant to enter given her uncanny ability to find trouble. *Still, it doesn't hurt to check it out.* She bends over and peeks through a bush to get a clear view of the area, careful not to be taken off guard. *Clack! Clack! Clack!* A brown horse shoots across her line of sight and races down a dirt road. "Huh! Whoa!" she squeals and falls backwards. She jumps back up and peeks through again to see if the horse is still there, but it's gone.

A beautiful white mare walks across the lane and heads over to a giant grayish brown bin full of water. This reminds her of when Cash used to take her horseback riding when she was eleven. He taught her so much about them. Riding horses was the only thing, aside from her mother, that could truly relax him. She misses him so much and hopes she can get back to him and Alexandria and see the new person he'll become without the chokehold of his father's evil presence hanging over him.

The mare takes a sip and looks in Amelia's direction. She stares in curiosity for a while and takes another sip. Once she finishes, she proceeds to walks towards the entrance. *Oh no. Can she smell me? Do I stink?* Amelia sniffs her armpits. Neeeehahaha! A black and white horse trots over to the mare and snorts. She turns around and walks next to him where they take off running far into the distance, leaving a cloud of dust behind them. *I don't see how this can be a harmful place to enter. Besides, my Stylot could be in there, so I can't back down now. But just in case, I'll transform into a horse so that I can blend in.* With careful concentration, she becomes a shiny black beast. She hops over the bushes and finds herself in the middle of the land. She starts running as fast as she can. Her long raven hair flows in the wind. *Wow, this is so cool. I would totally love to come back as a horse if I could.* She gallops through the hills and dirt roads. She feels so liberated and glorious that she finds it difficult to stay focused on why she's there. Once she reaches a dead end, she turns around and walks through the town, searching for Stylot. *He has to be here...somewhere.*

She walks over to a bucket of water and quenches her thirst. *Bark! Bark!*

She stops and looks around. "Stylot!" she shouts. *That's his bark, he is here!* "Stylot!" As she calls his name, nothing but the sound of a horse comes out. *Crap! He won't be able to understand me. I have to transform back.* She closes her eyes to focus when all of a sudden, someone jumps on her back. She shakes the intruder off and comes face to face with a man dressed all in black. His dark eyes are full of fear, like he's running from someone. She senses that he's mean and hateful. *He's a demon!*

"Damn you!" He screams at her. He jumps up and looks behind him. A blond man peeks from behind a tree and throws his spear at him. He barely misses the demon's face. Amelia quickly moves out of the way. *I have to get out of here.* She starts to run when the demon grabs her tail and pulls hard. Neeehahaha! Ahhh! She falls back on her hind legs where he quickly hops on again. He angrily strikes her with the spear, forcing her to cry out. "Run! You fool!" He yells as he hits her again. Neeehahaha! Argh! "Go! Go!" The pain is the worst she's ever felt.

She takes off running with the demon on her back and looks back at the blond man still hiding behind the tree. He steps out and reveals the rest of his body. *Oh my God! He's a horse too!*

"Go! Keep going!" he yells as they embark on the entrance. She tries to shake him off again, but he won't let her go. He hits her again and kicks her side. She pants and pants, hoping he'll have mercy on her, but he's persistent and aggressive.

Gosh! Just when I thought all the abuse was over. He and Leona could write a book. Evil comes so naturally for them. She wiggles and shakes, but the demon is determined to use her as has his escape plan. Warm tears run down her face as the pain gets more excruciating.

"Go through the bushes!" he screams while striking her once more. She speeds up and flies over the bushes. She's back in the town with the little people.

There's a huge crowd gathered around in shock by what they're witnessing. She brushes through the town and out of the main wooden door. As she makes her way towards the bridge, she realizes this may be her only chance to get rid of him. She shakes from side to side, but he stabs her over and over, causing her to slow down.

Blood pours out of her side and drips on the ground. "Help me!" she cries. She knows they can't understand her, but continues to plead as her consciousness slowly fades. She's lightheaded and exhausted. She slows down and endures the pain as he stabs her again. "Go!" he howls. Amelia musters enough strength to run faster and harder, giving it her all as her life slowly starts to diminish. Her vision is cloudy and she's having trouble breathing.

She finally collapses on the bridge, forcing the demon to fall into the water. His howling screams echo in her ears as she envisions him being eaten alive by something. She looks at her arms and even in her weakened state is glad to be back to her original self, if only for the last time.

Bark! Bark! Stylot is here.

He whimpers and licks her face. She touches his furry face and tearfully whispers, "Goodbye...."

Chapter Fifteen

When Amelia opens her eyes, the clear blue sky and the vigorous sound of her heart beating puts a big smile on her face. *If I didn't die, how on earth was I able to survive that brutal attack?* She slowly tries to sit up, but feels as though she's being weighted down by five elephants. *Oh no, am I paralyzed? This can't be.* She starts to panic as the air rushes out of her chest. Her face feels like it's going to explode. She's lying under a blanket of leaves as the sun peers down on her through the trees. She turns to her right and sees a mysterious man fast asleep.

Who is he?

His blond wavy hair brushes the top of his shoulders and his long sandy eyelashes are exquisite. His muscular arms are formed flawlessly and his abs looks as though they were painted on. He reminds her of Aaron, just a lighter version. She looks past his abs and sees… "AHH!" she…screams in fear.

His ocean blue eyes snap open with fright as he carefully puts his hands in the air.

Amelia shuts her eyes tight and puts her hands over her ears. "This is not real. This is not real," she says through tears. *He's a man and a horse. This entire time I was lying next to a man horse! This is the weirdest diversion ever. I have got to get away before he tries to kill me.* She sits up and looks down at her legs. "AHHH! No! What the hell!"

"Let me explain!" The man shows caution as he rises on four legs.

"I am a… HORSE GIRL! What did you do to me?!" Amelia scrambles to her feet and stands erect, barely keeping her balance.

He looks down and blushes with a big smile on his face.

She frowns and looks down at her very exposed breasts. "Holy cow!" She pivots and covers her boobs with her hair. While turned around, she closes her eyes and concentrates hard on transforming back to herself. After a few seconds, she opens her eyes and angrily stomps her hoof in the ground. Feeling abhorrent, she descends into the grass.

The man puts his hand on her shoulder and whispers, "Please, don't be upset." She can't stop the tears from flowing, but that doesn't keep her from jumping up and kicking him in the chest.

"Ouch! What was that for?" He wails while rubbing his ribcage.

"That was for doing whatever you did! What's wrong with me? The last time I saw you, you were throwing a spear at that demon's head!"

"Okay, I understand why you would be upset, but I saved your life."

"How? I was bleeding to death."

"Well, I saw him jump on your back and at first I thought you were just another horse, until I heard you cry for help. So I ran after you and found you, a breathtaking beauty, on that bridge. I couldn't stop looking at you," he explains. He looks down and shakes his head. "Anyway, much to my family's chagrin, I used some of my powers to bring you back. But… when we use our powers on someone, they come back as one of us."

"O-one of you?" she stutters as her heart hammers against her chest.

He nods his head and takes a few steps back.

She wants to rip his head off, but the only thing stopping her is the fact that he saved her life. *Maybe this is a temporary fix until my powers come back. They have to come back. I can't stay like this.* She inhales deeply and steps forward.

He flinches and guards himself as she holds out her hand. "Thank you for saving me. I don't necessarily condone *how* you saved me, but nevertheless I'm glad."

With relief, he grins and shakes her hand. "You're welcome. So, you're not mad at me?"

"Oh I'm still mad at you. But things could have turned out much differently if you hadn't been brave enough to do what you felt was right." He nods and gazes into her eyes. She scowls anxiously, wondering what his problem is.

He nervously taps his left hoof on the ground and twists his fingers.

Jeez, he's just like me.

"Soooo, are you hungry?" he asks.

"Yes, my appetite has suddenly become more apparent given my, um, circumstances."

He smirks and pats her on the shoulder. *This is so humiliating.* She sulks and follows him out of his part of the forest. *Why did I have to enjoy being a horse? I retract the thought of ever coming back as one, now that I really am one, kind of. And here I thought I was walking on safe ground.* She breaks away from her thoughts and notices he's leading her towards the land of the little people.

She grabs his arm and whispers, "Hey, is it safe here? Won't they get mad if we're trespassing?"

"No, they've already seen you."

"What! How? I was invisible when I walked through here before, even though I swear one of them smiled in my direction."

"They can see beyond powers Amelia. You haven't fooled anyone by coming here, especially them. We all share the fruit from the tree, its how we survive."

"I know but… wait, how do you know my name?"

"Stylot told me." He shrugs and continues walking ahead.

"Stylot! He's okay? Where is he? I thought I saw him before I was dying, but assumed it wasn't real." She hurries to catch up to him.

He sighs, turns around, and grabs her shoulders. "I need you to relax. We found him unconscious out in the storm and took really good care of him. Trust me Stylot is doing just fine. As a matter of fact, my little sister is having the time of her life with him. She's given him a bath and played catch with him. You name it," he says.

"Ha! Ha! Yeah if that's true I'm sure he's having a blast." She sighs with relief. Although she's not amused by the new turn of events, she's happy he's alright. She is also thankful that she doesn't have a horse face and still looks like herself. She cranes to look at her backside, which is now a cream colored creation mixed with specs of brown. *Not too shabby.* She looks at her new hero whose walking ahead of her. *He's a chocolate silk masterpiece. Oh my God! What's wrong with me? Why am I talking about him like he's a scoop of ice cream?* "Hey, do your powers also mess with a person's head?" Amelia asks.

He stops and turns around. "No, why? Are you feeling alright?" He looks at her with concern.

She turns away and blushes. "No, I was just asking." She nervously bites her lip.

He furrows his brow and smiles, indicating he doesn't believe her response. "So what's your pleasure, Miss Amelia?"

"M-my pleasure?" she breathes.

"Yeah, um, what fruit would you like to eat?"

"Oh! Yes of course. I'll have some grapes," she answers. She walks behind the tree to gather herself. He picks some fruit while holding back a laugh. Amelia quietly giggles at her odd behavior, knowing full well he probably thinks she's weird. *It doesn't matter; once I get my powers back, I can get out of here and find Aaron.*

"You okay?" he inquires. He gives her a handful of mouthwatering purple grapes. She nods and walks over to the grass. "Listen Amelia, I know why you're here and I want you to know that I understand your concern. But, I couldn't let you go." He puts his head down and munches on a green apple.

"Did Stylot tell you?" He nods without looking at her. She hopes she hasn't somehow hurt his feelings, because it's clear that he likes her. But she can only handle one thing at a time. "What's your name?"

"Joleus."

"Joleus, that's—different."

He flashes a smile and grabs another apple from the tree. He tosses it in the air and catches it with his teeth.

Why am I turned on by that? She finishes off her grapes and hoists herself up to all fours. *This is going to be hard getting used to. I hope I don't have to get used to it.* She wanders over towards the hills and stares off into oblivion, wondering if Aaron is somewhere close by.

"I'll race ya!" Joleus offers with a grin.

"Excuse me! I will do no such…" She dashes down the hills while he's still trying to figure out where she was going with her complaint.

"Ha! Ha! You cheated!" He laughs while racing behind her. She hears the thumping sounds of his feet against the ground as he sprints past her. She giggles aloud, not being able to stop. She speeds through the wind and follows his lead down the hills until they reach an opening behind some trees.

"Where are we?" she pants.

"We're on the border of Sigmount and Zerios. Just past these trees is the land of Zerios, where I'm from."

"Oh. So, Sigmount is where the little people are from? Where the fruit tree is?"

"Yes, and they're called Sigans. They are very powerful and are as pure as spring water. Like I told you earlier, they can see past any powers because their own powers are infinite."

"Infinite? Can they change me back?" Amelia questions with hopeful eyes. He shakes his head no. She runs her fingers through her hair in frustration. *That's okay. I know I can change myself back. I just need a little more time.* "So where were we a minute ago when I woke up?"

"Oh, we were at my place, so to speak. Sometimes I like to be alone and need my space. I like to live on the outer parts of Zerios," he says.

He lifts her chin. "Come, I have something to show you." He trots ahead of her and turns to see if she's game. "You comin?"

She produces a fake smile and trails behind with hesitation. *What if my powers don't come back at all? I'm so stupid. Carys gives me an amazing gift and what do I do? I wander into Horsemanville and get myself trapped.*

Ruff! Ruff!

"Stylot!" she shouts. She runs to him as he runs towards her with his tail wagging. *Bark! Bark!*

When she reaches him, she drops down in the grass and wraps her arms around his neck. "Hey boy!" She sniffs and rubs his ears and chin. "Are you okay, you're not hurt?"

Rrrrr! He licks her face and buries his nose in her neck.

"Ha! Ha! I missed you too."

He jumps up and runs around in circles, beaming with happiness.

Amelia stands and smiles at Joleus. He walks over to her and wipes a falling tear. "Feel better now?"

With a giddy smile she nods while Stylot shows her his new acrobatic moves. "I'm just glad he's okay. It feels strange seeing him so elated. Before I changed him he was grumpy and mean spirited, like his owner. Then he grew almost two feet taller and became my amazing protector."

"So this Aaron, what's he like? Stylot told me that you're in love with him and you have to find him." Amelia walks to a nearby tree and nestles against it. He follows suit with an uneasy look on his face. Stylot treads over with his tongue hanging out and plops down next to her feet where he quickly closes his eyes and starts to snore.

"I guess he wore himself out," she says, rubbing his ears.

"Yeah, I'm sure my sister had something to do with that," Joleus replies with a grin. He then faces her, patiently waiting for her to answer his question.

"Aaron is the love of my life." She pauses for his reaction but surprisingly he remains stoic.

"Please continue," he says.

"My Aunt Leona caused a lot of trouble for me and my family. She abused me more times than I'd like to count and made my life hell. When he came into my life, a weight had been lifted off my chest and I was finally able to breathe. He was my air. In the end, she kidnapped, beat, and poisoned him because he was the last person on earth who stood up to her and gave a damn about me. Before she was killed, she shot me in the chest. I suddenly became aware of what I had to do and why I couldn't die. I knew I had to find him and bring him back to me because we were born to be with each other. He fought for me and now it's my turn to fight for him. I know it doesn't make a lick of sense, but it's true. That's why I'm here."

"I'm so sorry. I had no idea."

She shrugs her shoulders. "How could you know? It's fine. Anyway, I've already been through much worse than this," she whispers while pointing to the other half of her body.

He laughs and grabs her hand. "I truly am sorry," he says again. She smiles back and removes her hand. "So what happened to your aunt? Have you seen her?"

"I don't know, but if I ever see her again… let's just say I'll make the most of our time together."

"Why did I feel a sudden rush of fear when you said that?" He snickers.

"You have no idea Joleus."

He looks into her eyes. "You make my name sound really nice. Amelia, you're the most beautiful thing I've ever laid eyes on."

She stands up and folds her arms. "You can't talk like that. I'm eternally grateful that you saved my life, but I belong to someone else."

Saddened, he looks down and throws a rock towards a tree across the way. The rock shatters into several pieces.

Damn, he's strong.

"You belong to yourself! You seem to have been through hell already and I'm pretty sure wherever this Aaron is, can't be a safe place for you. You'll be putting yourself in harm's way." He looks away and sulks, miffed.

"That's my decision to make," she says and walks away. *I have to get some distance to clear my mind. What is going on here? Why does he feel so strongly for me? We just met. And why am I so attracted to him? What's this about?* She finds a quiet spot by a lake and takes a drink and then eases herself down. She runs her fingers through her hair and bites her nails. *Lily said Leona was coming soon, but where is she? I don't want her wreaking havoc on Sigmount or Zerios. I have to tie up all my lose ends before I leave. I wouldn't want anyone to be held hostage because of my demented family.*

She finds it difficult to even come up with a rational way to fight anyone in this condition. *What am I going to do, kick her to death?* She shakes her head at the thought. *That witch needs to be put down like the animal she is.* She glares at her hands and smacks her teeth. Not too long ago she could touch someone and they would cease to exist. That was a great luxury she wishes she had again. *Maybe I should try again.* "Concentrate Amelia," she whispers, closing her eyes. "I wish I can be my true self again." With her eyes squeezed closed, she feels her body tremble and she becomes nauseous. *Oh, this is a good sign. This happened before.* She's excited that it's working. When she opens her eyes, her smile fades. "No!" she cries. "This can't be my true self, it just can't be." She sobs into her hands, destroyed by this revelation.

"Amelia?" Joleus whispers. She looks up with teary eyes and stands.

"Stay away from me! You did this to me! If you think I'm going to live here like some freak and be at your beck and call you're wrong!"

"I… I," he shakes his head with a confused expression.

"Just stay away from me!" she yells. She runs through the trees and out of the woodlands, desperately trying to get away from him, from her new self, and from everything. "Stylot! Where are you?!" she hollers, wide-eyed and frenzied.

Ruff! Ruff! He runs up to her and sits on his hind legs.

"Come on; we're leaving."

He whimpers and cries while staying put.

"NO! We have to go! This place isn't good for us anymore." She starts to walk towards Sigmount when he runs across her path and stops in front of her, blocking her in.

"Stylot what are you doing? They have trapped us here! We—I," she drops to the ground and cries so hard her face hurts. Realizing that she'll never lay eyes on Aaron again feels worse than dying. *If this is my true fate, then I was wrong about everything. Wrong about Aaron and the life we were supposed to share. I can't go to him like this.*

Stylot wails and cries along with her until her sobs abate. She sniffles and takes a few deep breaths to stifle her need to cry more—forever. She doesn't want to live without him, but killing herself would only make matters worse for everyone. Navid would be devastated if she didn't wake up, and her parents would probably end their lives just to come and find her. *I can't have that.* But moreover, she hates not being sure about anything anymore. Everything she thought she knew was now off balance and incorrect. *I can't even trust my own logic. It's time that I leave and never come back. Stylot will be safe here, safer than he's been with me.* She rises up and dries her face. She looks into his teary eyes and kisses the top of his head. "Stay," she whispers.

Without looking back, she treads out of Zerios and into Sigmount. A young man and an elderly woman are standing by the tree, gathering their next meal. They both look at her and smile as she walks by. She smiles back and continues walking until she's out of their enchanted land. She takes another deep breath and heads over to the cobblestoned bridge—the sky is getting dark. The dim water beneath the bridge is silent and still, and the light breeze feels good on her face. It reminds her of the first time she and Aaron kissed and danced in the moonlight. The breeze always felt so good from her backyard. They both loved it. She gazes at the moon and whispers, "Aaron, I'm sorry. I can't rescue you like this. Goodbye," she sniffs as fresh tears find their place on the stones, tainting them with her misery.

She breaks down again when someone touches the back of her shoulder. She whirls around and almost loses her balance now that she's half horse. She comes face to face with Joleus. *What does he want, to twist the knife deeper into my heart?* He puts his hands on her face and wipes her tears away with his thumbs. She realizes he looks as miserable as she does. He takes her hand and walks her closer to the other side of the bridge, where the moon is shining so bright they can see each other clearly. His bloodshot eyes match hers, blue against blue. *I really hurt him, but, I'm hurt too.*

He looks down at her hands and then into her eyes. "The last thing I wanted was to hurt you. I only wanted to see your face again, alive. When you almost died, I couldn't just stand there and do nothing.

You're this beautiful creature who wandered over to our land at the wrong time and I would not and could not let you die. Not just for my own selfish reasons, but for Stylot, and because of this addicting and extraordinary aura that follows you. You may not realize it, but you draw people in, Amelia. Unfortunately for you, the people aren't always good. But I am. If you stay here with me, I will never leave you no matter what. I will take care of you and show you how special you are every day, forever," Joleus whispers.

Another tear escapes and tracks down her cheek. She looks down and takes a deep breath, trying to process everything. He lifts her chin and whispers, "I'm not asking you to love me or be at my beck and call." She stares into his clear blue eyes. "I just want you to know that you no longer have to fight for anyone or anything. And that you can finally rest and be happy. I want to make you happy. I want to be your protector, your friend, your comedian, and lastly—I want to be your man."

Chapter Sixteen

Her mind is telling her to let go of her uncertainties and give him a chance, but her heart is telling her to run before anything escalates. *What am I supposed to do? He saved my life and all he wants in return is to make me happy. Is that so wrong? Am I a monster for being attracted to him?* Nothing makes any sense to her and it's draining. "Joleus, I don't know. I can't promise you I'll be the woman you want. I'm beyond distraught and extremely emotional right now because I just said goodbye to the love of my life. I need some time."

"I can respect that." He smiles and wraps his arms around her. For the first time in a long time, she feels safe. She takes in his sweet earthy scent and immediately starts to feel guilty. She steps out of his embrace and looks away, trying desperately not to break down in front of him. He frowns and holds out his hand. "Please, come." Without bombarding her brain with any more rationalizations, she takes his hand and walks over the bridge and back into sacred grounds.

*****

Early the next morning, she looks over and sees Joleus sleeping peacefully next to her. *This guy is not going to let me out of his sight. It's kind of flattering.* She stretches and walks over to the pond to gather some fresh water. While pondering last night's conversation, she can't help but wonder what could have happened to allow these chain of events to take place. *If Aaron and I are really meant to be together, why would I need to be rescued by someone whose powers are so limited that the only way to save me is to change me into his likeness? Does this mean I'm never going to wake up? There has to be some logical explanation for this.* She wonders if her life is that messed up or if the answer she's looking for is the reflection staring back at her.

Her hair is straight and shiny and her eyes are still vibrant and full of life, indicating that all is perfect. But it's just a veil, blinding others from the truth, hiding the morose feelings that rise from deep within her soul. Her facial features are still normal, but the other half of her body is a stranger, one that she has no interest in knowing. She wonders if this is what she saw in the dream at the hospital. She remembers looking into the river and feeling happy, but her reflection was sad and overwhelmed. *Is this what was meant to be all along? Was Aaron just a prop to get me here? Was bringing my parents back together my only purpose in life?* So many questions, not so many answers. All she's left with is the present and that's not exactly a gift. *So what's a girl to do?* "What do I do?" she whispers to herself and shakes her head in confusion.

"You live," Joleus murmurs, stepping closer.

"I didn't hear you come up," she says. He takes a step closer with one hand behind his back.

What's he hiding? She knits her brow and stares at him curiously. He slowly reveals his hidden treasure, a bouquet of long stem pink roses.

"Ha! Ha! Ha!" Amelia giggles, enjoying the irony.

Joleus frowns then smiles, not knowing which expression is appropriate. "What's so funny?" he says.

"Nothing, it's just that there was a time when I loathed the sight and smell of roses."

"Oh, I'm sorry. I'll go throw them away." He turns to leave.

"No wait. I want them, they're beautiful." He grins and turns back around, handing her the bouquet. Their sweet aroma rushes into her nostrils and lightens her mood. She offers a warm smile with gratitude.

"Your smile brightens my day. Please do more of it Amelia. I want to show you something."

"Okay," she replies. She loves how easy going he is. *Maybe he really does understand how hard and foreign all of this is to me.* She sniffs the roses again and walks side by side with him. "Where's Stylot?"

"I hope you don't mind, but my little sister came by and scooped him up for an early morning play date with her friends." Amelia laughs at the thought of gigantic Stylot entertaining his new horse friends. While walking in silence Joleus looks over at her and snickers.

"What?"

"You have no idea how captivating you are? Do you?"

"Looks aren't everything Joleus. Inside I feel like rotted flesh. I'm a shell," she states.

"I understand. But Amelia, give me a chance to prove to you that you will be cherished forever."

She huffs and grits her teeth. She doesn't want him to feel this way. He's a thoughtful and humble person who she happens to find very attractive, even on all fours. *How dare he come into my life this way and completely derail my plans. How dare he look at me the way he does, as if I'm some prize when all I am is broken glass. He should be running for the hills because I'll just end up hurting him like I've hurt everyone else in my life.* "Why don't you have a partner of your own? No other horse girl was interested?"

He sighs and throws his hands up in the air. He stops in his tracks, scowls at her, and confesses, "I have no problem finding "horse girls," as you so eloquently put it. As a matter of fact, there were several women in waiting."

"In waiting?" She looks down and wiggles her hoof in the grass, embarrassed that she just insulted him.

"Yes. When we become a certain age, we have to find our mate and marry them. If we don't, it can mean trouble for our families and for the town. When little girls are born, they're trained to be a suitable mate so that when they become ripe at twenty, they'll be ready for a husband and a family. If they don't do it by that age, their insides will dry up and they'll lose out on children and a family forever. We need children in order for this place to survive, just like in your world," he explains.

"That seems a little harsh. What if a girl decides she doesn't want to be married?"

"That has never happened. By the time the girls turn eighteen, they're ready to get away from their parents and find the love of their life. I know it sounds crazy, but it's true. Not to mention there are certain needs they can't ignore. It usually starts at eighteen and it gets pretty insane from there." He blushes.

Tell me about it. The moment I met Aaron my hormones went into overdrive. Damn I miss him.

"Anyway, I had several girls to choose from, but I haven't made my decision yet."

"I bet you do Joleus. You're a handsome guy." Amelia finds herself staring at his chest and abs. She swallows hard to keep her salivating to a minimum. A tiny bead of sweat glistens on his forehead and runs down the side of his face. She quickly looks away and sighs, hoping he didn't see her gawking at him with desire. *I bet he would have sex with me, no questions asked. Maybe there is a bright side to this situation.*

"A compliment from you?" he smirks, interrupting her maddening thoughts.

She rolls her eyes. "Listen, I don't think you should keep those girls waiting because of me. They've been waiting patiently to be your wife for goodness sakes. Hell, they were born and trained to be your wife."

He shrugs his shoulders and grimaces. "When I chose to save your life, my parents almost threw me over that bridge." He ponders that day and shakes off an unfriendly vibe. "As far as choosing them, well, I'd rather not. At least not right now," he says in a low, sensual voice.

Amelia exhales and covers her face with her hands. *I have got to calm down.* She can just imagine what he's thinking because an uninvited thought just assaulted her mind, leaving her breathless. *Jeez, maybe I should go jump in that lake.* "Hey by the way, what's in the water below the bridge? Before I blacked out it sounded like that demon was being eaten alive."

"Oh. Well, he was."

"By what?"

"Millfish. They're purple fish the size of a small watermelon. They eat mostly the algae and residue from the river, but they won't turn down a good meal if given the opportunity. That man was probably the best meal they've had in a long time. Their sharp teeth permit them to tear flesh into fragments."

She shivers. *That could have easily been me falling into the water. I'm glad he landed there instead.* "Who was he and why was he running from you?"

"He was a demonic soul. He wandered over here probably looking for a leader of sorts. I guess I frightened him, being half horse and all. Anyway, he tried to devour one of the babies in our land, so my friends and I were running him out when you showed up. We try to keep to ourselves because other souls can pass through and tell others about our sacred grounds. The last thing we need is some devil running wild and condemning everything we stand for. They would kill us all no questions asked."

"No! That would be awful. This really is an amazing place to live. Zerios and Sigmount would be a wonderful place to spend eternity," Amelia says. She breathes in the sweet scent of the air. Although she's only been there a short while, she finds herself quite attached.

"Then will you..." Joleus inquires, biting his bottom lip.

Amelia crosses her arms and faces the lake. *Will I? Can I? He's so easy to like and I really do feel safe with him. Why does this have to be so complicated?* "Can I ask you something?"

"Whatever you want Amelia," he answers. He stands behind her. She can hear the enthusiasm in his voice. His will to oblige her at every turn is nice. She can feel his warm breath on the back of her neck.

He's closer than I thought. Dammit! Focus Amelia! Without turning around she asks, "Will I ever wake up?"

"I don't know. Your heartbeat is strong and loud. It's beautiful."

She turns around to look into his eyes and is startled by them. They can light up an entire football stadium with the way they glow in the sunlight.

"If you don't know, then why would you take a chance of being with me if one day I can wake up and be gone forever?"

He walks closer to her and touches her shoulders, igniting an electric force of desire she didn't know still existed. "I don't care about that. You're here now, and that's enough for me. If you wake up one day and leave, I'll be crushed, but until that happens, I want you with me every second of the day."

Oh my God, he's really serious.

His breathing has quickened and his eyes are glistening with tears. *What the hell is going on here? And why do I want to kiss him?* "Joleus I..."

He quickly puts his index finger over her lips to stifle her words. "Please, don't say anything right now. I want you to see something. It's the perfect time of day." He takes her hand and kisses it. "Come on!" he yells and speeds off through the forest.

She's completely breathless and shaken up. She's so confused, but ignores her better judgment and runs behind him, enjoying the wind in her hair. Joleus moves quickly, like lightening. If it weren't for his

sweet earthly scent, she wouldn't know where to find him. She
follows his aroma all the way up a large hill where a giant bush
surrounded by millions of tall green trees sits atop it. Flashes of
colorful lights penetrate through the leaves and into the immaculate
green grass. The area looks like a disco ball, illuminating everything
in it's entirety. She walks past the bush and find Joleus standing
directly in front of it, gaping at something remarkable. His face is
practically glowing as he looks on, smiling graciously. She's eager
to see what could have him so taken, so she climbs out further and
stops.

As she joins his side, she blinks twice to confirm what she's
seeing. They're standing on a steep cliff where everything far
beyond and beneath is glowing. She's never seen so many colors in
her life. There are mountains and mountains of blue, purple, green,
and red rock. It's a landscape made of shiny colorful stones. An
indigo waterfall connects to a vast body of clear water as the
chartreuse green patches of grass ignite the environment. She has no
words for what she's looking at—none could give this scene justice.
Crystal yellow and lavender rocks graze the bottom rim below,
sealing in the masterpiece. She wishes she can run down and grab
one, to remind her of the simple and elegant things that life has to
offer. To remind her that something as plain and minute as a rock
can make you forget about your troubles and enjoy being... well,
being.

Without saying a word, Joleus takes her hand and squeezes it.
They continue to marvel at the magic unfolding in front of them. The
sun shines down at the perfect angle and makes it all stand out even
more—perfection at its highest. She doesn't know why Joleus
brought her here, but is happy he did. It's just what she needed.
"Thank you," she whispers. He looks at her and smiles; his blond
waves rustle in the breeze. He squeezes her hand a little tighter and
brings it to his mouth, caressing her palm with his lips.

As she gawks at him, the fact that she's standing on the edge of a
cliff hits her like a ton of bricks—she's afraid of heights! She lets go
of his hand and steps back. She gets closer to the bush to keep her
balance. *This half horse thing is still a little tricky.* Plus, she's a lot
heavier than she used to and tired all of the time.

Cah! Cah!

"Oh no!" she yells. She looks for the bird, it sounds close.

Cah! Cah!

She turns to look behind her but can't see it. Suddenly, everything is silent. Her heart is thumping because silence is not always a good thing. She peeks through the leaves to see if it's gone when it abruptly flies out towards her. "Ahh!" She flails her arms in panic and accidently steps back, over the cliff.

"Amelia!" Joleus shrieks. He lunges for her and falls to the ground. She's barely hanging onto the edge of the cliff. An old stick that's poking out of the grass is all that's keeping her from falling to her death. The tighter she grasps it, the more it begins to break. She's suddenly blinded by fear and adrenaline. She knows that at any given moment she'll fall. She silently prays that it won't be painful. Tears start to trickle down her face, not because she's about to die, but because she thinks she's ready to die. *Maybe it's the depression talking but this would be a justified way to go. It's not like I chose to be attacked by that bird. And I don't want to be the reason that Joleus doesn't pick a mate. My presence is hindering him from a good life.* As the stick continues to bend, she pauses and stays very still. *If it's meant to be, it will be.* Joleus is frantic and trying desperately to get to her. *Crack!* She closes her eyes.

Joleus instantaneously reaches out and grabs her arm. For a split second, Amelia saw her entire life flash before her eyes. *I thought that only happened on TV.* She saw her parents' horrified and distraught faces, Navid's uncontrollable breakdown as they stood and watched her body being lowered into the ground. She didn't see Aaron but, she heard his voice whisper, "If you die, I die." She doesn't understand a lot of things, but now she knows without a doubt that she has an obligation to at least try harder to stay alive. It's not just about her anymore, and for some reason, she keeps assuming that every choice she makes only affects her. *Even if Aaron and I can't be together, I know he'd be content knowing that I'm alive somewhere in my mind.*

"Hold on to me, baby. I'm going to pull you up," Joleus grunts while pulling on her arm.

Amelia inhales deeply to clear her mind. She focuses on saving her life and not the beautiful colors that await her death. *I guess it's time I give it my all.* She swings her other arm over and uses it to help pull herself up.

"Almost, you're halfway there," he coaxes.

She reaches a little further into the grass and wraps both arms around his neck as he pulls the rest of her body over the cliff. Once they are successful, she slams into the grass and onto her side, out of breath. *In retrospect, that would have been a terrible way to die*, she considers. She'd have to watch his horrified face as she slipped from his reach and anticipated slamming into the beautiful yellow and lavender rocks. *And if I didn't die right away, I would've suffered tremendously, begging for an end.* Joleus drops down, panting, clearly exhausted. While trying to catch their breaths, they stare at each other in silence.

When she wakes the next morning, she realizes they've slept on the cliff the entire night. *Either we have a death wish or we were more tired than I thought.* His long blonde eyelashes remain closed. She loves how peacefully he sleeps and feels guilty for waking him, but it's too dangerous to stay there. "Joleus, wake up," Amelia whispers.

He opens his eyes and smiles. "Hi," he yawns. She smiles back and reaches over to remove a single leaf that landed in his hair. He catches her hand and brings it to his mouth. She blushes and rises to her hooves.

"I'm sorry for waking you, but we're still on the cliff."

He jumps up and looks around, shocked. He scoots back and grabs her hand.

What's his deal? "Are you okay?" Amelia asks.

Joleus hurries her far behind the bush and back into the colorful forest. She can't help but admire this place, again. Without warning, he puts his hands on her shoulders and wraps his arms around her waist. His chest is heaving and she notices he's trembling. Without knowing what to do, she hugs him back for what seems like eons before they both let go. She sees fear in his eyes, something he was trying to hide for some reason.

"I'm sorry but, forgive me for bringing you here. I'm such an idiot. You almost died. We could have both easily rolled right off the cliff last night and ended our lives forever. My family would've been inconsolable if they learned of my death or whereabouts," he explains.

"Joleus, don't apologize for bringing me here. This is such an amazing place and I don't regret a moment of it." He smiles and shakes his head in disbelief. "Okay well maybe the part where I almost died," she giggles.

He puts his arm around her. "Yeah, I thought so." He smirks. They walk out of the woods with his arm still around her shoulders. "But seriously, we shouldn't have come here. No one from Zerios is allowed in these parts. Besides, if you died, I probably would have lunged over the cliff myself."

Amelia stops walking and faces him. "You can't say things like that. Do you think I would want you to end your life for me? What happened up there was a mistake, but to hear you say those things to someone you just met is alarming."

"I don't care how it sounds, that's how I feel. When will you understand that my feelings for you are real? I've lived here my whole life and I have never felt more alive and important until you came along. Everything we do and stand for is such a routine and there is no real excitement. But you, you're what I needed."

She sighs; she realizes there's no use trying to get through to him. He's clearly got it bad. She's too confused to know which end is up, let alone trying to define her own feelings. "Well, let's get out of here since this place is forbidden. Why is it forbidden?"

"Well for starters, it's highly dangerous. Of course we figured that out the hard way. But the other reason is because it can leave us vulnerable for attacks from outsiders. They prefer if we stay within the vicinity just in case."

"Yeah it was dangerous, but aside from the slip up, it was so worth it," she admits. "Um, thank you for saving my life—again." She leans over and kisses him on the cheek. His face turns bright red and he licks his lips. He moves closer to her and looks into her eyes. She can see the longing for more in his face. He pulls her closer to him and stands very, still. She doesn't want to move. Instead, she stands there, trapped in his warm embrace. He slowly kisses her cheek and then her forehead. His lips are soft and inviting. He leans down and gently kisses her nose. She closes her eyes and waits for the touch of his lips, but nothing happens. When she opens her eyes he's gone.

Chapter Seventeen

"Joleus!" Amelia shouts. She turns in a fierce circle, completely thrown as to what just happened. *Where could he have gone so quickly?* Suddenly she's catapulted back into that dream she had about Aaron disappearing right before they kissed in the greenhouse. "Joleus this isn't funny! Where are you?" She starts running through the woods. When she reaches an area she hasn't seen before, she cautiously walks through. She hears someone whispering and stops to listen.

"Son, what do you think you're doing? You can't just do whatever you want with no concern about consequences. You have a responsibility to this land, to your family, and to your future bride."

"Mom, this isn't fair. Why would you take me away from her like this? You shouldn't use your powers just because you need to speak to me. Now she's going to think I just vanished into thin air. Anyway, I'm not doing anything wrong to anyone. And I haven't even chosen a bride yet."

"That's my point! Why haven't you? You're nineteen years old. You know you're supposed to be married and have a child on the way by now. I just don't understand your logic, and—I only used my powers because you were about to make a mistake kissing that girl. I had to act fast." She sighs.

"Listen, Amelia is different. I really want to be with her and maybe with some time she'll get over that guy and want to be with me. I mean, she's one of us now, so that should make her decision a little easier."

"Ugh! Don't even remind me of that day. The day you betrayed your family and everything you stand for. I didn't raise you to disrespect our way of life. Now you've brought this stranger into our lives!"

"That's enough! Don't talk about her that way. She's everything I ever wanted in a mate and since when is saving someone's life a bad thing. You know Mom, you also raised me to do the right thing and to follow my heart. Well, I couldn't let her go and maybe if you would meet her, you could see what I see."

Whoa, this conversation is intense, Amelia thinks.

"I doubt that son. You have three beautiful girls who are eagerly awaiting a decision from you and you're wasting your time with someone who's not even in love with you. I don't want you to get hurt, and I think that's exactly where you're headed."

Amelia peeks from behind the tree and stares at him as he drops his head in disappointment. She sees how frightened he is by his mother's admonishment and she's afraid that his mother may be right. She has no answers for him right now. *Everything has happened so fast since Dad was shot. I need a steadier pace.* She hates that she's not used it by now, but Joleus is a curveball she didn't see coming—*a gorgeous curveball.* His muscular frame is glowing in the sunlight and his blond hair mimics a yellow halo. Being around him is making it hard to concentrate—on anything.

"Well, if that's true, I will enjoy every moment of the risk," he says.

Why do I feel relieved to hear him say that? In the pit of her stomach she knows the truth. She's ashamed to admit her feelings for him, even in her mind.

Joleus's mother shakes her head and walks away with her arms folded. Her long blond hair swings in the wind as she picks up speed towards the sun. The other half of her is pure black silk. He watches her run in the distance and then turns around with a sorrowful look on his face.

Amelia is heartbroken for him. *He's practically turning his back on his way of life for me. Have I been selfish all this time? I need some time to think about this.* She turns to walk away, hoping he won't hear her, but her loud traitorous hooves have given her away. *Damn this half horse crap!*

"Amelia? Is that you?" Joleus calls.

She stomps her hoof with frustration and turns around with a straight face. "Um, hi," she whispers, feeling guilty. She bends over and picks a yellow daisy from the ground and tucks it behind her ear. *I'm so nervous. Why do I feel like a child in trouble? I hope he's not mad at me for eavesdropping. Maybe I should try to explain.* "Listen Joleus…"

He holds up his hand to stifle her words. He walks closer and removes the flower from her hair and throws it behind a tree.

Oh great! He's mad.

She frowns with bewilderment when he says, "Those are Drius flowers—they're poisonous." His serious expression transforms into a polite smile.

"Oh. Good to know."

Without saying anything else, he takes her hand and motions for them to run far down the hill, away from the most beautiful place she's ever laid eyes on. They never speak of the conversation between him and his mother. Amelia assumes there's not much left to say about it anyway and that he might be embarrassed. They make it back to his part of the forest, and without saying a word, jump into the lake to wash the dirt off their bodies. When Stylot jumps in and makes a loud splash, it forces them to relax and break away from the somber looks and depressed feelings they both share.

The sparkling blue water is much more refreshing than she thought and everything in the vicinity is breathtaking. The yellow and pink flowers are in full bloom and the bright green plants flourish in the sunlight. Being in the water reminds her of her sixteenth birthday, when everything in her life changed dramatically. She remembers seeing Aaron's beautiful green eyes on the beach for the first time, and learning that her dream about him didn't do him justice in real life. He was so gorgeous. The second they looked at each other, they both knew in that moment they were meant to be together. *What I wouldn't give to be back on that beach. If I knew then what I know now, I would've made better choices. Of course I'd become a murderer in the process, because Leona's life would have ended a lot sooner than it did… if I could go back.*

"So what do you think?" Joleus asks.

Amelia breaks out of her reverie and stares at him. "What?"

He swims a little closer and splashes water in her face. "Hello, earth to Amelia," he snickers. She splashes water back at him and swims further away, but he's right behind her, splashing more water on her back. "You can't get away beautiful girl!" He laughs and grabs her waist. She tries to break free but he's so strong. He pulls her closer and touches her shoulders. "Are you okay?"

She nods yes and smiles while wiping some of the water out of her eyes.

"Here let me."

She closes her eyes in anticipation, hoping he doesn't disappear again, but this time she can feel him caressing each of her eyelids with his plush lips. Everything inside her body awakens. She's bursting with hormones and longing for more. Her better judgment is once again clouded with his intensity. She hates him for making her feel so good and needed. She doesn't want to desire him, but he is so attractive and warm. *This is so not fair. If I hadn't seen every inch of this place with my own eyes, I'd swear he was a pawn conjured up by the Beast. But I know that that disgusting thing is long gone, at my hand no less. Boy, if he could see me now, like this, he would be jumping for joy. Although, it seems as though my virginity is no longer a requirement.*

Joleus's lips have disappeared from her face and it prompts her to open her eyes. Their faces are inches apart. He's staring at her with hunger and raging with need. She can practically feel the heat emitting from his body as it trembles next to hers. Whatever is going on between them is mutual in every aspect. *How can I fight it when it's so evident to me; I want him and he wants me.*

"I think your eyes are free of water now," he says and dunks his entire body beneath the water.

Amelia breathes in and out and forces herself out of water. She runs behind a nearby tree to wring out her hair in private. The last thing she needs is for him to see her exposed chests while they're both in heat. *This horse thing is not for me.* Once her hair is back in place and strategically covering her boobs, she comes from behind the tree as he's about to step out of the water.

He slowly eases out as the sun highlights every bead of water on his body. He shakes his head from side to side to rid the moisture from his face and hair. "Where did you go!" he yells, looking around.

"I'm here." She strolls closer. "I thought we could get something to eat. Also, I need a tank top or something. I can't keep walking around like this."

He nods and holds out his hand.

"Come on Stylot, let's go!" Amelia commands. With a loud bark he rushes out of the lake and shakes his body, splashing water on them. "Real nice, thanks a lot," she giggles.

When they make it to tree, they pick off oranges, grapes, and pears. Some of the Sigans come out to greet them while gathering fruit for themselves. An older woman toddles out of her dwelling and hands Amelia a tank top to put on, which she accepts with gratitude. She runs behind a bush and pulls it over her head—it stops at her midsection. *Good enough.* When she comes back, she points to her small shirt and Joleus gives her thumbs up.

As she eats, she can see how much the people really love Joleus. Their faces light up whenever he's around. "You know, you say I have an aura that draws people in, but what you don't realize is that you have one too."

"No, people are just nice to me because my father is the King."

"What!" *That's an interesting piece of information he forgot to share. No wonder his mother is freaking out, he's a freaking Prince!* "Why in the hell didn't you tell me this?"

"Well… I have no answer for you." He laughs while twirling a strand of her hair.

She pulls away and crosses her arms. "No Joleus! It's not fair that you've kept this from me. You're, a prince. You are next in line to keep this place going. You *do* have a responsibility to everyone. Your mother is right. And the Sigans, they must also count on you for their safety. You have to understand that."

His face hardens and he stomps off towards the tree. He yanks a pomegranate and chunks it at a nearby tree trunk; red juice splatters everywhere. "I never asked for any of this! I don't think I can be King. The responsibility alone would drive me insane and it would force me to become someone I'm not. My father is a strong domineering Zerian. He's cut out for all this, not me."

Amelia treks closer to him. "Joleus, this is much bigger than just you. Think about your little sister and all the other Zerians who dwell in this sacred land. Do you want them to be damned because you don't feel like being King?"

He shakes his head no and looks away.

She takes his face in her hands and whispers, "You definitely have what it takes to be King one day. And don't get so worked up about it right now, it's not like it's going to happen anytime soon. It's just something that has to stay in the back of your mind because you are the one who'll have to lead." He runs his index finger down her cheek and kisses it softly. *I wish I knew what he was thinking.* He stares at her and shakes his head again, almost as if he's forcing himself to abstain from speaking.

He leads her to the grass and beckons her to sit down. Stylot joins them while still chewing on an apple. "The Sigans discovered this land long ago. They've been here since the beginning of time it seems. Like I said before, their magic is so powerful and pure that I've never seen anything like it. I'm in awe of them because they're so humbled and appreciative of us. Most creatures of such powers do more harm than good, but not them. They created Sigmount as a place where they can all be accepted in their own right without having to answer to anyone. As long as they keep the grounds sacred from evil, they're allowed to stay. I think it's some kind of gift from God. Anyway, they created us so that we could fight off demonic spirits or whoever comes to cause trouble. Now the only drawback to the deal is that they had to make a ruler, which is my dad. Even though they created him, he still gets to make the decisions," he explains.

"Why couldn't they just use their own powers to fight off spirits?"

"They tried many years ago, but someone always ended up dying, especially the children. They needed a distraction, someone to catch them off guard. They made us half human so that we can communicate easily with others and because it makes us less threatening. The other half was created to be powerful and bold to scare off anyone with malicious intent. Luckily, they can sense when trouble is near and it gives us an advantage to be ready to fight. I must say, it was pretty clever of them to shape us in this manner. I can't tell you how many times we've been able to trick our enemies with our innocent faces alone. It's almost comical the way their arrogance sends them right into our hands just from one look at us. Then, when they get closer, they realize we're not what we seem and it always throws them for a loop." He smirks and tosses a grape in his mouth. "They don't have a fighting chance at that point. We use our powers on most of them, but there are instances where my friends and I get bored and let them think they're getting away. Then we go in for the kill. It's just a game."

"So I take it no one has ever gotten away?"

"No, and luckily because of us, no one has been harmed for decades. At least not until you showed up. You threw me off my game."

"Oh, well, excuse me for ruining your ego trip. I was only being stabbed to death by a demon," she mocks.

He chuckles and grabs her hand. "Trust me Amelia, my ego is perfectly fine. I'm just glad I was around to save you."

"I'm glad you were too."

He smiles and pulls off several oranges and mangos from the tree. "Who are all of those for?"

"I'm taking you to meet my family, and I thought I would bring them some fruit." Amelia's smile fades and she stands up to protest when he says, "Before you object, it's going to happen. I need you to meet them."

She shakes her head no and runs towards the green fields, running harder and faster than she has before. She hears his laughter in the wind as he chases after her. "Will you stop!" He pants, catching up to her. Eventually he grabs her arm and pulls her closer to him, forcing her to slow down. "Please, don't run from me."

"I—I can't meet your family. I can't go into your village and pretend like I have all the answers, because I don't," she huffs.

"No one expects you to have any answers."

"Ha! Yeah right! Your mother is going to grill me into oblivion about my intentions and I'm sure she's informed the entire clan about our… whatever this is between us."

He grins and lifts her chin. "So, you admit there is something between us."

She waves her hands in the air. "Well isn't it obvious?"

He walks closer and attempts to wrap his arms around her. She scoots back and raises her hands to block him, imploring him to give her space. He puts his hands up and sighs.

"Since you're obviously not going to let this go, I guess I have no choice. Just give me a minute to mentally prepare myself for this disaster."

"Trust me, there is no way you can mentally prepare yourself my family. Just be yourself."

*****

When they get to his village, Amelia's reluctant to hear what his mother has to say. She sucks in some air and puts on a brave face. Their town is hidden deep within the forest and appears to have its own majestic ambiance, which is different from what she's seen thus far. For starters, the sky's cerulean hue is hypnotic and the foliage is almost glowing with magic little creatures crawling about. She's never seen a yellow worm before and the ladybugs are purple with orange spots. Everyone here is just as beautiful as Joleus. His friends Eric, Maceus, and Zul greet them the moment they step onto the grounds. She has to force herself to look away from their mesmerizing gaze.

"So Amelia, what do you think of Joleus here?" Zul asks while putting him in a headlock. Joleus squirms to try and break free while turning beet red.

"I think he's awesome," Amelia giggles, trying not to blush.

Finally he breaks free and pushes Zul away.

"It's nice to meet you Amelia," Maceus says while kissing her hand. "These two are constantly going at it so you'll have to excuse their testosterone contest."

Amelia laughs in agreement, while observing, *Wow, such a gentleman.*

"Hey baby," A girl mutters and kisses Maceus on the cheek. He wraps his arms around her and kisses her on the lips. They immediately start making out and fondling each other.

Okay, get a room... or forest for that matter, Amelia wants to chide.

"Excuse us lovebirds," Joleus says. He grabs Amelia's hand and leads her to another area. "They just got married. I guess they're working on that baby," he jokes.

"It would appear they are. Hey your friend Eric seemed a little quiet, what's his deal?"

He rolls his eyes and whispers, "I'll tell you later."

Amelia spots Joleus's mother over by a tree with a much smaller blond-haired horse girl. *Uh oh.* Stylot barks and runs across to greet the little one.

"Stylot!" the girl screams. She runs towards him and squeezes his neck.

Joleus's mother walks over with her arms folded. Her powerful glare forces Amelia to look down. But then she thinks about her position in all this and becomes angry. *I never asked to be rescued or wooed by her son, so if she wants to give me hell, then bring it on!*

"Mom, I'd like to formally introduce you to Amelia." Joleus is obviously nervousness.

She gazes into his eyes and smacks her teeth. Without looking at Amelia, his mother holds out her hand and shakes Amelia's. Amelia gives her a firm grasp, hoping she'll at least look at her, but she doesn't. Joleus scowls at his mother and looks away, annoyed. Amelia rolls her eyes and stoops down.

"Hi, you must be Joleus's little sister."

"Yes, I'm Briseus," she replies with a grin.

"What a beautiful name."

"Thank you." She pets Stylot. "I love your dog."

"I think he loves you too," Amelia whispers. "Isn't that right boy?" He barks and turns over, prompting them to rub his belly. Briseus giggles and begins to tickle his side. Amelia looks up and notices a hint of a smile on his mother's face and Joleus beaming with compassion.

"She's lovely," Amelia says to his mother.

"Yes, she is." She looks at Joleus and then back at Amelia. "I'm Chara."

"It's nice to meet you ma'am."

Joleus kisses Amelia's hand as his mother looks on.

"Amelia, why don't you stick around? I'd like you to meet Joleus's father."

Amelia nods her head with a smile, but her insides are churning. *I don't know if I'm ready to meet the King.* Joleus gives her an apologetic smile and puts his arm around her shoulder.

"Come Briseus, it's time for us to take a nap," Chara says.

"But, can't I just stay here with Stylot," she begs.

"No young lady. We go through this every day." Briseus stomps off with her arms folded as Chara shakes her head and waves goodbye to Amelia and Joleus.

That evening, the town of about fifty Zerians gather together for King Jordan's call. Amelia glides down in the grass next to Stylot while Joleus and his family walk out behind the king. She found out that these calls happen once every month and it was just her luck to be present for such an unnerving and terrifying event. She's surrounded by the large crowd as they all cheer in sync as the king takes his seat on the throne. Amelia notices Joleus gawking at her.

She smiles back and he shoots her a wink. *He makes me blush. I really like him, God help me.* As King Jordan makes his speech about marriage and upcoming events, she can't help but feel out of place. *I shouldn't be here. I'm an intruder.* She considers this would be a good time to try and escape because everyone is preoccupied with the king and there is no way Joleus would be able to leave his father's side to run after her. *Okay, I can do this. I can leave now before my feelings get any stronger. Why can't I get up? Why can't I move my legs?* She wants to get up and walk away, but the thought of never seeing him again has her perplexed. Is it possible that her feelings for him have traveled far beyond her imagination?

She looks up at him. He is staring back at her, as if she's the only one in the large crowd. He looks nervous and uneasy, like he knew what she was thinking. Then it dawns on her. Her traitorous heart has pulled the rug right out from under her. Everything is starting to make sense. She and Joleus have this deep connection that can't be broken. Sure she can try to run away and tell herself that everything will be fine, but it won't, because she won't be fine. *I have to see where this leads, for my sake and for Aaron's. So that I won't have any regrets. I know what I have to do, and I'm finally ready to make my decision.*

As King Jordan wraps up his comments, everyone starts to scramble and go about their business. Joleus makes a beeline towards her and she stands to greet him. When he walks over, she grabs his hand and says, "Joleus, we need to talk."

He drops his head; he looks so sad.

"So this is Amelia?"

Amelia freezes and looks behind Joleus. His father is standing three feet away, patiently waiting for her hand. While trying to put one hoof in front of the other and ignoring her ever pounding heart, she stands firmly in front of the king—frightened. *With one thrash, he can probably make me disappear forever.* She holds out her shaky hand to greet the giant grayish-blond haired creature. His blue eyes look into hers with warmth. She immediately starts to feel relaxed. *Thank God, he's got good vibes.* Although he's extremely powerful, she's relieved he has a sweet side.

"It's nice to meet you, sir," Amelia whispers, shaking his hand.

"Likewise. Please, feel free to roam about."

"Thank you sir, I will."

With a puzzled look, Chara grabs the King's arm as they walk away.

Joleus wraps his arms around Amelia and kisses her cheek. "Oh and Amelia?" The king shouts.

"Yes?" she replies.

"You're not an intruder!" he hollers back. Her mouth drops open and she's suddenly frozen.

He laughs aloud and strolls away.

Holy cow! He can read minds!

Chapter Eighteen

Great! His dad must have heard every crazy thought I just had. How embarrassing. I hope he doesn't hold anything against me. Her heart pounds in her ears, but she calms down when she realizes what's done is done and there's no point in panicking. *The king was pretty understanding and very kind. Chara must be the tough one.*

"So, you thought you were an intruder?" Joleus laughs.

Amelia shrugs her shoulders. "You should've told me he can read minds. What's with you today? Do you enjoy keeping secrets from me?"

He shakes his head no and smiles, but then his smile fades. "Well, let's find a quiet place to talk." After they've eaten and found a quiet spot by a flower garden, they look at each other in silence. Amelia bites her bottom lip and stands. Joleus reluctantly stands with a somber face.

"Joleus, I… um…"

"Before you say anything, I want you to know that I just want you to be happy. Every moment I've spent with you has been amazing. You make me excited about life and because of you I'm not afraid of tomorrow. I can't thank you enough for everything you've done or said, especially your words of encouragement." He walks closer and takes her hands. "Amelia, I Love You."

Amelia's mouth pops open and all she can think about is his lips.

"I'm sorry. I don't want to pressure you…" She covers his lips with hers before he has a chance to finish his sentence. The warmth and deliciousness of his fruity breath takes her to a place she hasn't been before. And the way he holds her seals all her emotions inside this envelope of desire. He breaks away and puts both his hands on her face. Their breathing is in sync as they try to catch their breaths. His eyes are filled with intensity as he pulls her closer and kisses her harder—more passionately.

Their heavy bodies fall to the ground and transform into something else, something otherworldly. They're not people or half horses, they're just beings. She feels light and free, and the aura around them is a yellow haze. She closes her eyes and enjoys his kiss. *I love this feeling and I love the way he makes me light up with life. Is this where I belong? I'm so scared. What does this all mean?*

"I want you Amelia, forever," he whispers.

Her eyes well up. She pulls him closer and kisses again. After moments of being wrapped in each other's embrace, Amelia realizes they can't let themselves give into temptation, as hard as it may be. The yellow haze slowly fades and they're back to being half horses, facing each other, longing with need and desire.

"I thought you were going to leave me," Joleus says, while wrapping his arms around her waist.

"No. I was going to tell you that I want to stay here with you."

His face lights up and he squeezes her tight, sighing with relief. He looks back into her eyes and kisses her tenderly.

"I love you," he whispers as their lips still touch.

Amelia nods her head and caresses his golden hair. "I know."

*****

In the following weeks, Amelia and Joleus have become inseparable. She can't think of a time when she's been happier. They laugh, play, and on occasion they even fight, but by twilight they're back in each other's arms. A small part of her feels guilty that she's happier with Joleus than she was with Aaron. And that may have a lot to do with a dark thunderous cloud named Leona who constantly roared her ugly head. They tried to make the most of their time and love, but in the end, she broke them. Amelia still loves Aaron very much but she finds herself entranced with Joleus and this new life, one that is stress free. Allowing herself to think about Aaron is much too painful because she can't go to him like this. Her decision is to put him in the back of her mind permanently, and only think of him on occasion. On the bright side, Joleus is a dream come true, a perfect distraction. Every day she finds herself growing closer to him.

He tells her he loves her all the time, and each time she says, *"I know."* She knows it's breaking his heart and he tries to hide it, but she can't bring herself to say it unless it's true.

*****

One day, she finds herself daydreaming about the time she and Joleus went to the forbidden side of the forest and when they almost kissed. He's saved her life in so many ways that she will never be able to repay him. In such a short time, he's given her a happy life and an escape from being constantly tormented. At this very moment, she can't imagine her life without him. He adds something she didn't have before. She's not sure what it is, but knows she'll be empty without it, without him.

"There you are. I've been looking for you," Joleus says.

Amelia turns around and wraps her arms around his neck. "What is it my sweet?" She kisses him on the lips.

"What was that for?"

"Joleus—I love you," she whispers.

He breaks out into a boisterous laugh and squeezes her so tight she can feel his heartbeat. He continues to hoot while caressing her face.

"What's so funny?"

"Nothing, it's just that I've been waiting to hear those words even though I know you've loved me since the first time you kissed me."

"You didn't know that. I didn't even know until this moment," she replies.

"I knew because I felt it. You wouldn't allow yourself to admit it because of your feelings for Aaron. But I knew the moment you kissed me that you felt the same."

"Hey, I've been meaning to ask you something? How did you know that by saving my life would in turn transform me into a Zerian?"

He drops his head and admits, "It happened before."

"To you?"

He shakes his head and runs his fingers through his hair. "Eric went through something similar and it destroyed him. He's a different person now because of it."

"He seemed distant and annoyed when I met him. I thought he had a problem with me."

"No, he saved a girl once. She was a mortal, like you. She was dying when he found her and used his powers to save her. She immediately transformed into one of us and it provoked an outrage.

168

Everyone went into shock. I mean, we've never seen anything like that before. Dad was beside himself and you can just imagine what Mom was thinking. But Eric guarded her with his life and wouldn't let anyone go near her. At first she was grateful and appreciative, they were even thinking about getting married. But then something inside her changed. She became volatile and mean. She grew to despise him and all of us. She even kidnapped a baby and held it hostage, demanding that Eric change her back into her original self. But he didn't know how to change her back," he explains.

"So what happened?"

"My father had no choice but to kill her. We couldn't ask the Sigans to interfere, so our only option was to exterminate."

"Oh my. Why couldn't the Sigans just use their powers to transform her?" Amelia probes. As the words flutter out of her mouth, she wonders: *Why haven't I gone to them?* Then she remembers Joleus told her they can't help her.

"It's a mutual respect sort of thing. They don't interfere with our issues and we don't interfere with theirs."

"I know, but that girl was going to kill a baby. That takes precedence over a silly rule."

"That silly rule has kept all us all alive and strong for many years. We can't go around asking them for help every time a situation arises. They would lose respect for us and could possibly deem us worthless. They gave us these powers so that we can take care of ourselves and be great protectors, and it's worked thus far. The only time they help is when a massacre happens, and in that case, we all have to band together and use our powers as one."

"A massacre?" The thought of harm coming to any of them is unfathomable. A chill runs through Amelia's spine and makes her shiver.

Joleus pulls her close and lifts her chin. "Don't worry; we haven't had one in at least fifty years," he murmurs and kisses her nose.

"How old is your dad?"

"He's one hundred and fifty-two." He sees the surprise in her eyes. "We age very slowly, which is beneficial. Then, on our fiftieth birthday, we stop growing altogether."

"That sounds about right. I was expecting your dad to be this old gray haired man with a long white beard that dragged the ground. But instead he looked really handsome and in his prime, if you will."

"Old man with a white beard that dragged the ground? My dad would get a good chuckle out of that one," he laughs.

"Is that all you heard?" Amelia giggles, smacking his arm. "I said he was handsome."

"Oh Miss Amelia, I was just kidding." He kisses her again and wraps his arms around her waist. She nuzzles her head under his neck and breathes in his mouthwatering earthly scent.

She looks up and stares into his sparkling blue eyes. "So does Eric think I'm going to wake up one day and go nuts, like that girl?"

"Yeah, I think so. Ever since that disaster, my dad forbade the village to save anyone's life ever again. He said we couldn't afford another event like that one, however unfortunate. That's why they were so upset when I saved your life. They saw history repeating itself and they didn't know what to expect. My mother was livid. When Dad read Stylot's mind, we knew that you would be harmless. They felt horrible about the things you've been through and I think that's what saved your life."

"So, your dad was going to kill me?" Amelia asks.

Joleus nods. "They were going to do it while you were unconscious, but I wouldn't let you out of my sight, I couldn't. When my sister found Stylot and nursed him back to health from the storm, they saw what a beautiful and fragile soul you are. They saw that you came through here looking for someone you loved." Amelia pulls away and walks towards a tree, slowly kneeling towards the earth. Joleus walks over and sits down next to her. "Amelia, you don't have to hide who you are for my benefit. I know you love him too." He puts his arm around her. She nods with a smile and lays her head on his shoulder. She couldn't ask for a more understanding creature to spend eternity with. He saved her life and he loves her. He's also easy on the eyes.

"Thank you so much for every act of kindness you have shown me. I know your mother had other plans for you and although she's accepted me into the village, I can see that she's still hesitant about our relationship. To be honest, she has every right to be. I don't know what tomorrow holds. I don't know what I can give you, but I know that I've fallen in love with you."

"Amelia, that's all I want from you. Just you being yourself," he breathes. He pulls her closer as the yellow haze forms and flourishes around them, igniting newfound electricity. As she feels his touch all around her, she can't help but feel herself getting more and more out of sorts. The intensity is becoming unbearable and satisfying. The feeling is indescribable. His breathing has become more rapid and she feels herself getting hotter and hotter, as if she's heading right towards the sun.

Wait a minute! Are we? "Stop!" she screams. She jumps back. The haze disappears and their bodies return to normal.

"What is it my love?" he says. He kisses every inch of her face and neck. It feels so good that she's having difficulty remembering why she stopped him. Then she opens her eyes and sees the haze again. She quickly pulls away and stares at him.

"Joleus? Were we just… making love?" She returns to her nervous habit—biting her nails. "I mean, we couldn't have been. right?"

"Well, we were on our way. I mean, we could've been if you would stop interrupting," he whispers. He kisses her hand.

She jerks away from him. "You could have told me that's what we were doing? I don't know how the other horse girls are, but I want to know if I'm about to make love to someone. I thought you do it like regular horses. You know where I turn around and…" She can't stop blushing. *This is so embarrassing.*

Joleus laughs and scoots a little closer. He grabs her by the shoulders and tries to kiss her.

"No! I can't trust you! You can't just have sex with me and not tell me!" She stomps off.

"Amelia! Come back!" The louder he calls, the faster she walks. "We didn't make love! At least, not yet!" he muses.

She stops, turns around, and folds her arms. "We didn't?"

He strolls over to her and tucks a strand of hair behind her ear. "No, we didn't." He lifts her chin. "Trust me, if we made love, you would feel it and believe me—you would know it."

She blushes again and puts her head down. "I'm sorry, I didn't mean to accuse you of anything. It's just that when we're together, everything is so intense. I felt hot and full of desire," she admits.

"I know. That's how we make love. When we have a strong mutual desire with a partner, we become this entity of passion, and the longer we're in the mood, the more passionate it becomes. I'm sorry for assuming you were ready, I just want you so bad Amelia. It's like you have a magnet attached to you, drawing me in. I can't pull myself away. I have never felt this before," Joleus says.

"Me neither. Don't get me wrong, I desired Aaron on a daily basis, but with you, my feelings are foreign—and in a way—I get a sense of relief. I feel like I can finally relax and be myself. It's nice to not have to worry about you or your safety. I'm able to enjoy everything I feel without being afraid that you'll be taken away from me. I don't know what's happening to me. I can't think when I'm with you—all of my logic dissipates."

"Same here. I've never had these feelings for anyone. The crazy part is, it should've happened with the other girls, but it never did. As of now, I just want to love you and cherish what we feel. I'll try to control myself, and when the time is right, it'll be more special and I know it will be amazing. Especially if it's anything close to what we were feeling," he says while holding her. "I can't wait! This is new for me, too!"

"New for you? Are you a virgin?"

He looks behind him, grabs her hand, and pulls her behind a tree. "You can't just ask me stuff like that out in the open, but to answer your question—yes."

"Oh, I'm sorry. Wait, if you've never been intimate before, then how do you know we didn't just do it?"

"My friends sort of described the feeling to me and let's just say, it gets way more intense. When you get to a certain point, you can't stop and you don't want to stop. I think we'll both know when we're there." He yawns and rubs his tires eyes. "Let's go back to my place and get some sleep."

"We're not staying in town with your friends and family anymore?"

"Amelia, we've been here for weeks. I've seen enough of my family for a while and to be honest, I want you all to myself. There's a festival next month, we can come back then." He leans down as she wraps her arms around his neck. They enjoy one more fervent kiss. The fact that he's a virgin like her makes her fall deeper in love with him. *He's just like me.*

*****

"Good morning my sweet?"

She opens her eyes and looks up. "Hey, how are you?" she yawns, blushing.

"Good." He softly touches the curves of her face. "I have something for you."

She rises up and stretches her legs. As he pops a red berry in his mouth, she can't help but appreciate his beauty and his gorgeous smile that brightens up the forest. She takes his face in her hands and kisses him. "So what do you have for me?"

"Close your eyes and hold out your hand." Reluctantly, Amelia follows his request. Joleus gently takes her hand and kisses her palm before placing something with sharp edges inside. "Open them," he whispers in her ear.

Her eyes flutter open, and so does her mouth. Without blinking, she gapes at the sparkling yellow rock. "When…How did…?"

"I saw you gawking at the lavender and yellow rocks at the bottom of the cliff. The goofy look on your face was priceless. I watched the way you enjoyed every moment of the breathtaking array of colors and how they glimmered in the sunlight. But when you looked down and stared at the rocks, I was surprised by your sudden interest. You seemed more intrigued by the simplicity of the rocks than anything else. So I waited for the perfect time to grab one for you. I hope the yellow one is okay."

"It's more than okay. I was thinking that I would love to have one of those pretty rocks to remind me of how the simple things in life can put a smile on my face, regardless of the horror unfolding around me. I can't believe you knew I wanted one. This was so thoughtful of you. You're pretty remarkable. I will keep this forever," Amelia says.

"I hope so. I'm going to hold you to that, and you're pretty remarkable yourself."

"Tell me about the festival," she says.

"On the first day, everyone from both Zerios and Sigmount will come together to celebrate the purple moon, which only comes around every ten years. It's a big event and folks party from sun up to sun down. They make wine from the grapes on the tree and on occasions like this they roast small gorks." She raises and eyebrow. "They look like baby pigs, but they don't have a snout, and their entire bodies are covered in fur. There are no rules and everyone is allowed to do as they please, within reason.

*****

Joleus and Amelia wake up early and head into town to help prepare for the big event.

When they arrive, Amelia's immediately greeted by Stylot, whose been traveling back and forth for the past month to check on her and then heads back to Joleus's family. She still can't believe how happy Stylot and she are there. She knew he was miserable with Mortis and is honored to show him a good life where he can be himself and enjoy what it's like to be loved. As much as Amelia misses Aaron, it's gotten a lot easier to push her feelings for him aside for the sake of her sanity. Joleus has made it so easy for her to relax. He kept his promise about ensuring her happiness every single moment. *I never thought I could love anyone as much as I love Aaron but…I truly love Joleus. I'll probably never see Aaron again, so I should let go and give Joleus my heart, which he deserves.*

"Hey, what are you thinking about?" Joleus asks.

"Oh nothing, just about how much I love you," she replies and kisses him.

He holds her in his arms. "I love you, too, Amelia." He twirls her hair around his finger. "So much."

She hugs him tight as fresh tears fall. She listens to the sound of their heartbeats battling it out. *I never want this to end.*

He pulls away and notices her face is wet. "Why are you crying?"

"I'm just so happy. I feel like something bad is going to happen because for the first time in my life, I'm at peace and it's with you, with someone completely unexpected. "

"Nothing bad will happen, and no one can ever take you away from me. I will protect you as I promised. You're just used to having everything you love violently removed from your life, so you don't know how to be happy. But it's okay. You'll be okay, even if I have to sacrifice myself," Joleus declares.

She shakes her head and steps back as her heart pounds. "No! Don't you ever say that again! Aaron said the same thing to me and he was taken away. I can't live through that again, not with you. Promise me that no matter what—you will live."

"Amelia please? I love…" he sighs and drops his head.

"Promise me! If you don't, I will walk away right now and never come back. I will leave before I allow you to get hurt or killed because of me." She staggers towards him, sobbing. "So you need to promise me."

He looks up teary eyed and says, "I promise." He squeezes her waist and kisses her hard and fast. Their faces are wet with tears and their hearts are beating so fast they may as well be on a treadmill. They stop and stare at each other while trying to catch their breaths. "Tonight, after the festival…be with me?"

She nods her head and answers, "Yes, I will."

He runs his fingers through her hair and hugs her tight.

Chapter Nineteen

Amelia can't imagine how special and amazing her night with Joleus
is going to be. She's intrigued by the notion that it gets more intense
and passionate. From the moment they first met, she found herself
highly attracted to him and wants this experience because it's the
first time for them both and neither knows what will happen
tomorrow. *I could wake up and never see him again, or I could die
and be lost forever.* She knows that both scenarios would leave them
devastated for eternity. She's spent every waking moment with him
for months and has grown to love him and their time together.

"Okay love birds, stop making out!" Zul shouts while strolling
over with Maceus. Joleus and Amelia pry their faces apart to greet
his friends. Amelia is relieved that Eric is nowhere in sight. He
glares at her constantly and she assumes he's wondering if or when
she's going to lose her mind.

"Hey guys, how goes it?" Joleus says and shakes hands with them.

Zul and Maceus each kiss Amelia on the cheek. *They're so sweet
here. I will never get used to being surrounded by so many gorgeous,
godlike figures—but I'll try.* To keep from staring, she looks at the
ground while they converse back and forth about the festival. When
they walk away, Zul and Maceus turn around and wave at her in a
flirtatious manner, which makes the blood drain from her face.

Joleus rolls his eyes and puts his arm around her waist. "Miss
Amelia, do I have a reason to be jealous?" Joleus smirks.

She turns to him, wide-eyed. "Why of course not, just be on your
best behavior." She giggles and sprints towards the woods.

"Oh is that so!" He laughs while playfully chasing her. He pulls
her behind a tree and kisses her zealously, finishing what they started
earlier. Eventually, he opens his eyes and confesses, "I have to go
and get ready for the festival with my family. It's a ritual that we
walk out into the crowd together to kick start the ceremonies. Once
that's over I will make a beeline to you, my sweet love."

"I look forward to it. I'll go find Stylot and hop in the lake to
freshen up."

He caresses her hair and runs his index finger down her cheek,
electrifying her insides.

*Is it always going to be like this? Every time he touches me I feel a
new sense of yearning and passion for him, and we haven't even had
sex yet.*

"I'll see you soon, I love you," he whispers and kisses her hands.

"I love you." She smiles and runs away in search of her beloved
friend. As she rushes through the forest, she takes time to reflect on
what could lay ahead. *This is by far the sweetest dream I've ever
been given, if it is a dream.* She thought Aaron was just a dream, but
he was real. *What will be the outcome of all this?* She asks herself
these exasperating questions over and over but knows that all she can
do is wait and see. As she slows down to catch her breath, she gets
the feeling that someone has been following her. The muffled
stomping of their hooves are getting closer. She sluggishly turns
around and comes face to face with Eric.

"I'm sorry. I didn't mean to frighten you. I just wanted to talk to
you in private," he says, and walks a little closer. Without taking her
eyes off him, she takes a step back to keep her distance. He holds up
his hands in submission and grins, then laughs at her anxiety. "I'm
not going to hurt you Amelia, so you can relax."

*Well, he does seem pretty harmless and I sense that he's a good
guy, even if he is a little peculiar. It's good to know I haven't
completely lost myself.* "What do you want to talk about?"

"I want you to understand my reluctance regarding Joleus's and
your relationship. He's my best friend and I don't want to see him
get hurt. So if you really care about him, maybe you should just
leave," he suggests.

Where does he get off telling me to leave? "I don't think our
relationship is any of your business. Joleus told me about the girl you
saved. I know you were uneasy about him saving my life, but I'm
not her, you don't have to be concerned."

He drops his head and inhales, trying to relieve the tension. "It's not just that! We know you're not a threat. But we also have no idea what your intentions are because *you* don't know what your intension are. It's hard to see him so happy and in love with you when we know you'll just leave one day. Amelia please, we want him to have a fulfilling life and I don't think he can have that with you. No offense."

"No offense! How can I not take offense?! You're accusing me of taking Joleus for granted! I would never do that… I love him too much."

"I'm not contesting your love for him because I can see that you two are crazy about each other. But what about the other guy, Aaron? You loved him too, you came here searching for him, and now all of a sudden you're all about Joleus? It's a little alarming the way you switch…"

"Stop right there! I don't want to hear another word out of your mouth! How dare you judge me or my actions? You think I want to feel this way? I don't know what the hell is going on, but I feel like a new person with Joleus. And for your information, I begged him to let me go and even offered to leave on numerous occasions, but he wants me here. He would rather spend every moment with me for however long than to not have me at all. That's what love is, it's messy and complicated and none of it makes sense…but it's real. One day you will experience it again and you'll understand where I'm coming from. And you're right, I do love Aaron more than anything. But I can't be with him. Things change, and there is nothing we can do about it. All you need to know is that I will make Joleus happy for as long as I can and that I love him. I know you're a concerned friend, but that's the only answer I can give you."

"Well, I respect your honesty and I'm sorry again for offending you. But please, try not to break his heart. It would be hard for all of us to witness." He walks closer until he's inches away and offers a smile. "You know, for what it's worth, I can see why he loves you."

Amelia shakes his hand. "Thank you. And Eric, you will find love again. I can tell you're still beating yourself up about what happened in the past, but you know, the good thing about the past—is that it's gone. You still have a chance to be better, better than you ever were before."

"You think so?"

"Absolutely, you're a good guy. You also have something about you that radiates leadership. I can see you being something great one day, something powerful. Just wait, you'll see," she declares.

"Really? I don't know. I've messed up in the past. I doubt the village wants me to do anything," Eric whispers.

"Don't be so hard on yourself. Everyone makes mistakes. I'm glad we had this talk."

"Me too. See you later," he mutters and picks up speed towards Sigmount. When he's out of sight, she runs into town to find Stylot.

*****

The festival is about to start and she has to admit, she's pretty excited. *Just a few months ago I sat in this same crowd and felt like an imposter but now I feel like I'm part of the family.*

King Jordan walks out first. He looks powerful and magnificent with his silver and blond hair and solid gold crown. Chara is right behind him—beautiful and poised. Her long blond hair brushes the back of her black hindquarters as she holds her head high and waves to the crowd. Briseus is a mini version of her mother. Amelia can see her maturing and becoming a wonderful Zerian, and last but not least, Joleus appears behind his little sister. His hair is shiny and neatly combed as it flows to his shoulders. His flawless face looks smooth and clean and his sparkling blue eyes are hypnotizing. *I'll never tire of looking at his rippled chest and muscular arms.*

He finds her in the crowd and grins. For a split second, she feels her heart stop. The magnetic charge between them is so strong and powerful that she wants to throw herself towards him. He winks at her as he follows his parents to the top of the royal hill. As the king gives his very lenient rules about safety and behavior, he does something that she's never witnessed before. With one quick movement of the hand, he waves what looks like sprinkles or magic dust all over the crowd. Amelia looks at her hands and stares at the substance, then—it begins fades away.

"That's his way of giving us his blessing," A Sigan informs with a smile.

Suddenly, there's music and laughter. The Sigans and the Zerians have all come together and are enjoying every second of the party. Gorks are roasting on an open fire and there's enough fruit to last an eternity. Stylot and Amelia enjoy a pomegranate while the Sigans embark on making wine. Amelia notices the King and Chara headed in her direction with goofy smiles on their faces. *What's that about?* Chara walks up and does something completely out of character for her—she gives Amelia a hug and a kiss and King Jordan embraces her with a warm hug.

"So Amelia, how are you dear?" the King asks.

"Don't you know?" Amelia teases.

He laughs aloud as does Chara. "She got you on that one honey," Chara says, still laughing.

"You're alright with me Amelia. Most people, especially girls, don't like the invasion of privacy, if you will. I try not to intrude unless it's necessary," he says.

"Well that's good to know," Amelia replies with a smile. She feels awkward and bites her bottom lip and twists her fingers. They continue to smile and stare at her, as if they're hiding something.

"There you are," Joleus whispers in her ear. She quickly turns around, relieved by his presence. She looks back and sees his parents walking away. "I missed you."

"I missed you too. It seemed like you were gone for a long time." She lifts up to kiss him. The touch of his lips on her sparks a long awaited need that's finally getting fulfilled. She forcefully pulls herself away from him to spare the crowd of an unwanted scene. He kisses her cheek and takes her hand. With Stylot clinging close to her side, they walk around eating, drinking, and laughing. She can't remember the last time she laughed so much.

The purple moon has come into the night sky and it's breathtaking. Amelia can definitely see what all the fuss is about.

"I'll be right back. I promised Maceus I would show him how to skin a Gork."

"Okay, hurry back." Amelia strolls towards Sigmount to gather more fruit, although she feels stupid going there alone. The town is completely barren—not a single Sigan is in sight. She quickly grabs a few peaches and turns to leave when from the corner of her eye she sees someone walking towards her. A very old Sigan toddles in her direction. Her tiny, fragile body looks like it could break at any second. Her face appears tired and worn but she manages to produce a lovely smile.

"Hi, I'm Amelia."

The woman nods and bows her head, knowingly. The old woman steps closer and holds out her hand. Amelia offers to shake it when the woman swats it away.

She's a feisty little thing.

The woman holds out her hand again and motions for Amelia to come closer. Amelia sets the peaches down and kneels down so they are eye level. The woman's tiny right hand covers Amelia's eyes. Amelia flinches and leans back, shocked by the coldness of her fingers. The woman lets out a small laugh and whispers, "See." Amelia leans forward again and allows the woman to show her whatever she wishes. She covers her eyes again and at first, all Amelia can see is darkness, but then she sees herself.

I'm not a horse girl. I'm me again and I'm happy. As Amelia looks on, she realizes she's standing in front of an older man who's wearing all black and holding a bible. She's donning a white veil with flowers in the form of a crown on her head and Cash has just given her hand to someone, but she doesn't know who it is. *Could this be my future? Am I looking at my wedding day?* Amelia pulls away and looks into the woman's gray eyes.

"Is this real?" she asks.

The woman slowly nods, yes.

"But, I wasn't like this?" she says, pointing to the other half of her body.

The woman shrugs her shoulders and stares back at her, confused. Amelia's eyes fill with tears. "Can you change me back?" she whispers

"Yes," the woman croaks.

Amelia stands and gathers the fruit. *Joleus said we're not supposed to ask them for help. How can she change me back when this is supposed to be my true self, my fate? I think this old lady is mistaken. Maybe she's senile and doesn't understand. I can't get my hopes up and allow her to take away my happiness. I have to ignore it. If I couldn't change myself back, then I don't see how she can. I had powers too, powers that were strong enough to kill a Beast.* Amelia no longer has the desire to change back. She wants to stay here with Joleus, happy and free.

"Where were you? I was getting worried," Joleus says and runs up to her.

"I went to get some more peaches, we were out."

He kisses her forehead and then holds her close. They stand together for a while, holding on for dear life and savoring the way it makes them feel. *How could I even think about being away from him? I would be miserable. A feeling I'm all too familiar with.* Joleus pulls back and looks into her eyes; moves her hair out of her face. She smiles at him as he admires her silently. She doesn't have the heart to tell him what the older Sigan told her. "Is the party almost over?" she whispers. She has sensual things on her mind.

"I bet I know what you're thinking. I can't wait either, but just a few more hours, okay?"

Later that night, Amelia has come to realize that the Sigans can't hold their liquor very well. They're stumbling all over the place and running into anything that stands still. It's entertaining to watch. A few of them have even flown straight up into the sky and crashed back down to the ground. *Clearly they're going to be writhing in pain in the morning, or not. Maybe their powers will take care of that.* She refuses to take a single sip of wine because she wants to enjoy every moment of her night with Joleus, when they give themselves to each other. She's not sure if she's ever looked forward to anything more. Normally, she'd feel guilty about her desires, but not with him. Not with the way things have turned out.

While he rushes off to gather more grapes for the wine, Amelia notices the water tin is almost empty. She walks through the forest and heads for a spring just down the way. The further away she gets from the party, the quieter it becomes. The peace and quiet is so relaxing—she can finally hear herself think. There is a nice breeze and the fresh scent of roses fills the air. It's another reminder of her backyard and how it was always so peaceful and quiet.

"Oh no," she whispers. She feels her eyes welling with tears. An overwhelming bout of depression and anxiety run through her. Her buried feelings for Aaron race through her mind like a runaway train. She's tried to keep them hidden, now she feels the same pain she felt when Navid brought his lifeless body into the house. *I vowed to find him and promised to never give up.* She can't stop herself from crying. Then suddenly, she hears something walking towards her, forcing her to quickly turn around. Green eyes are staring back at her with curiosity.

I know those green eyes. I'd recognize the distinction of that color anywhere.

A green-eyed black panther paces back and forth while keeping its eyes on her. She feels naked and exposed, almost as if it's reading every thought she's ever had. *It's Aaron! It has to be him...his soul.* This animal reminds her of him in an eerie kind of way. She puts her hands over her mouth to stifle her urge to weep. She sniffles and crouches down to the ground, crying desperately for his forgiveness. She hopes he doesn't hate her for being half horse. *What's happening to me?* "I'm sorry Aaron," Amelia cries. A lurid growl from afar makes her jump up and she stumbles. Even the leaves from the trees are trembling from the roar. The panther slowly drifts away from her and sprints into the dark night.

"Wait! Come back!" she shouts and starts to chase after it.

Bark! Bark!

She stops and turns around. "Stylot! Hey boy," Amelia yells. She kneels down to him. "It's okay, I'm okay." She sniffs and wipes her eyes. She does not want him to see her upset. *He's been so happy and content that it would be a shame to break his spirit. No one can see me upset. It would break Joleus's heart.* Stylot looks down and begins licking her feet. Amelia giggles as his tongue tickles each one of her toes. *Wait! I have toes!* She rises and looks down at herself as if in slow motion. "I'm back! Oh my God! I'm myself!" Amelia screams. She is so happy that she grabs Stylot's neck and holds him tight. He licks her face as she laughs with relief. She vigorously rubs her legs, hoping this is for real.

"Amelia! Are you out here?!" Joleus hollers. *Oh no! I have to change back.* She runs behind a tree as Stylot follows behind. She quickly changes back into a Zerian and grabs the water tin.

"I'm here Joleus!" she shouts. She runs out from behind a row of bushes. "I was getting more water." She wipes her face.

"Come here you," he says. He wraps his arms around her waist. They quickly kiss and walk out of the forest hand in hand.

How am I going to tell him what just happened? That I think I saw Aaron's soul in a panther and that I have my powers back. She's afraid he'll panic, but knows she can't keep secrets from him either.

He stops suddenly and puts her face in his hands. "I love you so much Amelia."

"I know. I love you, too. Please don't ever doubt that," she says.

When they get back to the party, she notices his parents and a few others from the village are standing around. *What's going on? Did something happen while I was gone?* She looks up at Joleus. With a huge grin on his face, he kisses her cheek and stands directly in front of her. She glances over at his father, whose mouth has just dropped open. *Oh no! He's reading my mind. Crap! Now I have to tell Joleus what happened. Damn him!*

"Son! A word please!" King Jordan shouts from across the way, but Joleus shakes his head and focuses on Amelia. *Thank goodness, that will buy me some time to explain.* Before she realizes what's happening, Joleus has circled around her twice. She can't help but giggle at this newfound game he's come up with. He proceeds to do it two more times and stops directly in front of her, grabbing her hand in the process. He pulls out the yellow rock he gave her earlier. It's now attached to a strong green material. He's made it into a necklace.

"Amelia, I want you to know how special you are to me and that I will spend every moment of my life in love with you. You're the love of my life. Will you marry me?"

Oh my! That's what he was doing, proposing? She opens her mouth to give him her tearful reply when someone screams, "Ahhh! Help us!"

Chapter Twenty

Demons raid the village with alacrity. They are beastly monsters with razor sharp spikes on their capes and pitchforks in their hands. Amelia's completely frozen and horrified as her worst fears are coming true. *A massacre!* The thought of any of these amazing creatures being harmed is frightening. She snaps out of her paralyzed state and runs to help as many Sigans and Zerians as possible. Since everyone is drunk and incoherent, her quest is a challenge. She doubts their powers will be of any use at this point, and is certain that this disaster must have been planned out. She's convinced the demons heard about the Purple Moon Festival.

"Amelia wait!" Joleus screams. He's frantic. "You can't just run and leave my side! I'd die if you got hurt." He grabs her hand and together they help hide the Sigans. Most of the Zerians have run off to take cover and some are coherent enough to disappear. As they run towards the forest, Amelia is horrified to see that a lot of them didn't make it. Slaughtered remains of fellow Zerians are lying in pools of blood. "No! This can't be!" she cries.

A few of them are still alive and wailing, but death is imminent. Joleus runs over to them and touches them briefly. A lightning force emits from his fingers and silences them forever.

"What did you do? Can't they survive this?" she implores.

With teary eyes he confesses, "It's too late. When we get hurt, we have to be cured right away. I put them out of their misery." He takes her hand and leads her further into the forest. "We have to get out of here before they close in on us."

"No. Where's your family, and Stylot?"

"They're okay, my father is hurt, but they're safe for now. Stylot is guarding my little sister not too far away from my parents."

How does he know this? Amelia looks at him with curiosity.

"Dad can telepathically talk to me and my little sister." They find a dark spot between a set of bushes. "Let's stay here." He slowly disappears while holding her hand. The problem is that Amelia's still visible.

Joleus reappears and glares at her.

"Joleus, my powers came back. I am back to my original self again. Amelia carefully closes her eyes and transforms back to two legs. Joleus lets go of her hand as the tears fill his eyes. "Please, it doesn't mean anything, I still love you."

"When were you going to tell me this?"

"I was going to tell you tonight. I just wanted us to be alone so that I could break the news to you. Please don't be mad at me," she whispers.

He pulls her close and holds her. "I'm not mad, I'm just disappointed. I really thought you were going to stay like me, forever. Now that you're back, um…have your feelings changed?"

Loud roars followed by footsteps are headed for them. Joleus starts to panic; he doesn't know what to do.

Amelia takes his hand and closes her eyes, which makes them both invisible to the outside world. She feels a soft kiss on her cheek. "I love you," he whispers in her ear. She squeezes his hand tighter as the demons approach them. They look around in wonder as they wave their pitchforks in the air. Joleus and she quietly scoot backwards to keep from getting stabbed. The demons finally leave their area, but a loud rumble from the right jolts fear into her. She looks up at a monstrous lion running into the forest. An insanely large demon quickly follows behind and gazes through, searching for someone to destroy. The lion seems to be on a mission, as if it knows exactly where it's going.

It cruises through every inch of the forest and stops directly in front of Amelia and Joleus. Amelia stares into its golden eyes and instantly knows who it is. Her whole body shakes as anger rises from within. Amelia steps forward, ready to attack, but Joleus squeezes her hand tighter and quietly pulls her back to him. The lion stares at their invisible bodies without moving an inch. Finally, a demon runs up and says, "The town is completely empty. Even the fruit tree is dried up. I think we got them all."

The lion's gaze finally leaves Amelia's eyes as it slowly steps backwards and walks away. It takes off, running out of the forest and out of the village. When Amelia can no longer feel its presence, she reappears and runs out of the forest. "Stylot!" she shouts.

"Amelia, what are you doing?" Joleus hollers.

"She knows I'm here. It was written all over her face. Did you notice how she looked into my very *invisible* eyes? I have to stop her before they kill anyone else," Amelia explains, still running.

"No you don't! Please my sweet; don't put yourself in danger. Don't leave me," he pleads.

Amelia stops running and turns around. "Joleus, I have to do this. There is no other way. Do you honestly think I want to leave you?" She caresses his face and kisses him. "I love you so much."

"I'm going with you," he demands.

"No! Absolutely not! No one else is going to get killed because of me. That's Leona! She's not playing a game, Joleus. She will keep coming back until she demolishes everything. I killed her father and her daughter. She wants revenge…and so do I." She leaves him and speed walks through the cemetery that used to be Zerios.

His loud hooves stomp behind her, picking up speed. "Stay the night with me and think about it tomorrow. I just want to hold you and maybe in the morning we can talk about this. Please," he begs. He reaches her and stands in front of her. His heart's about to jump out of his chest and the look of devastation on his face is something she never wants to see again. She sighs and shakes her head; she knows he's not going to let her do this. If she leaves him, she knows he'll follow her and get himself hurt.

"Okay," she acquiesces.

A grateful smile forms on his face as he lifts her off the ground. She's thrown by how light she is since she's in human form again. He kisses her hair and sets her back down. Stylot appears and nuzzles her side. She checks him over to make sure he's unharmed. They quietly follow Joleus back to his spot in the forest. When they reach his place, they find that they have no energy and just want to sleep. She curls up next to Joleus as her human self. He wraps his arms around her and holds her tight. Before she closes her eyes she turns over to get something off her chest.

"Joleus, I can't imagine my life without you in it. I can't even begin to understand why I feel this way, but I do, and I can't turn it off."

"Do you want to turn it off?" he questions, and caresses her hair.

She shakes her head no and kisses him tenderly. He leans back and says, "Neither do I."

She runs her fingers through his blond hair and kisses both his cheeks and then his lips once more.

"I asked you a question earlier that deems a response."

She looks into his eyes and smiles, without saying a word.

He laughs as she turns back around. "I will get my answer Miss Amelia," he whispers, kissing her hair. "No matter what."

She falls fast asleep with a huge grin on her face.

*****

Aaron is wandering around in a stunning place. The vivid colors personify every being in its vicinity. *It looks like paradise.* But he's not happy. He's afraid and depressed and doesn't know whether he's coming or going. He picks up a silver rock and throws it towards a gigantic waterfall and watches as the rock breaks into shattered pieces and disappears into the whirlpool beneath. He turns around and nods his head in submission, knowing that his time is running out. Three beautiful women are standing around him, guarding him with their life and waiting for the word to kill him. Each one of them has a specific power that is beyond compare.

They look at each other and say, "Time is almost near."

Aaron begins to tremble with fear. He steps back and leans against a tree.

*****

Amelia jumps out of the dream and looks around. Her body is shaking and her face is wet. Joleus is sleeping peacefully. Stylot opens his sleepy eyes and perks up. *They're going to kill him! I have to save him! I have to save Aaron before it's too late! But first, I have unfinished business.* She carefully removes Joleus's arm from her waist and scoots away from him, knowing it's the hardest thing she'll ever do. She softly kisses his cheek and grabs a stick. She finds a smooth patch of dirt and carves. *I'm sorry, my love.* She is filled with remorse. Stylot quietly follows behind her as she walks away from Joleus.

Once she gets out of the forest, she makes it to the nearest tree and drops to the ground, sobbing her eyes out. Stylot whimpers next to her. He feels her pain of having to leave. Her respite is over. As dawn approaches and the sun shines, Amelia dries her eyes and takes some deep breaths. *Gotta keep moving.* She and Stylot stroll out of Sigmount and quietly close the large wooden door. When they get over the bridge, she hugs Stylot's neck. "Are you okay boy, I know you'll miss Briseus." A lonely tear falls down his furry face. "We'll be okay, we're strong," she whispers.

*****

Navid

    Swish! Swoosh! The sound of the machines makes his insides turn. The constant beeping of her heart monitor is branded in his head as it continues to tweet on cue. After months on end, there's still no change. *Not one damn change. She deserved better than this, all of us did. But my conniving mother had other plans for us. I hope she's rotting in hell where she belongs, and if she's not, I hope Amelia is giving her every ounce of torture and suffering a person can stand.* Navid takes Amelia's cold, fragile hand and hopes she's fighting to come back to them.

"Come on Amelia. We need you here," he whispers. He moves her hair out of her face. "Sharon and I are getting married, but we won't do it without you. So you need to wake up, please." As he sniffles in silence, he hears someone turning the doorknob. He perks up and wipes his tears.

"Oh, hello again Mr. Jamison," Dr. Wallis says. He walks over and shakes Navid's hand and then examines Amelia carefully. He jots notes down on his medical tablet. He shines a light in her eyes and checks the reflexes on her hands and feet. From what Navid sees, there is still no change. *Her Glasgow coma score must be the same.* Navid has grown to learn more medical terms and procedures than he ever cared to know. But coming to the hospital everyday for hours can practically turn the biggest idiot into a doctor. "How long have you been here, son?"

"Since ten a.m. I can't leave her yet. I guess I have a feeling that there will be a change today," Navid replies.

Dr. Wallis pulls up a chair and takes a seat in front of him. "Navid, you can't let this consume you. It's five o'clock in the evening. For the past six months, I have seen you come here and spend hours in her room, hoping and wishing for a change. But what you have to understand is that comatose patients who have been in a coma for this amount of time will more than likely stay this way for a while.

She could wake up one day, but who knows when that will be? You
have to get on with your life."

"Doc, I appreciate your concern, but you don't know my cousin.
She's the strongest little thing I've ever laid eyes on. She will come
back to us. I know it. Besides, she promised me."

Dr. Wallis puts his hand on Navid's shoulder and smiles. "Well, if
she's as stubborn as you are, I'm sure she'll be with us very soon."

*****

Amelia

They've searched and searched for an entire day and can't find
Leona anywhere. *Ugh! I know that witch is taunting me.* A big part
of Amelia wants to run back to Joleus and forget this crap. It's
exhausting and hard and she's not sure she can do this. But like all
things in life, nothing is ever easy. Now that she has her legs and
powers back, it only makes sense for her to set forth on her original
plan. *I have to kill Leona and save Aaron. She took him away from
me in life, but she's not going to do it here.* She won't rest until she
sets him free, and hopes that once she sees him, she'll know for sure
what the future holds for her. Spending all that time with Joleus only
confused her and now she can't figure out what's right anymore. All
she knows is that she loves them both. She doesn't know how Joleus
did it, but he made her fall in love with him and the connection they
share is much deeper than she ever thought possible. She desperately
hopes he doesn't hate her for leaving. But she'll accept that if it
means he and his family will be safe.

Bark! Bark! "What is it? What do you see?" Amelia whispers,
yawning. She hadn't realized she fell asleep. She stretches and
stands, annoyed by yet another day of misery. *Aaron's in danger,
Leona's out there somewhere, and I can't be with Joleus.* After
minutes of self-loathing, she shakes it off and focuses on her current
goal. *I don't have a lot of time. Think Amelia. Where could she be?*
The only place left that Amelia can think of is the pyramids.
Although she blew up Lily's pyramid, she knows Leona has to be in
the area, sifting through the carnage. *I hope she's miserable. Grruff!*
Ruff! Amelia cautiously looks behind her. "Huh! Stylot run!"
Amelia screams. Two demons are heading for them. "Ahh! My leg!"
she cries. The painful slash of the pitchfork tore through her skin as a
knife to butter. She hops along and tries to escape as she
concentrates on what to do.

Her trembling body grows fifteen feet in the air. With one strong swipe, Amelia knocks the demons into a giant tree. Stylot chases after their remains and rips them apart before they have a chance to recover. Amelia closes her eyes to change back when she sees two bigger demons headed for her. She leaps forward and smashes them under her foot, twisting left and right several times to rid this world of their repulsive existence. Stylot trots back as Amelia returns to normal.

Together, they dash through the fields and into a forest that's infested with giant insects. Swatting away enormous mosquitos and wasps reminds her of Bram, a memory she hopes to never revisit again. Of course the fact that she killed Abraham is a reverie she will return to, especially when she's feeling low. A lizard the size of Stylot stops them and forces Amelia to become one. She battles it out, giving it her all while praying in the end that she never has to be a disgusting lizard ever again. When they reach the pyramids, Amelia's happy to see that only one still stands. She can't help but laugh at the idea that Lily actually thought she was going to trap her there forever. In retrospect, it wasn't totally Lily's fault because she listened to Abraham and assumed that things would be different. She was positive that everything he told her would come true, that she would spend eternity with her mother.

Amelia has made a point to never judge a person's thoughts or beliefs ever again. If it weren't for Stylot, she would have never met Joleus. She went inside Sigmount hoping to find Stylot so that they could leave and rescue Aaron. She *believed* Aaron was her all. *Instead, I met a great love of my life, a man who's half horse no less. The thought of me loving anyone more than Aaron seems absurd; but I can't deny what feels right, however strange. When I think back on that terrifying day when Joleus transformed me, I was ready to leave and never come back, but Stylot wouldn't let me go. Is it possible he knew what was best for me even when I didn't? Did he know I was meant to fall in love with Joleus? After all, he didn't stop me from leaving this time. I thought he'd want to stay and live with Briseus, but his remarkable loyalty to me has trumped everything else.*

He looks up at her and nuzzles her side. "I love you boy. Thank you for being my best friend and for saving my life countless times." She rubs his ears as he licks her face. "Now, let's go and find this monster."

Bark! Bark!

She rises up and walks slowly to what's left of the crumbled
pyramid. They both stand still and stare at the shattered masterpiece.
She can't see Leona anywhere, but knows she must be somewhere
near. While waiting, Amelia starts to think about all of the events
that took place inside the pyramid and it makes her start to shake. *I
could have died there, and Lily could have done her mother proud by
doing the dirty work herself.*

Before Amelia realizes what's happened, she's stepped back about
ten feet. *If Leona's out there somewhere, she can come to me.* She's
overcome with terrible memories of all that blood and Jordan's filthy
hands around her neck. Stylot begins to bark and growl ferociously.
She turns in a circle to see what the problem is. The large field of tall
weeds and flowers appears harmless, and the forest doesn't have any
critters crawling towards them. *What's he barking at?* She looks
straight ahead at the pyramid again and understands his anger. The
ever ready lioness has come from behind the dwelling to finally
show her face.

Amelia becomes enraged from just seeing Leona. Stylot tries his
best to guard her as she speed walks towards Leona without a care in
the world. Leona growls so loud the ground shakes, but Amelia
won't slow down. Her anger spurs her to run towards her with gritted
her teeth, ready for war. She slowly begins to morph into a massive
lion. Amelia leaps into the air just as Leona takes flight and crashes
into her. Amelia slaps her down and pounces on her so fast she
doesn't have time to react. She bites down on Leona's leg and tries
to tear out a piece, but Leona chomps down on her tail and it forces
Amelia to cry out. *Rah! Raaar!* Amelia jumps up and plunges herself
on Leona as she lunges for her. Bam! They roll around biting,
scratching, and clawing each other.

Grrr! Stylot gets close enough to bite Leona's foot, but she
carelessly kicks him across the field. Amelia furiously scratches her
face, leaving four red slashes in her fur. Leona pauses and scowls at
her and angrily goes in for the kill.

Amelia falls back and fights Leona off when something strange
happens and stops them both from moving an inch. They both rise up
and step back. Stylot limps across the field and manages to sit by
Amelia's side. Oddly, he doesn't seem bothered by the massive king
cobra that's positioned in front of them, the same one that she's seen
several times already. *What does it want?*

Ssssss. It hisses at them and expands its head.

With Stylot by her side, Amelia steps further away. Leona and she reluctantly change back into their natural selves. Amelia grits her teeth; she wants more than anything to finish her off. *If this snake is going to kill Leona; he better get in line.* Amelia faces Leona and crouches down, waiting for the right moment to strike. Leona scowls at her and says, "This time, I'm really going to kill you."

Without responding, Amelia leaps up and kicks her in the face. Blood shoots out of her nose and mouth. "That's for my father." As Leona tries to charge her, Amelia punches her in the stomach, stealing away her breath. "That's for my mother." While Leona's still bent over, Amelia picks up a sharp stick and grabs Leona by the hair; she pulls her head back so she can look into her eyes. "And this is for me." Amelia raises the stick high in the air.

"Stop!" A deep voice shouts from afar.

Amelia pauses and looks directly into the eyes of the man from her dream. *Roland?* "You—You're here. You were the snake?" Amelia asks. She still holds onto Leona.

He nods his head and grimaces at her. "Let her go Amelia. She's mine."

Amelia's eyes fill with tears. She shakes her head no. *I can't let Leona go, not after all of the things she has put me through; I can't let her breathe another second. All of the nightmares I'm going to endure because of her and what she's done.* Amelia tightens her fist around the stick.

"I know it's hard honey, and maybe I'm a little selfish, but I've been waiting a long time to put this witch out of her misery. It's my time to for revenge."

Leona maneuvers her way out of Amelia's hold and laughs. "Ha! Ha! Ha! You can't do a damn thing to me. You always were a weak bastard Roland; just admit it. I won! And the way I killed you was classic. How was spending your last few breaths in a plastic bag? Then I buried you in your precious desert that you loved so dearly." She giggles.

I can't believe her audacity, well, yes I can.

Roland's face hardens as he swallows hard, trying to hold his tongue. His hands are shaking and his lips are starting to twitch but he manages to look at Amelia and produce a faint smile. They've both waited so long for this day to come, and will relish the sweet revenge. "Amelia, it's time for you to go. Thank you for solving my murder and for caring enough to follow through with everything.

You need to go and save your friend. The way out is in the top of the other pyramid. If you make it to the ninth level, you'll be free."

Amelia takes a long deep breath and nods.

He walks closer and shakes her hand. "Tell my Navid that I love him," he whispers.

"I will," Amelia cries. "Goodbye Roland." She turns to walk away, but something stops her, something that can't be ignored as flashes of the past race through her mind. She whirls around and slaps Leona so hard she crashes to the ground, forcing it to crack. Tears flow from Amelia's eyes like a waterfall. Leona holds her face and stares at her, with sorrow? Her eyes begin to well up with tears. Amelia knows Leona has finally come to realize the hurt and damage she's caused, because at this moment, she has no other option but to face her wrong doings. *Now, I can finally walk away.* "She's all yours," Amelia whispers.

From the corner of her eye, Amelia sees Roland returning to a huge King Cobra. As she walks towards the pyramid Leona yells, "Amelia, don't leave me with him! Please! I'm sorry!" Sssss! Without turning around Amelia walks up to Stylot, who's still staring at Roland and Leona. His shiny black eyes are like a mirror. She sees the snake's body fly up in midair and bite down into Leona neck. "Ahhh! Help me!" she shouts. Amelia turns Stylot around and motions for him to follow her. They run towards the standing pyramid as the beautiful sound of Leona's death echoes in the wind. The constant striking followed by deathly screams has finally ceased. Amelia lets out a sigh of relief; she knows that Leona is gone forever; never to be heard of again.

Amelia puts her hand on her chest and smiles at the beating of her heart. *Who knew I would make it out of Bram, and now out of Felinity?* She doesn't know if she'll ever come back, but if one day she decides to find that wooden door, she hopes to see Joleus again. She misses him so much already and imagines him waking up feeling devastated that she's not by his side. It kills her to be away from him, but she had no choice. She knew Leona wasn't going to let up, especially if she found out about her love for Joleus. She would have made it her mission to kill him…and that would haunt Amelia forever. *I still can't believe Roland was waiting around all this time for Leona, but I'm glad he was there to finish her off. He deserved his justice.*

They reach the ninth level and stop to catch their breaths. "I can't believe how fast we got up here," she whispers to him. Her eager will to stay alive, pushed her and kept her moving. She shoves open the roof and gets ready to climb out when she sees a dark shadow in the corner. She stands up and looks at Stylot, hoping that she's imagining things. *Can he see it too?* As the dark shadow comes closer to the light her heart drops into her stomach. Grrr! *I guess it's not my imagination, he sees him too.*

"Mortis?"

BOOK 3
"Mortis"

Chapter Twenty One

Just when I thought I was free. He's the last person I want to see. He frightens the hell out of me. Sure, I can put on a brave face and pretend that's it's all good, but his powers are so much more complicated than anyone else's. If I hadn't been so busy with Abraham, I could have made sure he didn't escape the Crying Forest. But I have no regrets because Abraham needed to die and killing him demanded my undivided attention. The scary part about Mortis is that I have no way to defeat him. My only shot is to outsmart him.

"You look surprised to see me. Did you think I wouldn't come after you?" he says.

Stylot growls at him as the saliva drips from his mouth.

"Oh shut up you traitor!"

Stylot steps forward, but Mortis quickly jumps on top of the pyramid and closes his eyes. The ground beneath them begins to vibrate and Amelia's head suddenly feels like it's going to explode. She puts her hands on her head and tries to breathe slowly as something drips from her ears. It takes great strength to concentrate on blocking out the aches. Stylot cries loudly while scooting closer to her. A bright light shines in her eyes and the sound of a digital monitor beeps in her ears. *Where am I?*

*****

Navid

Beep! Beep! Beep! "Hey! Did you see that? Her face just moved! She's waking up doctor, she's coming back!" Navid shouts.

"No Navid, this is another false alarm. Comatose patients do this all the time. Sometimes a body part will move or you'll see a mouth twitch, but it doesn't mean anything, it's all nerves."

I know he's a doctor but he's so negative. I know her more than he does. "No. I don't believe that. I can feel it, she's going to come back to us." Navid gently takes Amelia's hand and pats it. "Come on Amelia, you can do this. Open your eyes, please."

"I'll be right back. I'm going to get my stethoscope," Dr. Wallis says.

Navid nods. He stares at Amelia. *Could he be right? Maybe I'm in over my head. Maybe I'm starting to lose my damn mind. I should probably go home and get some sleep.* He kisses her hand and proceeds to put it down when she squeezes his fingers. Navid looks up. His heart is racing. *Her eyes are open!* Riveting blue eyes are staring back at him. Navid is shaking and afraid to move, he can't do anything. He opens his mouth to call the doctor but his voice is mute, so with trembling hands he rubs her face and smiles. "H-hi," he croaks.

Amelia looks at him in shock as she stares around the room. She pulls the tubes out of her mouth and inhales deeply. She swallows hard and whispers, "Navid…Roland says…"

"Amelia no! Come back! What did my dad say? Come back, don't close your eyes!" Navid screams. He gazes at her inquisitively, hoping she stays with him, but her heavy eyelids take over, fighting her eagerness to keep them open. In the end, the darkness has won as it pulls her back under. "No! Come back!" He shakes her and falls down beside the bed and wails like a child. Everything has takens a toll on him. "Why is this happening?"

The hospital room door flies open and quickly closes. The sound of high heels echo inside the quiet room as he sits there, buried in his own thoughts. The soft touch of a woman's hands caresses his neck and shoulders. He looks up and squeezes her waist. "She was here Sharon, she came back."

"Navid, baby, you can't keep doing this to yourself," she whispers.

He stifles a moan. "You don't believe me. Look at the tubes, she pulled those out," he says and points to Amelia's hands. Sharon's eyes expand and she covers her mouth in shock. Her eyes well up with tears as the doctor walks back in and stops with his mouth open.

"She was telling me something about my dad," Navid says.

Dr. Wallis walks over and shines a light in her eyes and examines her body. "So…she woke up briefly and went back under?" he inquires. His dumbfounded expression tells Navid that this doesn't happen often.

"Yes, she opened her eyes and looked at me. She was trying to tell me about my dad, but something powerful pulled her back under." He looks at Amelia and yells, "Fight Amelia! Fight it!"

*****

Amelia

"Navid! Navid can you hear me! I'm trying!" she screams, crying. She opens her eyes and is back with Stylot, afraid of what's happening. *Mortis must have taken us out of Felinity and into his creation. Damn, I was so close to waking up and being free.* But the thought of Aaron being killed sends a lightning bolt right through her, so she's glad she still has a fighting chance to save him. She and Stylot cuddle together in the darkness as they wait to see what's in store for them. Glimmers of light finally pour through an opening, beckoning her to come out. "Are we still inside the pyramid?" She carefully crawls out of the hole and finds herself outside, in the snow. Stylot scoots out right before it collapses into slush. He jumps towards her and looks back in fear, realizing they could have easily been buried alive.

"Where are we?" she whispers. Her teeth are chattering as she pulls her arms to her chest, hoping and praying for some relief. They walk around in a winter land that's filled with tall oak trees and blankets of snow that cover every surface. She already hates it as she rubs the chill off her arms. She glances at Stylot. "At least you have fur," she says, annoyed. He looks at her and rubs his body next to hers. "Thanks boy, but I'll be okay. I think." If she didn't know better, she would swear she'd died and gone to Colorado in the dead of winter. The further they trek through the snow, the more nervous she becomes. A low howl of the wind adds more horror to the milieu. "I'm so c-cold I can't think," she utters, shivering. *Crap! I'm so not going to make it at this rate.*

Grrr! Ruff!

Amelia pauses and looks around. A man strolls from behind a tree and stops at a safe distance, eyeing Stylot with curiosity.

"So you're the infamous Stylot I've heard so much about. What a large animal he is." He puts his hands in his pockets.

"Yeah, I get that a lot," Amelia replies.

"Come, we've been waiting for you."

If I here that one more time. How the hell can everyone be waiting for me? I must be the most popular girl that ever existed. I wish I was this popular in school.

"Well?" The man smirks.

"Well what? I don't know you?" Amelia crosses her arms and stands her ground. She glances to her right and left to see if she's surrounded.

"I'm Joe, Mortis's brother."

"What is wrong with you people? You know, from what I hear Heaven isn't an awful place to be. Are you telling me that you chose to wait for your evil brother instead of going into the bright light?" she yells.

He frowns with confusion and shakes his head. "This is my Heaven, being with my family. You mean you've met others who's done the same thing?"

"You have no idea. Anyway, I'm not going anywhere with you and you can tell Mortis he'll have to come and get me himself."

She turns away as Joe speeds behind her. Without much effort, she transforms into a crow and flies away. Stylot quickly sprints beneath her, offering long strides to keep up. She peers down while soaring through the cold atmosphere, grateful for the warmth of the feathers. Joe has disappeared somewhere in the trees. She flies down once she is certain that the coast is clear. As she lands, she transforms back to herself. *I have to figure out a good plan to defeat Mortis. I can't drag this out and hide like I did in Bram. It has to end here.* She sits on a snow covered log and ponders how she can get Mortis to come to her.

She looks at Stylot, who appears to be preoccupied by something. He stares far beyond the trees. *Whatever he's looking at can't be good.* He steps away from Amelia and stops directly in front of a row of trees. Without saying a word, she walks backwards and leans up against a tree stump. *Aaarg! Poof!* Joe flies out of the tree and lands on Stylot's back. He pulls Stylot's ears and bites down on his neck.

"No!" Amelia shouts. She runs towards them, but Stylot looks into her eyes and lets out a loud bark, warning her to stay away. She reluctantly stands at a safe distance in sheer panic. *I hope he can get out of this.* While trying to block out the loud growls and screaming noises, she contemplates the best way to kill Mortis, but knows it's going to be tough.

She has a sick feeling in her gut that something terrible might happen.

Bark! Bark! Stylot is heading for her with blood on his paws. He tracks a perfect trail of red paw prints in the snow.

"Are you okay boy? Is that your blood?" She checks his paws and his body and can't find a scratch on him. She slowly goes towards where the fighting took place and is shocked by the amount of blood everywhere. Joe's mangled body looks unrecognizable. An arm lies frozen in the snow a few feet away and a hand is half torn off of his wrist. She feels bad for him. *What made him think he can fight a huge animal like Stylot?* As the blood continues to pour out of Joe's neck, Amelia can't help but think about Mortis and what he's going to do when he finds his brother this way.

"Come on boy, we have to get away from here. We have to be smart and figure out the best way to make it out alive. We will make it out alive," she says.

"No you won't. I've been planning this moment since escaping Bram," he says in a low, deep voice. He looks past them and eyes his brother lying in a bloody mess. Tears pour out of his eyes, but his calmness is what she's most afraid of. He's not even trying to kill them. "You will pay for that. I'll just add that to the list. You think you're so clever don't you Amelia? You came into Bram, pretending to be this frightened young girl, only to completely destroy what the Beast took so long to create."

"I wasn't pretending Mortis. I was terrified, but I wasn't going to stand by and watch you kill my friends and my father. That was not an option I cared to consider."

"You and Stylot will die today and there's nothing you can do about it."

"We'll see about that Mortis," Amelia replies.

"Ha! Ha! Oh yes, we'll see. The sooner you realize you don't call the shots here, the better off you'll be. I will have the last word!" he shouts. His deep voice echoes and rattles everything and forces snow to fall from the trees. Amelia inhales deeply and walks closer.

Grrrr! Ruff! Stylot trots in front of her and guards her as Mortis looks on in fear of him. "Sit!" he screams, but Stylot continues growling at him in disgust. Mortis curls his upper lip and scowls at him.

"He's not yours anymore!"

"Because you stole him from me!"

"Is that what this is all about, you're mad because I took your dog? Grow up!"

He grimaces at her and charges towards her. Stylot jumps up and tries to bite him, but he somehow dodges the attack and pushes Amelia down. She punches him in the face and knees him in the groin.

"Ahhh! You witch!" He slaps her, which draws blood from her nose. He stands erect and proceeds to kick her, but Stylot tears through his pants and slices his leg. "Dammit! You traitorous mutt! Amelia, you better call off your dog!"

"Stand down!" Amelia shouts, holding her face. But what he doesn't know is that she and Stylot have a connection. She looks at him. *Kill boy! Kill him!* As Stylot goes after him, Mortis quickly figures it out and runs in fear.

"Amelia, run into that tree!" He yells while running in a circle. Amelia cries and reluctantly follows his command. She rushes forward and hits the tree head on.

"Ahhh!" She falls backwards, dislocating her shoulder in the process. "No more Stylot!" she groans.

"Ha! Ha! Like I said, you're not as clever as you think. Now, stand up and follow me," Mortis commands.

Stylot licks her face and pulls on her pants, willing her to stand. As they follow behind him, she realizes this might be the best time to tell Stylot what to do.

With Mortis's back turned, she transforms into a Stylot look-alike. *Listen Stylot, Mortis is going to try and kill me. He knows he doesn't have much time because the longer he stays around us the more he's putting himself in danger. The moment you have a free opportunity, I want you to kill him. Don't worry about me, just make sure you do it successfully, okay boy?*

He looks up at her and quietly growls. *"Okay. Please be careful."*

Amelia transforms back. "Come here," she whispers as she hugs his neck and kisses his fur. She sucks in the cool, crisp, air and continues walking until Mortis stops in front of an ice covered pond that's surrounded by bunches of broken tree limbs. *Wow, he's really thought this through.* She can't help but wonder if this is the last thing she's going to see before she dies. She winces through the throbbing pain in her shoulder and puts on a brave face.

Mortis turns around with a big smile on his face and crosses his arms. He reads their expressions. "You look amused. Am I mistaken?" he asks.

Amelia glares at him without answering. He snickers and says,
"Oh Amelia, you never cease to amaze me. You know, you're a lot
like your grandfather. He wasn't afraid of a damn thing…except
you."

"Well, he should've been. And so should you."

He cocks his head to the side and smacks his teeth. Amelia
transforms in to a large buzzard and flies towards his face. She pecks
out his right eye and quickly removes a piece of flesh as he screams
in pain. He grabs a hold of her wings and throws her into a pile of
snow.

"Transform back right now!" he roars. She unwillingly transforms
back and immediately feels the seething pain of her dislocated arm.
She rolls over in the snow, utterly exhausted. "You will never pull
that trick again!" He holds his face in pain as blood gushes from his
eye socket.

"Oh come on, I thought we were just getting started. Did you
really think I wouldn't put up a fight?" She shakes her head from
side to side while smacking her teeth.

"I think I've heard just about enough of your voice for one
lifetime," Mortis says through gritted teeth.

She opens her mouth to reply but apparently Stylot has found his
opportunity. He flies over her, lunges for Mortis and knocks him
down. They tussle over each other as Mortis tries to get away. Stylot
bites down on his arm as blood shoots out onto the white ground.
Mortis screams to the heavens for mercy, but Stylot won't let up.
With his free hand he finds a stick and raises it high in the air.

"No!" Amelia screams and runs over to snatch it out of his hand.
She takes the stick and stabs him in the leg with it, hoping it helps
Stylot.

"Amelia! Walk into the icy pond and stay there," Mortis croaks.
Before she turns to follow his command, he rolls over and picks up a
tree branch and stabs Stylot in the chest.

"Ahhh! No! No!" she cries. Barely able to catch her breath from
the shock, she slowly walks into the ice cold water. She sinks lower
underfoot as the water rests at her waist. "Stylot!" she sobs. He
slumps to the ground and lies very still, barely breathing. She's so
consumed and devastated that she can no longer concentrate. Tears
pour out of her eyes. Mortis falls onto his back and breathes deep,
feeling the victory. Amelia looks up through tears and sees slight
movement. As Mortis looks at the sky with relief, Stylot jumps up
and bites down into his neck, tearing out a large piece of flesh.

Mortis gurgles and struggles to breathe while holding his neck in shock. Stylot carefully crawls towards the pond and takes one last look at Amelia before closing his eyes, forever.

"No!" Amelia wails. "Stylot come back to me!"

The icy cold water is starting to take its toll on her body, paralyzing her limbs. She stumbles to her knees as the water stings every nerve along the way. She's trying to focus on moving backwards. Once Mortis dies, his command will be void. *If I can just hold on until he takes his last breath, I'll live.* Her entire body is shaking from head to toe and it's getting harder to take a single breath. She looks over and sees Mortis bleeding out into the snow, knowing he's dying slowly and painfully. Tears continue to stream down her cold face and freeze before they hit the water. Her beautiful Stylot is lying on the cold ground. Her protector is dead. "I h-hope you know how much I l-loved y-you," she whispers in his ear.

Mortis gags one last time and finally dies.

Amelia closes her eyes and sniffles, trying hard to transform into a bird, but she can't. Her body is in shock and she's freezing, but she manages to rise up and take a step backwards. And then another. She picks up her weighted right foot and steps back, each step takes more effort than the last as she tries to back out of the water. She's out of breath. "Concentrate Amelia, c-concentrate on living," she grunts. Her heart is slowing down and her feet are frozen.

*****

Navid

"Dr. Wallis, why is she shaking like this? What's wrong with her? Her whole body is trembling!" Navid takes her hand and rubs it vigorously to warm it up.

Dr. Wallis walks over to the intercom and pushes the nurse's line. "Yes, bring our patient some warm blankets stat, her temperature is rapidly dropping."

Navid is getting scared. *This can't be good. What could be going on with her?* The next thing he knows, nurses are coming in and checking her heart monitor while Dr. Wallis checks her vitals and puts something into her IV. "What are you doing? What's going on?"

"We're just trying to calm her down before she goes into cardiac arrest," Dr. Wallis replies.

Navid falls back into his chair and rubs his forehead, contemplating on what to do. *I knew it! I knew something was going to happen today!*

"Navid, just breathe, baby," Sharon whispers while holding his hand. He can't look up. He's certain that the beeping sound of Amelia's heart monitor is getting louder and louder. It's almost ringing in his ears. The only comfort he has is that it hasn't stopped. It's like annoying music to his ears, because Amelia is still with them. Beep! Beep! Beep! Beeeeeeeeeeee

His head shoots up as it flat lines! "Huh! No! Amelia!" Navid cries.

Twenty Two

Misty, white fog has isolated her from everything. As she treks through a blanket of nothing, she becomes frightened to the point of immobility. She looks to her left and to her right, but can't find any hint of a shadow. Forcefully putting one foot in front of the other, she assumes there must be more out there somewhere. After taking ten diligent steps, she chickens out and pauses, refusing to move another inch. *What happened to me? How did I end up here?* Her mind is so clouded and she can't feel a thing. Without an explanation or a soul in sight, she can only assume something bad has happened. She's suddenly catapulted to the two worst days of her life, when she visited her dad in the hospital and when she saw Aaron's bloody body lying on her living room floor.

Out of the blue, a young boy, about four feet tall, appears through the haze and gawks at her. His black ringlets are perfectly curled as if on purpose and his immaculate fair skin glows in the white atmosphere. His beautiful brown eyes are fixated on her, staring as if he knows something about her that she doesn't. "Well? Are you just going to stand there or can we get going?"

"Excuse me? Who are you?" Amelia asks.

"Oh, pardon me madam. Ahem, my name is Anthony and I'm very pleased to meet you." His tiny hand quickly finds hers and squeezes firmly.

"I'm Amelia."

"I know," he replies.

A faint cry echoes from afar. Amelia nervously looks around. "Where am I?"

"You're in Heaven, well, almost."

"Heaven? No, this can't be right. I'm not supposed to die! I have to get to Aaron and save him."

Anthony's soft little hand finds hers again. "What exactly do you remember?"

"Not much," Amelia sniffles. "The last thing I remember is leaving Joleus and feeling utterly devastated. Um, my aunt Leona was finally killed. But everything from there is a blur." *Oh God, if he's right then why can't I remember how I died? I honestly didn't think it was possible because I had come so far.* Amelia covers her face and weeps. She feels lightheaded and kneels down. She tries to process her reality.

"Aww man, please don't cry. I'm ill-equipped for girls and their emotions. Please we have to go now." He disappears in the mist without so much of an indication of his presence. Amelia can't move. She's confused and distraught. *So much for thinking I was invincible.*

"I'm dead. Wow," she cries. *Everything I've been through, all that hard work was for nothing?* She has not one thing to show for it and the disturbing silence in her chest makes her feel even worse as it puts everything into perspective. No beating heart, no Aaron, and no Joleus.

"Hi, remember me? Yeah, we gotta go," Anthony demands. With little regard to her protest, he grabs a hold of her hand and starts walking. Before she can react, they immediately levitate and fly through the air, high above the thick fog that covers the ground.

The starry night sky is a brilliant welcome compared to being trapped in nothing but thick smog. The higher up they go the more the fog fades. Amelia looks behind them and notices two black shadows pierce through the white haze, picking up speed after them. "What's that?" she asks, pointing downward.

"Trouble," he answers as he flies faster. "They're demons waiting to capture you. If you had stood there a second longer, you would've been toast."

"Why do they want me?"

"They don't want you to finish your quest. There are certain things you don't know Amelia. You have been given a certain gift, one that will take you very far. Surely, you know that by now."

"I thought I knew. I don't mean to be a killjoy, but my quest is clearly over. I'm dead for goodness sakes. I'm no good to anyone," Amelia declares.

Anthony sighs and shakes his head with exacerbation. "Hold on tight, we're almost there."

The cool, fresh wind hits her in the face and dries her tears. As the demons pursue them, she forcefully closes her eyes and squeezes Anthony's hand tighter. *I can't believe my soul lies in the hands of toddler. Am I the butt of a joke?* All of a sudden, they shoot through a vortex and it jolts them forward at warp speed. Amelia's eyes fly open and she's relieved to see that the demons are no longer behind them. *At least we were able to get away.* When she turns back around, she can't allow herself to blink as she stares at…*Heaven.*

There is so much life and magic beneath a clear blue sky. It's a bittersweet moment as she accepts what is meant to be. This time she can't run away like she did before and she can't help but feel foolish for prolonging the inevitable. All that torture and heartache she endured in Bram and up until now only proves that she didn't need to drag this out. *If I'd only let the little creatures carry me away…into the light.* But, her conscious won't let her succumb to depression because she was able to save her dad and her friends. The bumpy ride pulls her out of her thoughts and back to reality. They shift back and forth in the wind and slam right into a patch of beautiful green grass. "Ouch!" Amelia shrieks. She rubs her back and frowns at Anthony. *Clearly he needs to work on his landing skills.* Falling flat on her butt was not what she expected on her first day in Heaven. She's amazed how being there makes every ache and pain cease.

"Sorry about the landing. I don't usually fly because Asa takes me wherever I need to go," Anthony says.

"Asa?"

"Yeah, my horse. She should be around here somewhere. My guardian Anita insisted I pick you up alone so you can blame her." He giggles.

"I'll be sure to do that. Listen little guy, I was wondering if…"

"Little guy? Let's get one thing straight Amelia, I'm over a hundred years old and I don't appreciate you treating me like a child. I know I'm not very tall and I look young but that is because I was just a boy when I died. But make no mistake, I happen to be an excellent weapon if need be." He stomps off with his nose in the air and disappears.

Great, now he's mad at me. She takes a seat by a giant rock and tries to contemplate her last whereabouts. "Come on Amelia think, where were you? How did you die? Who killed you?" she whispers.

She slams her fists in the ground. "Why can't I remember?" she
yells.

"Amelia?"

With teary eyes she turns around and smiles at Anthony. "I'm
sorry for insulting you. I'm just confused," she admits.

"Forgiven." He walks closer and throws something in her face.
Achoo! Achoo! "Hey! What did you do?"

*****

The warmth of the sun awakens her from a dreamless slumber and
the fluorescent blue sky is as bright as fireworks. The air smells like
fresh peonies and her skin has a golden shimmer in the sunlight. She
can't understand for the life of her what happened and why she's
wearing a white gown.

"How did you sleep?" Anthony asks with a grin.

She immediately remembers what happened yesterday. He threw
something in her face. She jumps up and grabs a fistful of his robe.

"You, you little creep! You drugged me!" Amelia screams and lifts
his body off the ground.

"Put me down!" He laughs while squirming to get away. "It was
payback for treating me like a child." He jumps down and lands in
the grass.

"Well I guess you sure showed me. What you did was childish and
wrong. How do you expect me to take you seriously?"

He shrugs his shoulders apologetically. Amelia shakes her head
with frustration when he breaks out into a laugh. As mad as she'd
like to stay at him, she lets out a giggle instead. *I guess it would be
taboo to be upset in Heaven of all places. I wonder why I was upset
in the first place?* She thought it was all about happiness and
laughter, but she feels like nothing has changed and that her somber
feelings and emotions are still lurking.

"I better get you to my home. I'm sure Anita will be looking for
us." He walks out towards a rainbow and shouts, "Asa!"

"I thought this was your home."

"No, this was just a stopping point, a safe haven if you will.
Heaven is an enormous place and I need Asa to fly us to where I
live. Trust me, you don't want me to fly us that far."

When she thinks about the crash landing they had yesterday, she
graciously concurs.

"Asa! I'm ready!" Anthony hollers again. Within a glorious millisecond, a sparkling white horse with wings strides towards them with water dripping from its mouth.

She's magnificent.

Asa's caramel brown eyes focus on Amelia as she trots forward. Anthony stares at her with confusion and finally says, "Asa, this is Amelia." Amelia nods nervously and walks closer to pet her long platinum blond hair. Asa cradles her head into Amelia's touch and lets out a tiny groan. Anthony rolls his eyes and floats up to get on her back. Amelia finds it alarming how fast he can elevate at any given moment. *What else can he do? Maybe I shouldn't underestimate him.* As Anthony positions himself on the amazing beast, he holds out his hand and motions for Amelia to climb up. They elegantly fly through the sweet smelling air and head towards the silver-lined clouds. *That breathtaking view I saw in Zerios looks like a dump compared to this.*

There are rainbows upon rainbows and puffy white clouds overlap like mounds of marshmallows, and the land looks like it's draped in the richest material known to man. Even the dirt looks like it was manufactured into perfectly scented powder. As for the vivid colors, she thought she had seen all the colors of the world, but none can compare to the colors of Heaven.

"We're almost there!"

"What did you say, Anthony?" Amelia asks.

"I didn't say anything. That was just Asa informing us that we're almost there."

Did I just hear him correctly? What does he mean? "Oh I get it. Ha ha, another one of your jokes," Amelia giggles.

Anthony shrugs his shoulders. Amelia looks on as they descend. The ride is as smooth as can be, better than when Anthony flew them.

"Hold on tight!" Asa screams.

"She just spoke!" Amelia yells.

"Yes, I can talk," Asa replies and turns to look at Amelia.

Amelia flinches back and falls off. "Ahhh! Help me!" As she descends from the sky, face up, she tries to ignore the fact that she has nothing to break her fall. *Is it possible to die in Heaven, I mean how exactly does this work? Maybe it won't hurt when I land.* She squeezes her eyes shut in anticipation for a life altering landing.

"Amelia!" Anthony screams. She opens her eyes and realizes that she's moving further up, towards the sky again. She wiggles and looks around. Anthony is floating in front of her with a concerned expression, which can only mean that…

"Ahh!" Amelia shouts, understanding that Asa has somehow broken her fall, midair.

"Are you alright?" Asa asks.

"Y-yes, I think so." Amelia's shaking all over with fear. "How are you able to talk?"

"Everyone in Heaven can talk. Don't worry, you'll get used to it." She laughs while moving forward to give Anthony a chance to climb back on. *This will be hard getting used to.* With shaky limbs, Amelia straddles Asa and wraps her arms around Anthony, hoping that this will be over soon.

When they finally land, Amelia spots a woman watering a beautiful array of colorful roses. She's youthful and pretty and is donning a white gown. Anthony runs up to her and squeezes her waist as she smiles in response, wrapping her arms around him. Asa walks over to a blue lake and takes a few sips while Amelia stands there. She feels completely out of place. A single tear falls down her cheek as she thinks about *her* mother and how much she misses her. She's overwhelmed with sadness because she feels like a failure. *Aaron is probably dead by now and on his way to Heaven.* She wonders if those evil women are closing in on him and ready to finish him off. *Maybe I'll get to see him soon and tell him how sorry I am.* She wipes her nose and tries to ponder what will come of her. Her journey has ended and she's devastated. She wants to feel great, but can't. *What's wrong with me? Am I that damaged that even a place like this can't lighten my spirits?*

She's trying hard to fight back the rest of the tears and stay strong, but her reality is hurtful and confusing. What plagues her most is she doesn't know how she died. *If I could remember, maybe that would give me the closure and peace I need to be at rest. Why did Anthony bring me here?* She looks around for angels, a gate, or St. Peter.

The woman strolls over to Amelia and smiles pleasantly. Her pearly white teeth bring out the perfection in her face. Her wavy black hair runs right past her shoulders and her skin is the color of milk chocolate. "Hey honey, my name is Anita."

Wow, even her voice sounds like a song in the wind. Amelia has an urge to embrace her and cry on her shoulder. Her calming spirit is magnetic and she feels drawn to her.

"I can assume you know who I am," Amelia whispers.

"I do. We have quite a bit to discuss, but first, I want you to be comfortable with us. Would you like a glass of milk?"

That's an odd question but I am a little parched. Amelia nods with a smile just as Anthony walks out of a mansion with a large glass. Amelia does a double take at the massive dwelling. She's been so distracted that she never noticed the huge masterpiece. Every brick and piece of wood has been perfectly structured to make the most beautiful house that ever existed. *Wow, they get to live here?*

"Here you are madam. One delicious glass of milk," Anthony says. Amelia closes her mouth and tries to hide the dumbfounded look on her face. With a small indication of reluctance, he hands her the glass and takes a step back. She drinks every last bit of it and immediately after, she begins to relax. This moment brings her to childhood when he parents brought her warm milk to calm her nerves. She hands him back the glass with tears in her eyes. His smile fades as he takes the glass from her trembling fingers. "Everything is going to be okay Amelia." Her eyes start to droop and she finds herself exhausted from the aftermath of everything she's been through.

"I'm so tired," Amelia whispers through a yawn.

*****

She wakes up with a start as the sun floods the luxurious room. Her bed is a silky plush work of art and the pillows are made of the softest material that ever existed. It's a wonder she awoke at all. Now that she thinks about it, she finds it weird that she *can* go to sleep. She thought being in Heaven meant that you can roam free to live for eternity, not needing sleep, rest or food. But here she is in the most beautiful place she knows and she's tired, confused, and hungry. Her stomach is growling as if she's never had a meal. She hops out of bed and walks over to the window, peering out at the extraordinary baby blue sky. As she stares out and imagines what her family must be going through, she gets deeply depressed. *What must Dad be thinking? I hope he's okay. I don't even know if he ever woke up or if Mom was able to get out of jail.*

She wishes she can wash her hands of the life she once knew, but something is keeping her from enjoying this sacred place, which brings her back to her theory about trying to figure out what happened to her. Since Anthony is her guardian, she wonders if he knows what happened to her. Just as she's about to look away, she

212

sees two cherubs fluttering by. Their chubby cheeks and hummingbird-like wings are even more precious than what she saw in books. There is so much to Heaven that she has yet to see.

"Hey, I see you're awake. How was your nap?" Anita asks.

"It was lovely, thank you," Amelia replies. There are so many questions bombarding her mind that she doesn't know where to start. "Anita, what's wrong with me? I feel so…"

"Help! Anita!" Anthony screams. They rush out of the room and head in the direction of his cries. Amelia trails her as she flies down the spiral stairs and out a set of glass double doors.

"Anthony! What's is it?" Anita shouts in panic, searching for him. They run past a large magnolia tree and out towards an enormous green field that's covered with vivacious orange flowers.

This feels like a dream. Everywhere Amelia turns, she finds herself enthralled by the beauty of life and laughter.

They find Anthony behind a tiny wicker house crouched down next to Asa.

"It's Asa, she's sick. We were out flying around when all of a sudden she started to gag. Then, she got weaker and weaker and fell out of the sky and landed here," he sobs, stroking her hair.

Anita and Amelia walk over to see for themselves and to their disappointment, Asa appears to look lost. The bright gleam in her eyes is gone and her metallic shimmer has faded. She barely lifts her head off the ground and tries to speak, but her weak body isn't strong enough to let her utter one syllable.

Anthony glares at them with red eyes and asks, "What do we do?"

Anita carefully puts her hand on Asa's side and closes her eyes. Amelia stares at her and then at Anthony, completely clueless as to what to do. *Are we going to watch her die or is she gonna make it.* Suddenly, from the corner of her eye, Amelia sees a luminous light emerge from Anita's hand. Anthony's eyes have grown two sizes larger in either shock or disapproval from what she can tell. He opens his mouth to speak, but stops when he makes eye contact with Amelia. She can sense that he wants to say more, but refrains from verbalizing his feelings. She wonders perhaps if it's the "not now" look Anita is giving him. *What is going on?*

"I feel like you two are hiding something from me," Amelia says.

"That's because we are," Anthony replies.

"Anthony!" Anita shouts. She gives him a stern look and stands to her feet. "You're obviously upset about Asa so I think you need to go and cool off."

"No I don't. Her being here is causing a problem. We have to do something before…"

"I said, go take a walk," Anita grunts.

"Hey, wait a minute! What are you two talking about, *my being here*? I deserve to know," Amelia demands.

Anita reaches for Amelia's hand and smiles. "Amelia honey, there is a time and place for everything. Right now is not the time." And with that, Amelia immediately drops the subject at hand. She's not sure if it's Anita's calming touch or her angelic voice, but she can't allow herself to argue or protest, not with her. *I'll leave it alone—for now.* Just as Anthony stomps off she notices that Asa has risen to her feet. She shakes her entire body and stretches. With a relieving smile, Amelia strolls over and pets her.

"What did you do?" Amelia asks Anita.

She shrugs her shoulders and says, "I just gave her a little boost."

"Amazing!" Amelia laughs while continuing to pet her.

"Let's go for ride. Hop on," Asa whispers. Her raspy voice startles Amelia, but she nods and hops on. She looks back at her and with a wink she jets off after Anthony, whose still clearly upset and has no idea that she's going to be okay. When they catch up to him, Asa speeds up and bumps his bottom, making him fly up with surprise. Amelia giggles aloud and waves; his face lights up like the sun when he sees Asa.

"Asa! You're okay?" He shrieks and flies over to hug her neck.

"Of course I'm okay. Now hop on, we're going for a ride." He jumps on and wraps his little hands around her neck. The three fly off towards the sun.

*****

Navid

"No! Help her! Please help her!" he screams. He leans over to her lifeless body and shakes her vigorously. "Fight Amelia!"

"Get him out of here!" Dr. Wallis shouts to the nurses. As they're carrying him out of the room, he sees a nurse doing CPR while the other one counts continuously. Dr. Wallis is holding up two electric pads. "Clear!" He hollers. The nurses move back as Amelia's body jolts up and flops back down like a dead fish.

Oh dear God, nothing is changing. The monitor is still flat lining. As they drag Navid out of the room, his whole body goes into shock. Vomit arises from the pit of his stomach and spews out of his mouth.

"I'll go get him a towel," a nurse's assistant says.

"Thank you so much," Sharon says. She cradles her arms around his waist and helps him sit in a chair outside the room. His stomach hasn't been the same since Leona poisoned him and his lungs are barely allowing the tiniest breath to escape. As Sharon holds him in her arms, he attempts to take a deep breath and concentrate on keeping his food down. His eager will to keep the tears from falling fails and only ends with him and Sharon crying together in sync. He can hear the sound of the machine outside the door as it continues to beep without a single break or interruption, which means that her heart still isn't beating. "Stay strong baby, Amelia would want you to stay strong," Sharon whispers.

"I know. They have to save her Sharon, they just have to." He pulls away and looks into her eyes. "I promised Amelia that I wouldn't let them give up on her, that I would make sure they kept her alive."

Sharon frowns in confusion as the tears flow down her rosy cheeks. He wipes them away as he can't bear to see *her* cry. "What? What do you mean you promised her?"

"Amelia made me promise that if anything ever happened to her, my job was to keep her alive no matter what, that she will come back," Navid explains.

"Did she know something like this would happen?"

He nods and holds her tight. Sharon only knows bits and pieces of the story. He can't tell her that Amelia was being abused since the moment her father was shot. He doesn't know how she would take that and he can't lose her. *What if she blames me for not doing more?* He squeezes her tighter as she rubs his back.

"Clear!" Dr. Wallis hollers. Hearing the faint sounds of the nurses continuing to count while doing CPR is all that's keeping Navid from running back into the room. As long as they're trying to keep her alive, he knows Amelia still has a chance.

Chapter Twenty Three

Amelia's enamored with every glamorous aspect of Heaven. It's
enchanting and the cleanest and richest place she's ever been. There
are no mistakes. In fact, the only mistake she notices is her. She
can't shake the constant feeling that she doesn't belong there and
hopes to someday feel differently. She realizes that whatever they're
keeping from her is paramount and it's only a matter of time before
she can no longer hold her tongue. Being at peace is very important
to her and it is pretty evident that she won't feel right until she gets
some answers. *For the moment, I'll keep my composure and enjoy
my surroundings because the more I contemplate things, the angrier
I become.*

"Over there is the highest mountain in Heaven," Anthony says,
pointing to the left. Once again he breaks her out of her reverie and
offers another wonderful creation that only God can conjure.
"Coming up on our right is the most fruitful garden you will ever
see. Everything in it is edible, including the grass. Even some parts
of the trees taste delicious. The fruit never goes bad and the taste is
indescribable."

"Sounds amazing. Is it the Garden of Eden?" Amelia asks.

"No," he retorts with a snicker.

Conversing about delicious fruit and trees reminds her of Zerios.
She misses Joleus so much that the notion of never seeing him again
makes her physically sick. She thought that somehow they'd cross
paths again, but now it's too late. *He must be so furious with me for
leaving him.* It hurt her soul to leave, but Leona had to be stopped
and Aaron needed to be saved. *Now that I'm dead, he'll never know*

how much I truly loved him and how I wanted to go back to him. He probably thinks I never meant anything I said. She takes out the beautiful yellow rock he gave her and brings it to her lips. She still can't understand why or how her feelings for him were so strong. She holds back her will to cry and looks up to keep the tears from dripping out. The wind is a refreshing gift as they soar through the sky in silence.

"Hey Asa! Why don't we take a rest in the garden?" Anthony suggests.

Amelia furrows her brow and wonders if she and Anthony have some weird connection because every time she feels like crying he tries to take her mind off of her burdens. *If it's true, I can't say that I blame him, this is Heaven after all. Who wants to feel someone else's burden in Heaven?* Asa nods and gracefully lands in a garden next to an apricot tree. Amelia climbs off and wanders about the magnificent orchard, hoping to get lost in the moment.

While noshing on a purple mangosteen, Amelia seizes the moment to ask Anthony about his past, hoping it will be therapeutic for her. She admires how free he is as he sucks the juice out of a pomegranate. He hasn't a care in the world. His charming boyish looks and sarcasm is magnetic. Although he's almost a hundred years old, in her eyes, he's just a child—an unforgettable child. Very few people have a way of making an imprint and Anthony is one of them.

"May I ask what happened to you?" Amelia whispers.

He stops chewing and looks at her like she just asked him to do a set of cartwheels. She looks down and bites her lip. *I guess it's too late to retrieve my query. He may not be interested in talking about it.* Nevertheless, she bats her eyelashes, smiles, and waits for his reply.

After dramatically rolling his eyes he leans against Asa. "I guess I knew it was only a matter of time before you asked me such things. I was in the wrong place at the wrong time. It was ninety years ago, but I feel like it was just yesterday," he sighs. He runs his little fingers through his hair and looks towards the sky.

"You know what, it's none of my business," Amelia says. She feels guilty for making him uncomfortable.

"No it's fine. It took me fifty years to let it go. Anita keeps telling me that it helps to talk about it. You know it's funny, dying and going to Heaven doesn't exactly wipe away your memories. I wish I

couldn't remember any of it. But I have forgiven them for what
they've done, so I guess that's what matters the most."

"They?"

"Yeah, unfortunately. I was ten at the time. It was in the summer
on a Friday. Dad woke me up around eight o'clock to tell me he was
going out of town for work and that he would return the following
Tuesday. He promised me that when he came back he would take my
three year old sister, Ella, and me to the circus. I was over the moon
and couldn't wait for him to come back. Later that day, my friends
came by and asked my mom if I could go play baseball with them.
Of course she was all too thrilled and practically forced me out of the
house. Whenever Dad went out of town, which was at least once a
month, Mom came to life. Don't get me wrong, she was always
pleasant, but the moment he stepped out of the house, she lighted up
like the Fourth of July. From what I could tell, they had a loving
relationship and Dad was the sweetest person alive. So I couldn't
understand why she was so ecstatic when he left."

"Back then, I heard that women had to be almost perfect. They had
to keep the house and kids in order while their husbands worked.
The Great Depression probably put a damper on things as well. I'm
sure a lot of their family and friends lost everything. Maybe once
your dad left out of town for work, it allowed her some time to relax
and enjoy *her* life," Amelia declares.

"You might be right. There was a lot going on at the time. But I
knew there was more to it than that. It's funny how parents assume
their kids don't know or understand what's going on, but little do
they know we know way more than they think. Probably more than
we should." He throws an apple core across the way.

*I can certainly appreciate that. Mom and Dad thought I didn't
have a clue about their relationship. What if I didn't know? Jeez,
they did a horrible job at hiding it the night he was shot.*

"So what happened?" Amelia probes, eagerly.

"It was the seventh inning and the other team was up six to one. I
was tired and hot; it must have been ninety-five degrees that
afternoon. We decided to take a break in the shade to reenergize
ourselves, but I chose to run home and get my lucky mitt. I hoped
that it would help my team make a comeback. When I opened the
door, I immediately knew something wasn't right, so I ran to check
on Ella. She was sound asleep in her crib, which was a relief for me.
After giving her a kiss and covering her up, I grabbed my mitt from
my room and was heading out the door when I heard a loud bang on

the wall. I thought, *oh my God, Mom must be in trouble*. When I
opened her bedroom door, everything I saw happened in slow
motion. I dropped my mitt, my mouth flew open, and my eyes were
in a trance. I'm not even sure I breathed. I couldn't move. Mom and
Uncle Will were having sex."

"Sex? You knew what sex was at that age?"

"Oh come on Amelia, of course I knew. My friends and I talked
about it all the time. Matthew used to steal his father's dirty
magazines and…"

"Okay! I get it! You don't have to go into detail." Amelia shudders
in embarrassment.

Anthony laughs without so much of a flush in his cheeks.
"Anyway, when I dropped my mitt, they both turned and saw me
standing there, in shock. My mom put her hands over her mouth and
started to cry, but my uncle had a different expression…anger. Now,
one thing to know about my uncle is that he was fearless and crazy.
When he lost his job the year before, his wife left him and never
came back. He got really depressed and lost sight of anything that
mattered. Dad had to go to his house on numerous occasions just to
help him get out of bed, feed, and clothe him. He tried his best to
encourage him to get back out there and fight for what he wanted,
but it was to no avail.

"When Uncle Will almost lost his house, Dad was able to talk to
some friends from the bank to save it. He even used some of *our*
savings to keep him from being put out. But some people are just
ignorant and don't see what's right in front of them. I knew he loved
Dad very much, but I also knew that he was jealous of what Dad had
and it started to consume him. My mom tried to tell dad that Uncle
Will wasn't very appreciative, but he refused to give up on his
brother. From what I could tell, she despised him and didn't respect
him, so I couldn't understand for the life of me why she would do
such a thing. It didn't make sense," Anthony says.

"Most of the things our parents do don't make sense. It almost
seems like we have more sense than they do. In our eyes, everything
is simple and can be fixed automatically, but what we don't see are
the shades of gray. I know that now. Life is way more complicated
than the obvious."

"Well aren't you the wise one."

"I'm not that wise. It's just that I can see things more clearly now,
now that it's too late. One of life's jokes I guess," Amelia
whispers.

Anthony's face hardens and he replies, "It's not too late Amelia."

What does that mean? Is he trying to make me more depressed? I'm dead! What more is there to say?

Anthony sees the misery in her face and pats Amelia's hand. "When I finally came back to reality, I started to run. I was headed right for the door when Uncle Will grabbed me by the shirt and pulled me backwards. Mom ran out of the room and told him to leave me alone. But he wouldn't listen and told her that I would tell Dad what they did. He said, 'Do you want my brother to throw you out on the street and get full custody of Ella? He'll tell the whole town that you're a whore and you'll be left with nothing. He'll never forgive you for sleeping with his brother.' As I struggled to get away, I begged and pleaded and swore I would never tell a soul, but my uncle called me a liar and slapped me across the face. He told her he has to get rid of me. I think those words rang in my ears over and over and over. He wanted to get rid of me, like…I was nothing. With tears in her eyes, Mom ran over and kissed me on the forehead. At that moment I started to cry like there was no tomorrow, because I knew tomorrow would never come. She was saying goodbye."

"I heard some horrific stories Anthony, but this is by far the worst. I'm so sorry."

"Don't be. In the end, everything panned out," Anthony murmurs.

"How so?"

"Once my mother gave me the kiss of betrayal, I fought and fought. I certainly wasn't going to make it easy for them. My uncle found a large cloth bag and wanted to put me in it. Can you believe the nerve of him? I punched and kicked and was lucky enough to scratch him on the side of his face. It was deep enough that I immediately saw blood. The next thing I knew, he punched me so hard it knocked me out. When I awoke, my whole body was aching and it was dark. My first reaction was to scream, but I felt it would be no use. Who was going to rescue me? Mom said her goodbyes and Dad was out of town. Something was weighing down on my legs, but I couldn't feel what it was. I felt around and noticed that I was wrapped in something, some kind of material. That's when I realized I was inside the cloth bag. I began to cry and press up against whatever was weighing me down. My air supply was slowly dissipating and nothing I was doing made one bit of difference. They buried me alive. I'm not sure how long I survived after that, maybe thirty minutes after I awoke."

"Oh my. Is that when you walked into the light?"

"No, I couldn't rest. I didn't go right away. I wanted to hang around on earth for a while to see if they were going to get away with it. I told myself to give it a month and if nothing came of it, I would go."

"Well something must have come of it."

"Oh yes, sweet revenge," he laughs. "When Dad arrived home the following Tuesday, Mom told him that I ran away from home and that I hated her. Even Uncle Will said he tried to talk me into staying, but I refused to listen and hopped on a boxcar out of town. Dad was furious and in disbelief of what he was hearing. He didn't consider a word of it. Much to my mother's chagrin, he called the police and told them that I was missing. Mom tried her best to convince him that I chose to leave, and even played the sympathy card. She told him how hurt she was when I left and that he should just trust her version of what happened. But I saw in his eyes that he knew something was wrong.

"For a week, there was a search party out covering the grounds, they even had dogs out sniffing around. Mom was beside herself and frightened that they just might find something that would contradict her story. Uncle Will hung around to create a diversion, but my dad ignored him. When the police came to take a statement from Mom and my uncle, Dad conveniently asked him how he got that scratch on his eye. That drew the officer's attention as well, and my uncle immediately became a suspect. But that wasn't going to be enough, although I hoped it would. When they took them down to the station for more questioning, Dad stayed behind and cried. He picked Ella up and hugged her tight. That's when my best friend Matthew showed up. Dad was a little puzzled as to why he was there. If I had run away, wouldn't I run away with my best friend?

"To test the theory, Dad asked him why he didn't run away with me, but Matthew looked confused and told him I didn't run away. He told him that I went home to get my lucky mitt and never returned to finish the game. When I took too long he went to the house to look for me but instead he saw my uncle running out of the house carrying a large bag into the field where he proceeded to bury it. Dad jumped up with Ella in his arms and got into the car. He told Matthew to come go and tell the police what he saw. That very night they dug up my body. I'm sure you can guess the rest of it."

"I assume your mom and uncle went to jail for the rest of their lives."

"Before they could arrest Mom, she ran into the house and shot
herself in the head. I think it was a mixture of guilt and the shame
she felt when they dug up my body. Everyone looked at her like she
was the worst person in the world. She couldn't take it. As for my
uncle, Dad asked the cops if he could have a few minutes alone with
him before they took him in. Back then, it was understood in such
circumstances for the cops to turn their heads and allow certain
things to happen. All I can say is that he got the worst beating of his
life and was eventually convicted and sentenced to death. Dad
wanted him to suffer just like he made me suffer. He was given the
electric chair a year later."

"Wow! Never in a million years did I expect that to be the
outcome," Amelia says.

"Yeah well, sometimes things have a way of working themselves
out. I guess Anita was right all along, I do feel better. Who knew?"
he smirks.

"Thank you for sharing that with me, I know it was difficult."

"Ah, don't mention it."

"So where to now? There's so much of Heaven I would love to
see."

"Why don't we go to the spring to get some fresh water?" Asa
submits.

"Sounds good to me," Amelia replies.

Like everything else in Heaven, the spring water was delicious and
exceeded her expectations. The water was the bluest and purest
liquid she ever laid eyes on. But the best part of the trip was when
Asa shared her many adventures with them. Asa's quite the
comedian.

Anita greeted them when they arrive back home, and offered them
a warm welcome. Amelia observed, *It's hard to stay depressed
because each of their personalities provides a perfect balance.* But
she still can't hide the fact that she misses her parents. She hates the
idea that this is it. *Will I have to wait for an eternity without seeing
them? If I could just find out how they are, then maybe that would
help.* She walks past the house and out towards the backfield when
she overhears Anthony whispering something.

"I don't know how much longer we can hide this from her. She's
depressed all the time and the dust isn't making her happy, it's
making her sleepy," he complains.

"I know. How is this possible? It was supposed to make her so happy that the last thing she would think about is her life. Maybe we should give her a little more of it," Anita suggests.

"MORE!" Anthony screams. "She'll be a vegetable! Absolutely not. We have to tell her."

"Keep your voice down, she can't know anything. Besides, it's not up to us, honey. We have orders to follow. Just keep giving her the same amount and hopefully, Amelia will know the truth soon enough."

I'm so tired of all the secrets. Amelia tiptoes away, brooding over her situation. She strides past the large field of orange flowers and down a hill. Deep between the large, magical trees she stumbles upon a little brook and sits down in the grass. She dips her toe in the warm water and wishes. When she dips her other foot, a memory pops into her mind. She sees a vision of her reluctantly walking into water. *But why?* Then, she remembers being scared, cold, and helpless. *But why?* Suddenly, more flashbacks flood her conscious and then it appears to her. "The water was freezing! Mortis! He commanded me to walk in. But…I never made it out." *Oh no, now I understand what happened.* "Stylot!" she cries, falling on her back. She rolls to her side and weeps, "He's dead, Mortis killed him." She sits up and draws her knees to her chest as her heart breaks all over again. Reliving every moment of what happened consumes her to chest pain and tears. She dries her face. She feels defeated and angry. *My life ended all because of that freak!* Crack! She turns around when she hears a stick break behind her. She jumps up.

"Amelia, you're going to be okay," Anthony assures her.

"Stay away from me! I can't trust you. I heard you and Anita talking about *the feel good dust.* I know you've been drugging me!" Amelia yells and wipes her nose.

"Feel good dust? Ha, ha, that does have a nice ring to it."

"This isn't funny Anthony! Just leave me alone!"

She runs past him and heads further down the hill. A mixture of tears and anger keeps her running. She ignores Anthony's fervent screams in the distance. She doesn't want to see him or anyone right now. She's running so fast she may as well be flying. When she reaches the end of the forest, she's out of breath, which she thought was impossible in Heaven. She stops and rests her hands on her knees to catch her breath when someone whispers her name.

"Amelia, is that you?"

She whirls around and looks up at a beautiful angel. Her bright eyes are full of life and she is so clean she's practically glowing. Her happiness brings Amelia to tears. *At least I have some proof that my life was not in vain. I see now that my purpose wasn't a total loss.*

"Carys?" Amelia whispers.

Chapter Twenty Four

"It's you? You're really here, you look so beautiful," Amelia says, stepping closer. She hugs her friend and for the first time in quite a while, she feels like herself. *Who would have thought I would have the luck of running into her?*

"Yes, of course I'm here," Carys says. Amelia's taken aback by the mellifluous tone of her voice. Carys pats Amelia's hand. "Thanks to you. Amelia, I can't tell you how happy I am. I never thought I would make it out of Bram and then you came along and put that monster to rest."

"There was no way I could stand by and let him continue to have his way with everyone. But, don't give me all the credit. I could have never done it without you. You were the perfect secret weapon, transforming into Grace and all. I'm just glad you guys made it out safe." She glances to her left and right. "Speaking of which, where are Langston and Mili?"

With a grin on her face, Carys points behind Amelia. Amelia whirls around and spots Langston and Mili flying down towards them. Their iridescent angel wings flutter through the perfumed air. A huge smile forms on Amelia's face. She can't help but be proud to witness such a great magic and elegance. She's stunned by their unique beauty as she watches them land gracefully in the grass. They don't look like they did before; even their skin is smooth and clean. She finds herself jealous and rubs the newly formed pimples on her face. She doesn't know if it's the stress or something else, but her face has been breaking out. *I know for a fact that angels aren't supposed to have acne, more proof that I shouldn't be here.* Mili runs up to her first and squeezes her waist, bringing her out of her horror.

She touches Mili's coiled shiny tresses and hugs her back. "How are you?" Amelia asks.

Mili looks up and smiles, showing pearly white teeth. "Do you even have to ask?" she giggles. She turns around and points to her glowing feathered wings.

"No I suppose I don't."

Langston walks over and picks Amelia up and swings her around. He plants a soft kiss on her cheek and sets her back down. "Thank you," he whispers.

"Don't thank me. Just…be happy," Amelia says through a smile.

"Oh, you don't have to worry about that. I've forgotten what being sad is like," Carys says.

Amelia drops her head and sighs. *I wish I felt like that.* Langston takes Carys's hand and kisses it. They all stare at Amelia with wonder.

"Hey Amelia, um, why are *you* here?" Mili inquires.

"I knew it was only a matter of time before one of you asked. Well, to be honest, I just figured it out myself. I couldn't remember what happened to me until a few moments ago. My guardian angel wouldn't tell me anything, and in the mean time, I've been driving myself crazy trying to figure it out."

"Well, what happened?" Carys probes.

With a huge sigh Amelia admits, "Mortis killed me."

"Mortis!" They all scream simultaneously.

She nods her head and tells them what happened. "You know the worst part? Stylot didn't make it. He—he died trying to save my life," Amelia mumbles as tears fall.

"Oh honey, I'm so sorry. I had no idea. I can't believe it was Mortis of all people. So, he made you walk into the water and you apparently froze to death?" Carys asks.

"Yes, I'm pretty sure that's what happened. I did wake up briefly though, I saw my cousin Navid. I just couldn't stay awake."

"So after Bram, where did you go?" Langston inquires.

"Oh man, I have so much to tell you guys. I found myself in a place called Felinity. Apparently it was another creation that I stumbled upon. I found out that my Aunt Leona had a daughter that was living there. Abraham put her there so that she could wait for her mother to arrive and rule over everyone. She tried her best to kill me, but in the end, a man helped Stylot and me escape. We were able to destroy her dwelling and kill everyone inside."

"Wow, so Stylot turned out to be an amazing ally," Mili says.

"He was better. He saved my life more times than I could count. I just wish I could have returned the favor. I shouldn't have taken him out of Zerios. If I left him there with Briseus, he would still be alive," Amelia grunts.

"Don't do that to yourself. Stylot wouldn't want you to blame yourself. You saved him too, Amelia. He was miserable with Mortis. With one touch you turned him into his true self again. Wait a minute. Did I hear you correctly? Where is Zerios, and who is Briseus?" Carys questions. A huge smile forms across Amelia's face when she thinks about Joleus. "Ha, ha. Now you have to tell me what you were up to missy."

"Jeez, where do I begin?" Amelia whispers with a smile. They all stare at her with amusement. As she looks at them, she can't help but feel a little exposed, almost as if they know what she's about to say. She rolls her eyes and grins. "Okay, guys, if you want me to tell you, you have to stop making goo-goo eyes at me," Amelia demands, stifling a laugh.

"Okay, okay. Everyone calm down," Carys giggles.

Amelia grimaces at their terrible attempts to keep from laughing. "Oh Carys, by the way thank you for your "gift" it was awesome and helpful."

"That's right! I forgot about that. You must have been a transforming nut," Carys says.

"Well yes, until I couldn't anymore."

"What do you mean?" Carys asks.

Amelia takes a deep breath and spills every detail about her long journey.

"I have never in my life met a girl more susceptible to finding trouble. But I must say, that Joleus is a very intriguing character. I mean, I know you hated being half horse, but wow what a ride," Carys whispers.

A tiny giggle escapes Amelia's lips when she recollects the massive freak out mode she was in after finding out she was half horse and then falling in love with her new life and Joleus, however awkward. "The whole thing was so crazy because I couldn't understand why that happened or why I was put in that situation in the first place. All I knew is that I wanted and needed to turn back into myself, but nothing I did worked. Once I realized that there was nothing I could do, I knew the only thing left was…"

"Was?" Langston inquires.

"Was to say goodbye to Aaron. I couldn't go to him and save him like that. I was useless and ill-equipped."

"I still don't understand how you were able to fall in love so quickly? You and Aaron were supposed to have some divine love that would last forever," Carys ponders aloud.

"That's what I'm still trying to figure out. I can't decipher how or why that happened, but it did. As strange as it sounds, it's like Joleus and I had a real relationship. We took our time and got to know each other, and in the end it made sense for us to be together. Oddly, my feelings for Aaron never really went away, but the love I felt for Joleus was different, it felt more real and I felt safe." Amelia grins. "He even proposed," she adds.

"Say what?" Carys giggles, holding Langston's hand. "What did you say?"

"Before I could answer, we were attacked by demons. Joleus and I had to help as many people as we could and then hide ourselves. The crazy thing is before he proposed, I got my powers back."

"How?" Langston asks.

Amelia shrugs her shoulders.

"So how did it end?" Mili asks.

"I couldn't risk Joleus getting hurt so I waited until he was asleep and used that opportunity to leave before he awoke. Stylot and I took off and went on a mission to find Leona. Leaving him was the hardest thing I've ever had to do, but I knew he would never let me go alone."

"It's weird hearing you say things like that about someone other than Aaron," Carys admits.

"I don't know guys; it's something I can't explain. I'm not sure if I'll ever see him again, but I really miss him. As for Aaron, I desperately wanted to rescue him and I was so close to getting there until Mortis showed up."

"Amelia, I'm so sorry you had to die before finishing your quest, but I'm glad you're here," Mili says.

"Thanks Mili, you know I just wish I could feel happy like you guys, but I'm so depressed. I don't know what to do," Amelia confesses.

Carys and Mili get on each side of her and fly her around Heaven. The one thing Amelia can't deny is her love for flying. It relaxes her and the beauty of Heaven will never cease from her mind. When she gets to their massive piece of land, she is once again dumbfounded by how extraordinarily lucky they are to spend eternity in such an amazing mansion. She can't stop herself from staring at everything. Carys offers her milk and honey as they walk around in awe.

"So, what's the status of you and Langston?" Amelia asks.

"We're married. I'm so happy with him and Mili I can't stand it. I honestly didn't think I was capable of loving him so much and being this content. I don't even remember what being sad is like, because now that we're here, nothing else matters."

"I'm so happy for you Carys. If anyone deserves to be happy it's you all. I mean, you'd been through so much already."

"You deserve it too, Amelia," Carys whispers.

"She's right," Langston adds, holding Mili's hand.

"I honestly don't know how. I love every part of Heaven and sometimes I'm happy, but other times I can't relax. I thought that once I figured out how I died that it would help my mood. Needless to say, it hasn't," Amelia says. "Although I must admit, running into you has made me feel a lot better. Maybe I'll just stay here and hang with you guys and things will change."

"Amelia, I think you should come back with us now honey," Anita says.

Amelia spins around and crosses her arms, silently protesting. Anthony steps closer to Amelia and holds out his hand. She stands firm and glares at them.

"No," she finally says.

Anthony looks up at Anita and shakes his head. "I knew she wouldn't listen," he sulks.

"I don't mean to be rude, but I overheard you and Anthony talking about the dust that's supposed to make me happy and quite frankly, I'm not amused by all the secrets. So if you're not here to tell me the truth, then you need to leave me alone."

Anthony and Anita both turn and fly away. Amelia faces Carys, Langston, and Mili and can see the disappointment in their faces. She runs her fingers through her hair and strides past them.

"Amelia wait!" Carys hollers, flying towards her. Amelia stops and turns around just as Carys glides down onto the grass. "I think you should give them a chance to explain. Maybe it will bring you peace."

"They've had ample opportunities to tell me whatever it is that they're hiding and they won't. I would've never known that there was a secret had I not overheard them," Amelia says.

"I understand that, but there must be a good reason for their anonymity."

Amelia rolls her eyes and bites her nails. *If nothing else I should apologize for being rude.* She nods her head. "Thanks for being my voice of reason. I guess I'll go to them."

"Don't mention it. I'm sure that once you find out the truth, you'll be at peace."

Before leaving, Amelia bids Carys, Langston, and Mili farewell and runs off to find Anthony and Anita. She promised them that she was going to be happy and that she would see them again one day, after she makes peace with everything. While racing through mounds of greenery, she somehow gets lost and finds herself stepping onto golden pavement. She kneels down and runs her fingers across the shiny, smooth street, marveling at the glorious work of art. As she ponders how to get the truth out of Anita, a big smile appears on her face as she realizes that it would be taboo to lie in Heaven, which can only mean that they have to come clean.

"Amelia?" A woman sings. Amelia stands up and turns around. She runs up to the woman and squeezes her so tight the woman laughs.

"Gisel, I'm so glad to see you," Amelia cries. She sniffs and looks into her green eyes, the same mesmerizing green eyes that Aaron inherited from her.

"I'm glad to see you too, dear," Gisel giggles and touches Amelia's face. "I have so much to tell you."

Amelia hugs her again and pulls away. "You do?"

"Yes. I realize I spoke in quite a bit of riddles when I was alive, but there was a reason for that. You couldn't know the truth, not until this very moment," Gisel says.

Amelia's head is spinning. She's ecstatic to see Gisel, but isn't sure if she's ready to hear the whole truth. It frightens her because as much as she thought she was ready, she's not. This is it. There's no turning back and for the first time she feels as though it might send her over the edge. She's certain that whatever Gisel is about to say…will change everything. She slowly sits Indian style on a patch of soft grass and signals for Gisel to continue.

"I believe that it's best to just come out with it and not beat around the bush. The reason I died is because I chose to."

"What do you mean you chose to? You died of cancer. I mean…it seemed inevitable."

"When I was alive, I would get these premonitions and I often knew what was going to happen before it did. Never in my wildest dreams did I think anything was going to happen to my son. As I told you the first day we met, I got terrible nightmares about Aaron. Each night was worse than the last and I knew that it was a sign. I knew that I was going to lose Aaron and I couldn't live with that. So, I chose to die in his place. But there's always a consequence to everything. The catch was that it wasn't going to be easy getting to him. And, he would be guarded by three very powerful women. You see, he had to be saved by someone who was powerful and had nothing to lose." She drops her head and confesses, "It also had to be a person who was in love with him."

Amelia's head shoots up. "In love with him? He had a girlfriend when I met him, Gisel?" Amelia stands up and paces. "Are you telling me that I was chosen? How can this be? I mean, I remember having that dream about him in the hospital and desperately wanting him."

Gisel looks down and then back at Amelia. "That was all part of the plan. You both had to be head over heels in love so that he would *want* to live and you would *want* to save him. Everything was foretold to me in the dream the moment I made a deal with God to take Aaron's place, and it happened just as it should. At least until that horse guy almost ruined everything. If I had gotten there a second earlier, he wouldn't have had to save you and put a ripple in the plan," Gisel says.

"What? Are you kidding me? You put a spell on Aaron and me? This whole thing was orchestrated because you didn't want to lose your son. Gisel I had a life!" Amelia yells.

"You don't understand Amelia. This was for you, too."

"How so?" Amelia grunts.

"Honey, you weren't going to make it either. Leona was going to kill you. You weren't supposed to make it out of Stillwater."

Amelia loses her breath and is overwhelmed by a vigorous cough. She pants and rests her hands on her knees to catch her breath. Gisel softly rubs her back and it instantly makes her feel better.

With tears in her eyes, Amelia huffs, "I, I wasn't going to live?"

Gisel shakes her head no.

"Wow, now it all makes sense. You know, I remember praying in the hospital for my dad to get better and asking God to help me survive living with them. I also remember feeling strange after leaving the chapel, like stronger. Shortly after that, I had the dream about Aaron."

"You were stronger, stronger and braver than you'd ever been. And I knew when I met you that you were the one. That's when I decided to die. I was supposed to beat the cancer, but you were the girl who was going to save my son," Gisel whispers.

Amelia rolls her eyes, feeling a little used. "If I were supposed to die, I don't understand why I didn't. I know God answers prayers, but it seems as though only your prayers were answered."

"It would seem that way, but there was a special person up here who was rooting for you to live, and if it weren't for him, you may not have been the right girl."

"Oh?" Amelia utters, crossing her arms. *I wonder if it's Mr. Wilkers.*

"No, it's not Mr. Wilkers, although he sends his love. He found out I was coming to see you," Gisel whispers.

Amelia's face lights up. "He's here! Well you tell him I said to stay outta trouble." A tiny giggle escapes Gisel's lips. Amelia laughs, but then her smile fades when she thinks about everything Gisel has told her. She can't help but feel like a puzzle piece in her plan.

"I need to know something. Are my and Aaron's feeling for each other even real? Because I can't help but feel like we're puppets."

"Of course Amelia. I think you guys genuinely love each other, but because you were chosen, it made you both fall in love very quickly."

"Quickly? That's an understatement. I wanted to jump his bones the moment I saw him, Gisel," Amelia complains. Gisel bursts out laughing and Amelia tries to stifle a laugh. "It's really not funny," Amelia giggles. "When I fell in love with Joleus, those were my real feelings weren't they? Is that why it was so easy for me to love him? Because I couldn't understand why I could love anyone as much if not more than Aaron, and now I realize that when Joleus saved my life it changed everything and opened my eyes. Our love was real," Amelia whispers.

"That may be true, but if your love for him was so strong, then why did you leave him?" Gisel asks.

"Because Aaron's life was in danger! I dreamed of the three women and I knew that time would be running out for him," Amelia says.

"Exactly. All I'm saying is that there must be a part of you that still very much loves my son."

"Of course. I will always love him. But I can't erase how I feel about Joleus."

Gisel takes both of Amelia's hands and looks into her eyes. "I realize how selfish I've been and I'm so sorry if you feel used. All I knew is that I wanted my son to be okay and I would do anything to make sure that he was. I love you sweetheart. You've been so wonderful and I couldn't have met a better girl. Thank you for keeping your promise and being there for him. I can't say that I regret any of this because that would be a lie. You lived and Aaron lived and that's what mattered," Gisel says.

"I appreciate you saying that, and there's no need to thank me. Aaron needed me and I needed him. By the way, I hate to be the bearer of bad news, but I'm not alive anymore. You know, since we're in Heaven and all," Amelia jokes.

"Oh Amelia. You haven't figured it out yet? You're not staying here. My Goodness, I have yet to see an angry person in Heaven." Gisel laughs.

Amelia suddenly feels better. *Does that mean I have a chance for a real life? But how is all of this even possible?* "How am I going to return to my life?"

"Listen honey, its almost time for me to go. There's something else that I think you should know. Selfishly, I wanted you to save Aaron, but, I know my son and I can honestly say that he would not want you to risk your life to save him. If anything happened to you, he would never forgive me. Having said that, this means that you have a gift not many of us have: the luxury of receiving. You have a second chance at life. This means that you can go and be with your friend or whatever you choose. I know now that my son will be fine no matter what. So whatever you do…I want you to live and live well. The choice is yours," Gisel whispers. A ringing of a bell distracts them. "Oh, that person who's rooting for you will be here soon. One more thing, it's okay to trust your guardian angels, they love you. Goodbye honey." Gisel kisses Amelia's cheek and starts to fly away.

"Wait! Gisel don't go!" Amelia hollers.

Smiling, Gisel flies away and disappears.

Amelia slowly sits back down in the grass, feeling mentally exhausted. *My God, all this time Aaron and I were…arranged! The choice is mine now?* She lies back and laughs to herself; she's elated that she has control over her own life.

What will she choose?

Waking Amelia,

coming Fall 2017.

Acknowledgements

I had so much fun writing *Monstrous Ties* and I must thank everyone who has been on this journey with me. God is such an important part of my life and I know my prayers are answered and that this is all possible because of him.

To my friends and family, you are such a big part of my life and I couldn't have done any of this without you. You give me strength and motivation to continue on my writing journey and I'm so blessed that you are in my life.

I am forever grateful for my reviewers, who not only read my books but also took the time to write me a review. I can't thank you enough for your support and for giving my book a chance.

I'd like to thank Danielle Hartman-Acee for believing in me and for being such a big help when I needed someone the most. I can truly call you a friend. I'm so excited to see what's to come and I really appreciate your words of encouragement.

To my editor, Mindy Reed, thank you so much for working with me and for doing an amazing job on making *Monstrous Ties* incredible. I'm so glad we crossed paths and I know without a doubt that it wouldn't be half as good without your expertise.

I have to give a special thanks to my book designer James Egan for the awesome book cover. I love how I can throw my ideas at you and you transform it into a masterpiece. You always exceed my expectations and I can't thank you enough for what you do.

SHINA JAMES is the author of *Like a Dream,* her debut novel that was published in 2015. She resides in Texas with her husband and two kids and loves reading and listening to music. Writing poems and working on her series is one of her favorite past times.

Visit SHINA JAMES at:
www.shinajames.com
facebook.com/authorshinajames
Twitter- @shina_j1